DAVID,

The Silencer

Thank you,

ARPAD HORVATH

The Silencer
Copyright © 2022 by Arpad Horvath

All rights reserved. No part of this publication may be reproduced, distributed, or transmitted in any form or by any means, including photocopying, recording, or other electronic or mechanical methods, without the prior written permission of the author, except in the case of brief quotations embodied in critical reviews and certain other non-commercial uses permitted by copyright law.

Tellwell Talent
www.tellwell.ca

ISBN
978-0-2288-8519-1 (Hardcover)
978-0-2288-8518-4 (Paperback)
978-0-2288-8520-7 (eBook)

SICILY 2005

A cool breeze wandered between a pair of open balcony doors making the long white silk curtains dance without care before entering the room. The breeze sauntered across the room and caressed the bed inside ever so slightly, a feeling that the occupant of the bed would never get tired of it made him feel alive. The occupant of the bed and the owner of the home for that matter was Don Benidito Laurenti, head of the Laurenti crime family for forty years the longest reigning Don in the history of crime families. He was loved by few, hated by most and feared by all. He lay in his bed with his hands behind his head staring at the white ceramic ceiling thinking to himself "it's good to be king". The sun outside was just starting to appear over the horizon. It was early. Now for a man with this much power and at his age (sixty- five) would consider sleeping in a few more hours, but not this man it was programmed into him a long time ago. Benidito grew up with little schooling but an extremely strong work ethic, which he got from his father Benidito senior. Working on his father's fishing boat he not only got a strong work ethic, he also learned discipline, trust, and teamwork, pity only the early rising was the talent that remained. Over the years his father's fishing business flourished and Benidito also was on the rise. As his father got older Benidito moved from the fishing boats to the office; it was there that he really began to become who he was today. He started making the fishing fleet bigger and stronger and with that came more profits and also started the corruption. Two years later Benidito's father passed away and six months after his mother passed and he had lost everyone and being an only child it was lonely, but profitable. He inherited the fishing fleet and the money his father and mother had been saving. After the loss of his family he sold the fishing fleet and his parent's house and his life made a steady spiral into the underworld of organized crime. Now forty years, one failed marriage and two daughters later here he was alone, wealthy, and powerful. It's funny how life works out. The Don sat up in bed, spun to his right and sat on the edge of the bed, his feet on the slightly cool hardwood floor. He stretched his arms up high as if to touch the high ceiling while doing this he made his standard male morning noises, he farted, burped and then lowered his right hand and scratched his crotch all normal morning actions (if you're male that is.)

Today would be a day unlike any other, What would happen today wouldn't be on television or on the radio, neither would it be in newspapers or talked about in small cafes but if you knew anything about the goings on in the underworld you would know that this day would only be comparable to a merger between neighboring countries during a conflict anywhere in the world. Today would be historic. The reason this day would be a red letter day was because four powerful crime families would unite, Rome, Milan, Venice and of course Sicily, the possibilities would be endless. Benidito then got up from the edge of the bed and started to walk over to his private bathroom with visions of a united plan between the families filling his mind with visions of casinos, racetracks and other great ventures. Flipping the switch on for the lights he entered his private bathroom. Now this bathroom was not ordinary, on the contrary it was as diverse as the don. It was part bathroom and part shrine all decked out in white. The floor and walls were all white ceramic tile and the ceiling was rough plaster. The sink, toilet and shower were all made from marble, all very expensive. Turning on the water in the sink he cupped his hands under the tap and filled them with ice-cold water then he splashed his face and slowly brought himself back to life. Now it was common knowledge that the don had four main interests and they were food, money, futbol (soccer) and absolute power. Smoothing the hair he had left around the edge of his scalp with his hands he looked upon the wall to the right of his big Broadway mirror as he called it because it had big round lights on every side. To the left was a framed picture of Italy's nineteen eighty four World cup championship team, then the don looked to the right there and was a picture hanging of the two thousand and six World cup championship Italy took in Germany, he smiled proudly. Then he heard a faint sound and paused for a moment to listen… he heard nothing then shrugged it off and removed his tank top, boxer shorts and quick response button which was on the end of a gold chain and had a direct contact with his top man, the heir apparent as it was, Vinchenzo while he was in the house incase of health emergencies or problems that may arise, after all, three attempts on his life made him a little edgy as he entered the shower. The hot water felt good on his old bones. The shower itself was big enough for four people and had a full sized mirror. The Don looked himself in the mirror; he certainly didn't look twenty-five or forty-five for that matter. He was your average senior male, he was five foot six balding and a rather big stomach and had a thin white mustache, which took the focus off his rather large eagle beak like nose. He looked at the image before him and sighed. Gone were the once rippling muscles, the beautiful head of hair and the energy of lightning, what was left was an old, fat, bald man an image no one had seen because he kept it hidden behind money, intimidation, and power and his image was still very much intact today as it had been for forty years. The Don knew if this image was exposed it could show a sign of weakness and more than that destroy the image the don had worked so hard to establish. The don reached for the taps and shut them off then opened the door and reached beside the door for two soft white towels and wrapped one around his waist and the other he simply put on his neck, after he put the necklace back on prepared to brush his teeth and dry off before selecting just the right suit, shirt, shoes and tie to stun the families to show them he still had a lot of class. The sun was now half way up. The don went over to the mirror and wiped the glass with his hand and with his other he pulled out a razor from the drawer and prepared to shave. As he applied the cream his mind could not help venturing back to what would result today: the power, the money and the piece of mind that he could retire somewhat because four heads would be better than one. The razor that was a cutthroat just like the one his papa had shaved so close that a shave wasn't required for at least a week after. As he pulled the razor down his face and felt it clean the stubble and the cream from his face his thoughts were of what clothes to wear and shoes with each stroke of the razor he grew worried that maybe it wouldn't come together then what? But like his father always told him "let confidence be your guiding light through the storm and you will always reach the shore". The sun was now in full view not high in the sky, just over the horizon. The don finished his shave and wiped off the access cream then applied some aftershave; the burning sensation really awoke him. He combed his hair and looked into the mirror again and smiled. He was ready for anything. He was ready to make history, not chronicled history but history nonetheless. He walked out of the bathroom and could immediately detect the aroma of freshly brewed cappuccino, God's coffee as he put it, it was his favorite. The object of his desire was at the far end of a very long, very old dresser. The dresser also had a mirror the full length of the dresser, but what lay across the top of this massive piece of furniture was really amazing. Half of the dresser had pictures on it of family, friends and great moments, the other half was covered with a thick velvet cover and on top was a king's ransom. The Don was very particular about his appearance and jewelry would have to compliment the clothes and on top of the dresser there were different styles of watches, gold chains medallions, cufflinks and tie clips. The Don picked out a tie clip, two gold cufflinks, a gold chain and picked out a crucifix and slid them all to the edge so he could put them on in a hurry. Meanwhile the families started to arrive which seemed odd because of the fact they were supposed to come an hour later, but you don't tell men of this stature to go home so the families were shown to the second floor meeting room and asked to sit at the long table then were offered coffee and told the don would be delayed due to the fact he was expecting them much later, the families stated there was nothing to worry about and sat patiently. Upstairs the Don, still clad in a towel, picked up his cappuccino holding the saucer and cup with his left hand; he slowly walked out onto the balcony. The view was breathtaking and the air was so fresh.

The Silencer

After a few moments he made his way back in because his feet were catching a chill from the tiles, which made up the surface. He started to walk towards his bed. He had not yet taken a sip of his beverage but he was waiting. He turned once more towards the balcony doors, smiled, then squinted as the sun was shining in all its glory and in his eyes. With his left hand holding the saucer and right hand using his thumb and forefinger to hold the coffee cup he picked it up and slowly raised it past his lips and under his nose so he could take in the heavenly aroma then lowering it to his lips he took his first sip. Downstairs the final of the three families arrived and were led to the room on the second floor when they entered they exchanged handshakes and curtain courtesies, acts of respect as it were. Up stairs a cup of cappuccino was being savored. Suddenly, after he had taken a second sip and started lowering the cup… it shattered and the pieces and remaining coffee fell to the ground with only his thumb and forefinger holding the tiny handle. The coffee was running down his chest but that didn't matter to him, what did however was how the cup seemingly exploded in his hand. The Don tried to contemplate what had happened and looked down at the cup once more but now he noticed red drops on the shattered glass and felt a warm sensation running down his chest, he was bleeding. He turned to the mirror and saw he had been shot in the throat. He tried to shout but nothing came out, his mouth started to taste like blood. He dropped the saucer and the tiny handle from the cup before the saucer touched the ground he was on his knees. The towel from his shoulders fell onto the ground he quickly grabbed it and wrapped it around his neck to stop the bleeding, which by now was flowing. He applied pressure with his one hand and with the other started to crawl to the side of the bed that was facing the balcony. He managed to crawl to the side of the bed. His hands bloody he reached up onto the bed so he could stand up. The once white silk sheets now had crimson handprints adorning them as he laid his one arm on top of the bed and stopped to rest for a moment. Benidito managed to stand under his own power. What happened next chilled him to the bone. As he stood there trying to breathe and stop the bleeding he noticed a shadow behind him, the sunlight from outside was being blocked by whoever was behind him. Then he froze as the figure behind him started to talk. His voice was low and flat, almost with the same tone as meditation of Buddists. There were no peaks or valleys to his voice; it was plain flat; he was impressed however that the assailant talked in Italian. It wasn't just the tone, it was what was being read… last rights. He had not heard last rights since before his father died. He thought to himself: I' am not dead and I will not cower when death rears it's head for I' am a Laurenti and we fear nothing and no one. The Don decided he was going to see his tormentor, so he gathered all the strength he could, stood erect and turned around. He couldn't make out a face. He only saw a silhouette and it was slightly to the left so the sun shone right into the Don's eyes. He narrowed his eyes, squinted and tried to block the sun with one hand. While doing this the figure kept his words constant. All of a sudden the words stopped as the figure still silhouetted against the sun made the holy cross sign and said "amen". The man in front of him who fifteen minutes ago was powerful and intimidating was now an old, bloody man who was cowering and fearing his life. The figure then pulled a small remote from his pocket and turned on the stereo to his left. In less then a second opera music came blaring through the speakers and he dropped the remote to the ground. The second floor below could hear the music but the families and his men paid no attention. All they knew was their host was preparing to come shortly and he liked opera music to get ready. Benidito knew his time would soon be up and he had to do something, then it occurred to him he could call his men with the button he wore around his neck and his assailant would not know what hit him. He looked at the figure as he took several steps toward him and gave a crooked smile as he reached down and pushed the button. The smile soon disappeared from his face when nobody came crashing through the door to his rescue. Reaching into his pocket the shadowy figure produced two batteries and taking one step back he stood them on a small end table just inside the balcony doors then looking back at his mark he pulled his gun from his holster with the right hand and with his left he removed a silencer from his pocket and started to affix it to the end of the weapon and with every turn of the silencer he took a step closer until he was almost standing over the Don who had since dropped to his knees. The bloodied old man looked up as the silencer was being tightened on the end of the barrel he gulped and looked at the face of the man who was going to end his life, not that it would matter. His assassin's face never really registered with him, what did matter was the cold blue eyes he was sporting that at that precise moment looked at him and gave him a burning feeling in the pit of his stomach. Then the Don saw something that he didn't want to see in front of... a silencer pointed at him. His executioner with weapon pointed looked directly into the eyes of the frightened blood soaked old man and started to recite The Lord's Prayer (in Italian of course).

All the time while keeping close watch on his prey. The prayer soon ended, the Don after taking one more look around stood up and stared back into the cold blue eyes of his soon to be killer and as a sign of solidarity and with the little strength he still possessed the Don erected his fore finger and flipped his assassin the bird then swore at him in Italian. The gloved hand of the assassin tightened on the grip of the weapon as he slowly squeezed the trigger... without even flinching. In the meeting room on the second floor the families were starting to get restless. Even when Vinchenzo looked at his watch he reassured the families that everything was fine and that the don was a little older and a little bit slower. The families smiled and chuckled and understood. Vinchenzo told the server another round of coffee for the guests and that he was going upstairs to help the Don along. Vinchenzo knocked on the door out of respect, there was no reply, he knocked again a little louder, this time still no response. He scratched his head and asked if everything was all right, only silence. Vinchenzo then broke with protocol and entered the room. Nothing seemed out of place at first until he took another step and something crunched under his foot, he looked down and discovered the remains of a coffee cup and a vague hint of cappuccino in the air. Knowing the Don as he did he thought nothing of his first discovery because the Don was a bit of a klutz sometimes, people always said it was a good thing he played futbol because he never had to use his hands. Then taking a few more steps forward he saw blood on the floor and he followed the trail with his eyes until he discovered the source of the blood: it was the Don. Vinchenzo rushed over to the bed, the Don with his feet on the ground was lying on his bed facing the balcony. His heir apparent looked at him and noticed that he had taken a single shot to the head and after removing the bloody towel which was totally saturated he discovered there was another single shot, this one to his throat, whoever did this was a professional. Vinchenzo fell to his knees and closed his eyes, he held the hand of the Don and stroked his head while a single tear ran down his cheek. Vinchenzo's eyes then opened and a rage came over him that would make a rabid grizzly bear take a few steps back. He stood up and realized as morbid as his succession had come to him… he was now the Don and his first act would be to kill the individual that did this. The illusive intruder was almost at the gate. He had hidden a pair of overalls, a cap and a tool satchel in the hedge directly under the Don's balcony then stated on the back of the coveralls that he was an electrician and this made him invisible and in a few moments he would be gone. Up in the room the new man in power picked up the telephone and pressed "1" which called the gateman. Vinchenzo asked if anyone besides the families had come past him. The guard answered immediately that besides the families yesterday an electrician came by and replaced the old fusepanal in the basement with a breaker panel and as a matter of fact he came by early this morning to finish up and pick up his tools and he was approaching the gate right now. Vincenzo nearly dropped the phone, he opened the balcony doors, walked out and saw hanging from the edge of the concrete balcony… a grappling hook and a long length of cable all the way to the ground which was used to escape, he then picked up the receiver shouted into it "kill him" then from the balcony he had a view of the driveway and the gate. He was going to enjoy this. The disguise-clad assassin stopped a little ways short of the gate and watched the guard in the booth as the guard raised one finger as if to say one moment please. The guard then lowered the receiver and looked out at a figure standing in the driveway wanting to exit the premises. He slowly reached into his jacket and started pulling his gun out all the while watching his target standing there not moving. The figure in the driveway stood still with a Zen-like calmness as the guard nearly had his gun drawn. The guard then pulled his gun, but before he could even think where to hit the target a single bullet exploded into his skull, he fell back, gun still in hand and slid down the wall behind him all the while maintaining a surprised look on his face. The assassin obviously being in this situation before didn't even draw his gun instead he had it in his right hand all the time he simply shot through his coveralls from the hip. Up on the balcony Vinchenzo slammed his fist on the thick, hard concrete edge of the balcony, he then pressed "3" on the cordless phone. Two rings and one of the men inside the front door picked up. He couldn't even respond, Vinchenzo verbally unloaded on him telling him about the situation and ordering him and the other three men at the door to go outside and take down an intruder. The guard put down the receiver and signaled the other three men to follow him outside. He pulled on the handle, the door wouldn't open again he pulled and the door would not open. They kept trying in futility because there was no other exit out of the front of the house. The assassin was ahead of the game. He put a piece of rebar through the handles on the outside so they would be in there for a while. Calmly he reached in the window of the booth and pressed the button to open the gate. A low buzzing noise sounded out and the gates slowly swung open. Vinchenzo, watching the intruder, was almost salivating like a mad dog at the sight. The assassin, knowing full well he was being watched, reached in his coveralls and produced a cigar, which he proceeded to light. The smoke rose in the air as he reached into the booth and picked up the receiver and dialed "o" the phone was ringing. Vinchenzo, in a state of rage, already tried to contemplate where the men were and why this intruder wasn't being gunned down. He went to push

"3" again when the phone rang and he pressed the answer button. A voice on the other side quoted the bible, more specifically the Ten Commandments one in particular although the number eluded him, "do unto others as you would have them do to you, amen and good-bye". Vichenzo didn't quite grasp what he meant. The assassin then put down the receiver and walked to the center of the two gates, turned and pulled out a small remote with a numbered keypad and above it a red button. Vinchenzo did not understand what the assassin was doing but in a second... he would. The assassin looked at the old structure in front of him and gave a sigh, a long drag off his cigar and with the finger he pressed the button. Suddenly the entire foundation of the structure exploded, then fell silent. Vinchenzo had a twisted smile on his face after the explosion because nothing happened. The assassin failed and now he would pay... dearly. The smile would soon disappear. The intruder looked up at the balcony, then looked at the building, took a deep breath and blew at the building. Suddenly the building started to rumble and then collapsed into itself and all that was left was a pile of rubble. He then reached in the booth and pressed the button to open the main gate, as the gate started to open he looked back one last time for any signs of life but all was silent. He then walked to his van, got in and left, the fact the road to the main gate was a mile and no traffic came down the road gave the intruder a slight edge because news would travel fast. Once on the main road, he drove for ten minutes or so to a small farm he saw on the way in. He drove down a narrow dirt path to the top of a hill which overlooked a large pond, he drove to the edge and turned off the engine. Going in the back of the van he removed the coveralls and cap and then removed the shoulder holsters he stripped down to his boxer shorts and put on a black t-shirt, jeans, sandals and a black ball cap. After his wardrobe change was complete he grabbed his shoulder holsters and a small leather satchel, closed the back of the van, set the shifter into neutral and proceeded to push the van down the otherside of the hill to the large pond. Fortunately it was at least a one hundred yard slope or the van couldn't build up the speed to go into the water. The van rolled down the slope and hit the water with a big splash, and then as he watched, the van slowly, silently disappeared under the water, as a few small bubbles rose to the surface and then the water was smooth. All he had were the clothes on his back, his wallet, a passport, and a cell phone. A few hours later after traveling by horse and wagon, a ferry and an extremely long cab ride the assassin arrived at the airport. After purchasing his ticket, and clearing security (he had mailed his guns and shoulder holsters back to his home address on route to the airport) he made his way over to the bar, which was next to his gate. He sat on a stool at the very end of the bar and ordered a single malt scotch then he pulled out his cell phone and pressed the speed dial. After one ring the phone was answered. The call took no longer than a minute, information was exchanged and he ended the call, by now his scotch had arrived and he sipped it slowly savoring it to the full. The television above the bar showed his handy work and the line of body bags on the ground. He finished his drink, paid the bill and left for his gate. He was looking forward to the flight. It had been one very long day but it was all part of the job.

> "Why do people kill? Is it for money? Power? Glory?
> Since the beginning of time the strong have always
> vanquished the weak, whether it was the animal
> kingdom or the human race, killing was always the way to
> instill fear or dominance, if you will.
> Ever since Pontius Pilate sentenced Jesus Christ to
> be crucified, death has always been a way to appease
> the masses, but you see Pontius didn't want to sentence
> Jesus he was only doing it to save his job... but I bet
> It never paid as good as mine.
> Short-term risks long-term gains to me it's all the same
> It's just a job, it's just a means to an end... or so I thought."

"You can try and run from your past but it always catches up with you and bites you square on the ass... and you don't even see it coming."

THE SILENCER

Written and Created By
Arpad Andrew Horvath
2007

Sweetwater, Texas (THE PRESENT)

CHAPTER 1

I'M WHO YOU'RE LOOKING FOR... ONLY I'M NOT.

The door swung open on the small general store jingling the small bells attached to the frame above the door. Three men entered. One was dressed in a cream colored suit with a black shirt and ostrich skin shoes the other two were wearing black suits with white shirts and black ties and shoes. The man in the cream suit told the other two men to wait by the door while he approached the counter. He was a good-looking man sporting jet-black hair, a thin mustache and a well-tanned face. He addressed the person behind the counter. "Good morning". The person behind the counter turned around and returned the greeting, "good morning". The man in the cream suit introduced himself "I am Jose Sanchez and I would like to talk to the owner of this fine establishment". The person behind the counter was a man with shoulder length brown hair, brown eyes and was unshaven for at least a week. He looked at the man on the other side of the counter, smiled and answered, "yer lookin' at him, Wyatt Brown is my name". Sanchez put out his hand and exchanged a handshake with Wyatt. "What can I do ya' for?" Wyatt asked. Jose responded, "Is there somewhere we can talk in private, perhaps?" Wyatt nodded and pointed at a door at the end of the counter marked "office". Sanchez looked back at his men and instructed them to wait in the car, he wouldn't be too long. The men nodded and left the store. Wyatt showed his guest into the office and then entered, closing the door behind him. "Please sit". Sanchez sat down in a chair in front of a desk, which Wyatt seated himself behind. Wyatt folded his hands and placed them on the desk then leaned forward "now what is it exactly that I can do for you, Mr. Sanchez?" Sanchez answered quickly and decisively "you can tell me where Sawyer Briggs is, I have something for him". Wyatt replied" well, he's not here right now but if you have something for him I can surely pass it along". Sanchez paused for a moment then reached down beside himself he pulled up a black briefcase and laid it on the desk, he then opened it up and removed a package of some sort it was clearly marked "private and confidential". Sanchez handed the package over to him. "It's all yours" he said, "Make sure he gets it please." Wyatt placed the package in his desk drawer "you can count on it Mr. Sanchez." With that Sanchez got up from the chair and extended his hand and shook Wyatt's hand "thank-you you've been most helpful." Then Wyatt escorted him out of the office, to the front door of the store and watched as this suave man got in the back of his car and left.

Wyatt walked back and got behind the counter and it was business as usual. The day went by as it always did, quickly with brisk business as usual. The store itself was only one of its kind in this and the surrounding areas. It used to be an average general store but when Wyatt bought it seven years ago he kept the staff but renovated the rest. What made this store so unique was that it was like a Norman Rockwell painting, a moment captured from yesteryear. It had a pharmacy, deli counter and a small corner with a post office. It also had common general store items as well magazines, milk etc. Wyatt had carved out a nice little life for himself peacefully, stress free and he lived upstairs it was perfect… but that was all about to change. The open sign was turned to the closed side as the store closed for the day at six o'clock just like the old days and closed on

Sundays. Wyatt had a small staff that worked for small pay. There was Delores (clerk); her husband originally owned the store for forty years until he passed away and Wyatt bought it. Clancy (deli), Delores' brother in law. Bob (pharmacist) worked for the store since Delores' late husband opened it in nineteen fifty-five and Katrina all around assistant, she could do a bit of everything and she did considering the rest of the staff was considered retirement age, her parents came to the store a lot and she got the job right after high school and had been there every since. The whole store was a family and Wyatt loved it and he always felt wanted. Wyatt locked the door behind Clancy who always left last. Wyatt turned and started to walk to his office which was across the room, then he stopped for a moment and looked around. He always enjoyed the silence of the store. He then strode off to his office. Upon entering his office he went behind his desk, opened the drawer and pulled out the package he had received today for Sawyer he put it under his arm and walked over to a door in his office he opened it revealing stairs he proceeded to ascend the stairs. The upper level of the store was his apartment. It was very meager but spacious, perfect for one person. Wyatt went over to a corner of the apartment where a large desk stood; on top was a computer, a slim screen, a keyboard, a mouse and a printer complete with a very comfortable, very expensive office chair. Wyatt pulled a letter opener from the drawer and opened the package and put it on the desk then sat down and pulled out its contents. He sat down and looked at what he pulled from the package: it was a laptop. So Wyatt opened the laptop and turned it on. He waited for it to come on. Once it was on it printed a message "please insert disc" Wyatt looked into the package and found a disk. He inserted the disc into the laptop and sat back waiting to see what would develop. A few minutes went by and then four nozzles, one each corner came out. Wyatt looked closely at them and then without warning yellow gas spewed a kind of tear gas. For a moment Wyatt tried to get up but collapsed on his desk on top of the laptop.

CHAPTER 2
TRUTH AND DISCOVERY

Wyatt's eyes started to open slowly and he looked around, but there was nothing to see, just darkness and a bright light overhead. He then noticed he had no clothes on; he had in fact been stripped down to his briefs. Wyatt decided to get up but this appeared to be easier said than done. Apart from being almost naked he also realized that his ankles and wrists were bound to the bed. Two wires. He followed the wires with his eyes one set went to a panel box and the other set was hooked to a litmus test machine. In other words a lie detector. He then heard a door open and footsteps approach. A figure came into the light and placed a wooden chair near the bed. Wyatt studied the figure closely, white shirt, black tie black pants and expensive Italian leather shoes... stylish. The figure also wore a balaclava, which covered his face all except his eyes and mouth. The well-dressed antagonist sat down on the chair. There was silence for a moment. "Skipping the foreplay are we?" as he looked down at himself lying there. The figure smiled "that's cute, what do you do for an encore... Sawyer?" Sawyer's brief smile came off. "That's your name Sawyer Briggs" Sawyer stared back "no I'm not my name is Wyatt Brown" As he answered he heard the lie detector needles scratch wildly across the paper, a bead of sweat rolled down the side of his head. The masked figure stood up and showed Wyatt a small cell phone sized controller. "Do you know what this is?" asked the masked figure. Sawyer shook his head. "Well let me explain, if you don't give the answers I want to hear I'll shock you like this" His thumb came down on the button and a rush of electricity went through Sawyer's body. The figure sat down calmly and started a line of questioning. "Ok let's try it again shall we?" He then asked his first question "name?" Wyatt didn't respond and a surge of electricity went through his body. "Name?" Sawyer paused then answered "Wyatt Brown" The masked figure sighed and pressed the button again. Sawyer shook from the shock. The masked figure looked at Sawyer "why are you being so difficult? All I want is your name, so what do you say? C'mon tell me your name and this will end." The masked figure waited for a response from Sawyer and all he got was Sawyer's head going from side to side. The masked figure was clearly becoming frustrated "ok look stupid I'm now going to set this sucker up on high and you will be electrocuted slowly and painfully is that what you want?" Sawyer looked at the masked figure with a hard look "bring it on bitch" The masked figure looked at Sawyer and from underneath the mask came laughter "I'll be a son of a bitch, you are him, no one can take that much torture and not crack." Sawyer, realizing that his tormentor used reverse physiology, gave up trying to hide his identity and told the masked figure "yes... yes I am Sawyer Briggs" The needles on the lie detector traveled straight for the first time.

The masked figure put down the small gray box with the button and reached over and shut off the lie detector then sat back down... Sawyer then asked, "How do you know I'm the real thing? I mean anybody who gets shocked like that would say yes to anything" After a short pause "yes I suppose you're right," said the masked figure. Sawyer was on a roll... or so he thought. "You don't even know me," Sawyer said with an air of confidence. The masked figure got up and picked up a file from a table behind him and returned to his chair and leaned back, opening the file. He cleared his voice as if he was going to address the nation. He started to read the file "Sawyer Samuel Briggs born July fifteenth nineteen sixty-seven in Billings Montana, your father was killed in nineteen sixty-eight on his third tour of Vietnam and your mother passed away in nineteen-eighty of a brain tumor you moved in with your aunt. In nineteen-ninety two you worked as an intern at Interpol. Within two years you were a field agent, one of the youngest in the history of the agency and three more after that you were a director". He looked over at Sawyer "Quick study, huh" He took a sip of water and continued "a year after that you married one of your team, Gwenith Hillery Boyd unfortunately she was killed two years later in a routine sting operation" Sawyer sighed. The masked figure read on "shortly after her death you resigned and dropped of the face of the earth, until a year later when you resurfaced as The Silencer, a gun for hire and for the next twelve years you carried out contract jobs to the highest bidder anywhere in the world" He stopped and took another sip of water "and your last job in Sicily, a real work of art, you wiped out four major crime family heads setting back the mafia at least a decade and then you went into hiding as a lonely shopkeep in Sweetwater Texas... and we had a hell of a time finding you" he looked at Sawyer and asked "Am I scratching the surface?... Seriously, what happened?"

Sawyer looked over and took a breath "I just got tired, and after Sicily I knew eventually the law of averages would catch up so I retired at the top of my game." "How would you like to put an exclamation point on your career, end it the right way?" The masked figure started to sound like a salesman. Sawyer looked at him with a small smirk "I think Sicily spoke for itself, top that" The masked man stood up "I went through a lot of trouble to find you, I want to hire you for one last job it's big but the pay off will be phenomenal" Sawyer began to show interest he raised an eyebrow. The masked man continued "and after it's all said and done you will never have to be the hunter again guaranteed" Sawyer went over the whole offer in his head "after it's over I'm done right?" "Right, that's it" The masked man, having made his pitch, sat down and waited for a reply. Moments passed until finally Sawyer replied ' I'll need some time to think about it, alright?' The masked man got up and walked off into the darkness "you have one week I'll meet you at Ish's Deli forty-third street New York city two o'clock sharp I'll be sitting at a table outside number seven, see you then" and he was gone "Sawyer laid his head back "now what?" All of a sudden he heard a hissing noise and then a light green haze floated across the light which was shining down on him "oh not that gas again…" and with that Sawyer passed out.

The sun slowly started to rise in the sky and with it the promise of a new day and through the curtains of Sawyer's apartment a sliver of light made its way across the floor. Within minutes the sliver of light was shining across the desk where Sawyer lay, motionless. Still in the chair his upper body strewed across the desk, his head sideways, hands laying on both sides and eye's shut. One eye opened, and strained to see if the room was clear then Sawyer slowly lifted his head and looked down before him was… a pizza box. Sawyer looked at the box with bewilderment the laptop that had gassed him was gone and so was the reality of what had transpired hours ago with that Sawyer got up out of the chair and looked at the windows in his apartment for any sign of forced entry but there was nothing to indicate that there was anyone in there last night. Sawyer made his way downstairs to the store. He opened the door slowly with a slight creak and peered into the store he didn't see anyone. He walked in and stopped. He sighed he had really found a place he liked and if what last night was in fact real he knew that this peacefulness he had discovered would soon and ultimately come to an end. Sawyer then noticed Clancy cleaning the windows outside and realized it was Sunday he just shook his head and went back upstairs and slept the rest of the day away.

The next day everything was going as usual at the store and Sawyer was feeling guilty as he watched his small but loyal staff working. He would have to go soon and he didn't want to leave them hanging, he signaled Clancy to come over to him. Clancy came over, stood at attention "yes sir" he said in a very military fashion this was attributed to the fact that he had served in the second world war and military protocol was all he knew and he took great pride in it. Sawyer looked at the rigid old man

7

in front of him "at ease" he replied. "Clancy can you call a meeting after we close I need to address the troops" he said with a small smile "yes sir consider it done" and with that the old soldier snapped around and went over to each member of the staff and told them about the meeting and in turn they looked at Sawyer to make sure Clancy wasn't just gathering them for nothing like the time he called a meeting so everyone would look for his dentures which were in his pocket. As soon as the store closed and the tills were counted everyone sat on a stool in front of the deli counter. Sawyer could see them all through the tiny hole in his office door. He took a deep breath; it was time to come clean. He came out of the office with his hands behind his back and paced back and forth twice, pulled a stool in front of them and sat. He cleared his voice and said "for the last seven years I've been living a lie". Everyone looked at each other with puzzled expressions. Sawyer continued "my name isn't Wyatt Brown my name is Sawyer Briggs, I've done a lot of things in my life some good some bad and I came here to escape that past, but the past somehow found me and I have to go for a while and I didn't want to leave all of you hanging" he sighed "I' am sorry I didn't mean to hurt anyone". Clancy stood up "permission to speak, sir?" Sawyer nodded "granted" Clancy walked over to Sawyer "do you mean to tell me that you've been lying to all of us for seven years?" Sawyer looked at Clancy and nodded slowly, Clancy looked behind him at everyone "I see... well myself and my comrades will have to give some thought to the situation and will be right back" He turned to Sawyer then to everyone once more and jerked his head towards the door and everyone got up and headed for the door and then outside in front of the store. Once outside, Delores and Katrina sat on the bench in front, while Bob and Clancy lit cigars. Sawyer could hear the muffled voice of Clancy and watched as he spoke with his hands behind his back pacing back and forth like general Patton and every so often he looked at Sawyer through the glass and squinted while Bob another veteran of world war two puffed on his cigar and added his two cents now and again, the ladies sat silently and usually just nodded. After nearly fifteen minutes his small staff came back inside and the distinct smell of Cuban cigars followed close behind. Everyone sat back on the stools in front of the counter all except for Clancy. Sawyer sat on his stool at the deli counter opposite the others, he felt like a man convicted. Clancy in his red Hawaiian shirt, blue jeans and black shoes walked into the middle between the two sides. Clancy always reminded Sawyer of Popeye; he was short stocky with faded tattoos on both forearms and a military style haircut and if you made him angry he could be meaner than a junkyard dog. "Now it is the opinion of me and my esteemed colleagues that in spite of your past you have always treated us with respect." He put his hands behind his back and started to pace back and forth and took on the demeanor of General Patton. He then walked over to Sawyer "we thank you and are behind you whatever the circumstances" then snapping to attention and giving Sawyer a salute he went over and took his seat. Sawyers stood up "thank you, all of you" he said with a gleam in his eyes and with that he went up to his apartment and everyone went home.

The next morning, when the store opened Sawyer went over to Katrina and asked her to book him a flight to Los Angeles with a connection to New York he needed a few hours in L.A, when Katrina asked him why? Sawyer responded, "I have to see someone important". So Katrina set right to work booking the tickets as Sawyer went around the small store talking to his staff at each department for a short time then walking back to Katrina to see if everything was set up. Katrina had his tickets set up via the Internet. Sawyer then walked over to Clancy and in military fashion asked Clancy if he had permission to speak to him, when Clancy granted permission Sawyer asked him "Clancy, can you provide transportation for me and my cargo to the airfield by eleven hundred hours today?" Clancy cracked a sly smile "sir yes sir" and saluted. Several hours later Sawyer and Clancy arrived at Avenger Field airport where Sawyer would take a connecting flight from Sweetwater to San Antonio to Los Angeles to New York it was the best Katrina could do but Sawyer had time even when he would arrive in New York he would have the comfort of a few days. Sawyer

9

looked at Clancy "make sure you keep the operation running smoothly and keep the troops safe" Clancy saluted and shook hands with Sawyer then left in his nineteen forty seven army jeep. Sawyer looked at the doors to the airport terminal and under his breath he muttered, "Here I go again" and entered the terminal building.

CHAPTER 3

BELOVED REUNION

Los Angeles International Airport

Sawyer stepped off the plane and walked to the check in counter and confirmed his connection to New York and since he was in transit he had no luggage to claim until he reached his final destination. So Sawyer went out the terminal doors and hailed a taxi. After a short drive the taxi pulled up to the Chapel of Pines Cemetery. Sawyer told the taxi driver to wait there after the driver refused. Sawyer pulled out a twenty-dollar bill and handed it to the driver. The driver then shut off the engine, pulled out a newspaper and started to read. Sawyer walked down a wide path intended for cars but since he didn't see any he walked right down the center of the path. The wind blew slowly shifting the leaves around as well as Sawyer's long black coat. He finally reached the spot he was looking for and sat down on a small bench in front of the gravestone. Sawyer looked at it for a moment and sighed it was his wife Gwen's grave. He looked at the picture on the head stone she looked so happy, he hung his head and closed his eyes as flashbacks of his brief time with her came flooding back, the first date, the wedding, the laughter, the tears and the funeral, he opened his eyes the pain of it all was too much to bear.

Sawyer put his hands over his face and wept. He then composed himself and started to speak "hi baby, sorry I haven't visited since the funeral… It's just been hard," he said as he wiped the tears from his eyes as more flowed slowly behind. He took a deep breath and continued "I'm up to my neck in it as you'd say but this will be the last time I swear, after you died my life had no meaning, no joy, it was empty and I vowed to kill every son of a bitch who tried to hurt anyone and I did… well maybe not everyone of them but as many as I could" Sawyer took a quick glance back to make sure his cab was still there then he looked back at the head stone in particular Gwen's picture. He kept talking "after a while I started to feel no remorse I had started down the path to being just another killer for hire and that's not who I' am so I quit and for seven years Gwenny I really lead a normal life… 'til now" He stood up and pulled a package of jelly beans out of his pocket and placed it by the headstone "I remembered you really liked these" he wiped a single tear running down his cheek "god, I miss you so much" he then leaned forward and kissed the picture then standing upright again he winked "see ya' soon baby" turned and walked away. Sawyer had a small smile on his face, through all the grief he was happy he felt at peace but that was not to last. As he started to approach the cab he noticed a big man leaning on the driver side window talking to the driver. Sawyer thought he was trying to take his cab and intervened "sorry buddy but this is my cab, just then the big man turned towards him and pointed the barrel of a gun directly at Sawyer's head. "You got a problem motherfucker," he said as his voice started to rise "I'll blow your fuckin' head off now gimme your wallet!" Sawyer looked at the big man who was wearing a nylon stocking over his head "ok, ok, just relax big fella I'm getting it" the assailant became jittery "hurry the fuck up!!" Sawyer produced the wallet and just as he was going to hand it over he dropped it, this made the big man very angry. He looked at Sawyer for a moment, Sawyer gave a small grin "butterfingers" and then he raised his gun, pointed it once again at Sawyer's head. Suddenly without warning Sawyer went on the defensive, with the speed of lighting he wrapped his left arm round the arm holding the gun and with his right he brought down the big man's head to meet his knee which he raised and firmly planted in his nose breaking it instantaneously. Sawyer next pulled his head up and shoved it through the passenger side window on the driver's side. The gun fell to the ground Sawyer picked it up and tossed it into a nearby trash can. The big man was now on his hands and knees on the ground bleeding from the front and back of his head. Sawyer kicked him in the stomach, opened the passenger door and placed his head between the door and the frame. Sawyer grabbed the door and pulled back with the intent to slam it and break his neck. He looked down at the bleeding mass "your not worth it" an air of disgust in his voice and with that he grabbed him by the collar and pulled him backwards he laid on the asphalt not knowing how lucky he was. Sawyer picked up his wallet and pulled out a ten-dollar bill "go clean yourself up and get a job" and let the bill fall onto the big man's chest then he got in his cab and told the driver at the airport "airport please" as if nothing had happened and settled back in his seat. The cab arrived at the airport, Sawyer got out and went to pay the driver who shook his hand and told Sawyer "no charge". Sawyer then entered the terminal building to catch his flight into the unknown.

NEW YORK CITY

CHAPTER 4
TWO SIDES... ONE COIN

"Excuse me sir... sir?" Sawyer awoke to find a female flight attendant trying to wake him up. He looked up at her "sorry I must have dozed off, are we in New York yet?" She smiled at him "aren't you precious" and she turned and started toward the front of the plane. Sawyer wondered about the comment and then realized he was the only person left on the plane they must have landed while he was asleep. He put his hand on his head as he prepared to get up "no more scotch... well at least for a while." A few hours later after checking into a hotel, a shower and a fairly lengthy nap Sawyer pulled out the phonebook from the night table drawer next to the bed and flipped through to the restaurant section. He scanned the page until he found what he was searching for "Ish's Deli" the address checked out forty-third street. Sawyer looked at his watch. It was nearly ten o'clock, it was getting late so he decided to take a shower and get a good night's rest because he knew tomorrow was going to be a long day but as the bathroom began to fill with the hot steam from the shower Sawyer noticed a message on the mirror. Could it be a code? Or some kind of signal? Sawyer looked closer as the message became clear "Welcome to New York" Sawyer smiled and shook his head "nice"

14

The next morning Sawyer awoke early he felt kind of like it was his first day of school, he was nervous then and he was nervous now. It had been seven years, seven long years since Sawyer had been in the position he was in now. He missed the quiet life he had back in Sweetwater running his general store, the friendly faces, the atmosphere where people treated strangers like friends not having to worry about being shot at, poisoned, beat-up or otherwise, a place where life was cherished not squandered and killing time was a lot more common than killing people. Sawyer got dressed in nothing fancy, a black t-shirt, blue jeans, black cowboy boots and his long black coat. He looked at himself in the mirror, cracked his knuckles and reached in his pocket for the last element of his ensemble black leather gloves that, along with the coat, had been with him since day one. Still looking in the mirror he took a deep breath and looked into his own eyes searching for Sawyer Briggs he knew seven years ago, he looked the same perhaps a little older the gray was starting to show on his bristly head and his two day growth. Sawyer wasn't really concerned with the outside; it was the inside that had him pondering if he still had ice-cold blood? Would everything be as natural as breathing again? Could he kill again? He looked for another moment in the mirror. He felt kind of naked, he was unarmed without a single weapon, excluding his fighting skills but he told himself it was just an interview, it wasn't a job he didn't need to be armed… he hoped. The morning flew by at a rapid fire pace as Sawyer walked the streets most of the morning taking in the sights and sounds of the city, he had done a few jobs here before mostly for small time mob guys not really skill testing but very profitable nonetheless.

1:45pm

Sawyer looked at his watch as he stood at the door of "Ish's Deli". He figured he was early so he'd go sit and have a coffee. He entered the deli and decided to ask the waiter, a slim tall kid where table seven was so he would know where to look when the time came around. He tapped the waiter on the shoulder "excuse me where is table seven?" The waiter looked at him with a confused look on his face. Most young people today have one but he was honestly confused "sir?, this is a deli we don't have numbered tables" Sawyer looked at the ground to hide his embarrassment not just from asking the question but realizing he had just been duped. The waiter then told him "but…" pausing for moment "a gentlemen came in here about a half an hour ago and told me that if some guy would ask me if there was a table seven to direct him to his table over there" and the waiter pointed to a table that was outside the deli to the side inside a white metal picket fence where there were several other tables. Sawyer made his way over to the table, and as he got closer the person at the table motioned for Sawyer to sit down which Sawyer did. "Couldn't find table seven huh?" said the man as he took the last bite of his sandwich. Sawyer just stared at him for a moment taking in every detail of his appearance he looked to be about Sawyer's age he had brown hair slicked back a white shirt black tie and the pants probably matched as well as the shoes he also had on a light beige trench coat Sawyer could see all of his in a matter of seconds, Interpol training taught him observation is the number one reaction and every detail is not to be overlooked, but stored away for future reference. "and you are?" The man across the small table said "embarrassed because I hadn't finished my lunch, you're early". Just then the waiter came and asked Sawyer if he wanted anything and Sawyer waved him off he then looked at the other guy and asked but he shook his head and asked for the bill. Sawyer then asked "why did you tell me you would be at table seven if there wasn't one?" The man looked at him for second and gave a small laugh "trust" he then sat back in his chair "you see I was checking if you had been here before because you could have had someone set up to take photos and check me out but you didn't and it shows trust also your early, not really early but I like that it shows character" he said as he wiped the corner of his mouth with a napkin. The waiter came back with the bill and the man paid the bill then looked at Sawyer "let's go somewhere where we can talk" They left the deli and the man hailed a cab. As the cab drove them through town Sawyer's mind was processing everything he saw, especially the description of the person sitting next to him. The taxi finally pulled up to its destination Central Park. They both got out of the taxi and the man paid the driver and he looked at Sawyer and said "let's take a walk" and as a gentle wind blew the multi colored leaves around the two walk until they came up to a picnic table.

They each sat down across from each other. The man extended his hand across the table "Ron Fuller". Sawyer shook hands with him "Sawyer Briggs but you already know that" they stopped shaking hands and sat back down. Ron then took an apologetic tone for the moment "sorry about the cloak and dagger shit a week ago but I had to make sure you were... you". "No problem" Sawyer said "but how did you find me and how in the name of Harry Houdini did you get in and out without even leaving any sign?" Ron smiled broadly "a good magician never reveals his secrets and that's all I have to say on the subject". Sawyer looked at him and gave a small nod "fair enough but now that you have me here please explain what the hell I'm doing here? And who in the hell are you? I don't even know you ". Ron gave a small smile "well like I said before my name is Ron Fuller and I'm a contractor". Sawyer looked confused "a contractor?" Ron continued "yeah" Ron said, lighting up a cigarette, "what's that?" Sawyer inquired. Ron continued after taking a drag off his cigarette "you see I have an employer and he wields a lot of power and he also has several businesses, the last thing he wants is competition he absolutely hates it. He always says "eliminate the competition, out of sight out of mind no problem". Sawyer looked at him for a moment "So who is this employer and what does he do?" Fuller took another deep drag off his cigarette and leaned forward, the smoke coming out both nostrils "first what he does is none of your business and second who he is... is none of your business also". Sawyer shrugged. Fuller crushed out his cigarette on the picnic table "well Sawyer are you in or out?" Sawyer sat back a little weighing his options then after a moment or two then shook Fuller's hand "I'm in". Fuller looked relieved. "So it's a standard shoot and sack, right?" Sawyer asked. Fuller scratched his head "it's a little more complicated than that, here's the deal three hits three million a hit and then you walk away". Sawyer said "complicated what do you mean complicated? Three hits, three million bucks, what's so damn complicated about that?" Fuller unwrapped a piece gum and placed it in his mouth and started to chew slowly "well you see remember when I said my employer hates competition well he wants you not only to hit the marks but destroy their operations out of sight out of mind kind of thing... you don't have a problem with that do you?" Sawyer was silent for a moment "so you mean to tell me he wants me to destroy the operations and take out the marks?" "Yep," Fuller said. "For a million a head I'll get the job done but then I walk away like you said right?" Fuller answered him confidently "that's right you will no longer be the hunter" Fuller then reached into his trench coat and pulled out a small envelope "here is your plane ticket first class of course". Then he reached in deeper "he are the keys to your vehicle and oh yeah" He reached into his trench coat's other pocket and pulled out an envelope "here don't open this until you reach your destination or open it before you land I don't care, it will explain what to do once you are there after you've used it destroy it... well that's about it unless you have any questions?" Sawyer had no questions but Fuller still had a nagging one "Sawyer... you state you were born in Montana but you have a slight English accent now why is that?" Sawyer gave a sheepish grin "a good magician never reveals his secrets" Fuller raised an eyebrow "touché" Sawyer then asked a question of his own "what did you do before this contracting stuff?" Fuller paused for a second "a lot more for a lot less". The two then stood up, shook hands and walked in opposite directions. Sawyer hailed a taxi and went back to his hotel to get ready, Fuller on the other hand still had his own agenda. He climbed into a taxi and left the park for a darker side of town. The taxi pulled up to dive and Fuller got out and told the driver to wait. Fuller walked forward looking at the sign, which was only partially lit up, read "The Pimp". He walked in, it was dimly lit with a layer of blue smoke so heavy it almost looked like fog. Fuller lit up a cigarette and walked towards a booth in the back corner and upon reaching it he sat down. On the opposite side of the table a quiet figure sat. Long black greasy hair ran down his shoulders he had a tanned face with five o'clock shadow and a six inch scar on his chin he was also wearing a black shirt, black leather jacket, black jeans and a pair black well wore in cowboy boots fuller could see them because the guy's feet were up on the other chair beside him. Fuller took a drag off his cigarette then blew the smoke up to add to the already thick layer hanging in the air he then talked to the individual who was sitting across from him in a dimly lit corner booth "it's on can I call on you?" The shadowy figure nodded, then folded his black-gloved hands and leaned forward into the light "when?" he asked Fuller. Fuller leaned forward "when I need you a day in advance anyway now can I depend on you?" The figure ran his fingers through his hair then with his index finger tapped the table in front of him. Fuller smiled broadly "I know where this is heading and you don't get a fuckin' dime until the jobs done" he then took an angry drag off his cigarette and blew it out the corner of his mouth "you got that?" The shadowy figure replied, "Ok, you want to play it that way" Fuller nodded as he crushed out his cigarette in an already overloaded ashtray. The man in the corner continued "alright I'll deliver the goods but after I better see the payoff or…" he leaned closer to Fuller "I'll take it out of your hide and I'll go after this employer of yours and take a chunk out of him too then I'll really get nasty you got that big shot?" Fuller nodded, then got up and headed to the door and left, the shadowy figure sat back in his chair, put his feet up and lit a cigar with a confident grin. Fuller got into his taxi and instructed the driver to take him to the airport. He flipped open his cell phone and dialed one on the speed dial. He waited for an answer and finally someone picked but said nothing. Fuller made a simple statement "everything is in place the ball is in play" he snapped the phone shut, sat back and relaxed while the taxi took him to the airport.

Toronto, Ontario, Canada

CHAPTER 5

KNOW THY MARK, KNOW THYSELF

The landing gear was lowered as Sawyer's plane was preparing to land. Sawyer looked out the window at the city below and thought to himself "here I go again". The plane finally landed in Toronto at Pearson International Airport. After clearing customs and claiming his luggage, a small black suitcase (Sawyer always traveled light) he headed for a small café where he ordered a small sandwich and a soft drink. Sawyer tried to negotiate his handbag, suitcase and supper such as it was to the table. After getting settled he pulled out the envelope that Fuller gave him, opened it and prepared to read it. The letter was casual and to the point it read:

Sawyer, if you're reading this then you have arrived at
your final destination so read this carefully and after
destroy it.
Take the shuttle to terminal three, once there walk
across to the parking garage and take the elevator
To the top floor and proceed to the parking lot
Press your keychain the alarm will deactivate and the

The Silencer

the vehicle will reveal itself, go over and pop the trunk.
Inside is a leather briefcase a bit bigger than your
average, take it up to your room after check in and
examine the inside there.
You've been checked in already so just go in and confirm
your reservation.
The briefcase has an envelope in it that will explain the rest.

... Fuller

Sawyer did what the paper asked and within twenty minutes, briefcase in hand he entered his room in an incredible suite he felt like the C E O of some major corporation or a really exceptional athlete of some kind. After the bellhop had shut the door Sawyer went over and locked it. He picked up the case and placed it on the desk and took a seat at it. Sawyer sat back for a moment and took a sip from a bottle of water he bought in the lobby and contemplated or tried to contemplate why all the luxury, although he didn't mind it was a bit overwhelming not what he was used to at all but he really liked the car a midnight black two door high end sedan.

Sawyer unlatched the clasps and opened the briefcase and the first item he saw was another envelope he opened it and started to read the paper inside.

This is a brief guide to the content of this briefcase.
Read Carefully and Destroy!
In the upper part of the case you will find a credit card,
Gold class with a one million dollar limit, be gentle.
In the lower you will find a pair of 10x42 binoculars
They should come in handy but the most important item in
case is a dossier, which contains vital information about
all three marks. now lift the lower part up underneath
You will find two unmarked pistols with silencers and
Three clips for each (providing you need them).

When you have finished and you are ready to leave to
your next destination just place the pistols and clips in the
trunk under the cover my employer has clean- up guys
they will handle the rest.
Remember after this job you have to arrange your own
Vehicle as well as plane tickets, this one was
For free.   Good Hunting. Fuller.

p.s a gentleman will be coming to your room shortly to
deliver a garment bag containing two Armani suits
(black) two dress shirts (black and white), two silk
ties (black and red) silk socks and one pair of
shoes.
This is a small token from my employer. Enjoy.

Just then a knock at the door came and when Sawyer answered it sure
enough it was a man with a garment bag he walked in and hung it from
the closet. Sawyer tipped him and he left. Sawyer smiled slightly the suits
the first-class flight the incredible room it was still a little hard to swallow
but Sawyer didn't really mind he walked over to the window with a view
the Toronto skyline "where were these guys years ago" he said as he took
two steps back and flopped onto the bed "the perfect end to the day" and
with that Sawyer drifted off to sleep.

Sawyer awoke to a knock at the door; he grudgingly went over and
answered it. A fresh faced young man was standing there "good morning
Mr. Briggs". Sawyer rubbed his face trying to wake up "you'll have to
pardon me I'm not a morning person, what's all this about anyway?"
The young man answered him as he walked into the room "it's your
complimentary breakfast Mr. Briggs you'll receive one every morning
it comes standard with the suite where shall I have it set up?" Sawyer
stretched and smiled "just set it up over by the window please" The young
man signaled and another man pushed the cart in over to the window and

then stood over by the door, Sawyer pulled some money from his pants which were hung on a chair by the desk and a tip to each of the boys thanking them and asking them to close the door on the way out. Sawyer walked over to the cart and stared at the shiny platters he then pulled a chair which was by the window over to where the cart sat down, this was going to be good. After eating what could possibly have been the best breakfast he had ever had he poured himself a coffee and put the "do not disturb" sign on the knob and locked the door. He pulled the briefcase out from under the bed and placed it on the top of the bed and opened it up and took out the dossier then placed it on the desk he sat down on. Sawyer sipped his coffee as he opened it up and pulled out five pages, which were in a smaller folder earmarked with the words "mark # 1". He open it and saw a photo of a slim black male about six feet tall maybe forty-three years old with cornrow braided hair, a goatee and a suit which when against the very laws of fashion a light purple with a black shirt and pointy black shoes, Sawyer just shuttered and sipped his coffee again. He turned to the next page, which had a little information regarding who this individual was "Terrence Phillip Mackinnon owner of T MAC exotic auto sales incorporated purveyor of high-end automobiles, he looks more like a rap star to me." Sawyer turned to the next page, which put everything into perspective. He saw pictures of this individual shaking hands with some shady characters, some of which looked like militants and militia in different locations, alleys, parking lots, shopping malls, etc. Sawyer seemed a little more impressed with this colorful character. Sawyer looked over the last three pages; they were more of the same photos and such, the last page was a small map of how to get to the dealership. He wrote it down on a small pad which was lying on the desk. Sawyer closed the folder and put it back in the briefcase and left it open on the bed. He needed to prepare. An hour later after showering and shaving he put on his black leather gloves, new suit and all it beheld him then, before putting on the jacket slipped on his double shoulder holsters which he brought from home and slamming the clips into their respective weapons he slid them in smoothly and silently. Putting on the jacket Sawyer reached into the briefcase again and pulled the credit card out of the small slot in the top of the case. It shone in the light as he put it in his wallet. Sawyer, always being a stickler for being prepared, stood still for a moment and did a mental inventory list check then he snapped his fingers as if he'd had revelation. He picked up his carryon bag from the closet, placed it on the bed and unzipped it. He pulled out what appeared to be an ordinary deck of cards, which of course it wasn't. Sawyer may have left Interpol but he saved a few choice items and this was one of them. The seemingly ordinary deck card was actually a deck of business cards, aliases from his missions in the past or at least a portion of them. He flipped through them and found just the right one. He pulled it and the four other copies from the deck then closed the box and put it back in his carryon then back on the shelf in the closet. He once again stood still and did his mental inventory and after a moment concluded that he was prepared to his satisfaction. Now was his last and most difficult task. He took a deep breath and walked in front of the full-length mirror by the bathroom door, eyes closed and slowly raised his head and opened his eyes. Sawyer stood for a moment... awestruck. For the first time in seven years he didn't see Sawyer Briggs the Interpol operative or Wyatt Brown the shop keep he only saw The Silencer.

CHAPTER 6

BACK TO BUSINESS

"Rome wasn't built in a day" a quote that had been used in every walk of life, from professional sports to politics and this quote had never been more prevalent than in the work ethic of Sawyer Briggs. Sawyer was cool headed and since cooler heads almost always prevail so did he in his endeavors, it was never speed, it was the quality with which the job was or the mark was executed rushing wasn't his style. He slid behind the wheel of his car, turned the key and listened to the engine hum "sweet" then shifting it into reverse he backed up and then drove forward towards the ramp down to the exit. In a few minutes he was clear of the airport and accelerating down the road towards downtown Toronto. As he was driving he programmed the GPS system to guide him to the location of his mark. Sawyer entered the downtown core. He was amazed at all the hustle and bustle of people and automobiles moving in every direction. It was like one giant organism working and moving in one perpetual movement to accomplish one goal… astonishing. Sawyer looked at the GPS display and noticed that the location he sought was out of the main core; it was more on the outskirts of town. As Sawyer got closer he now knew why the display showed the location further out because the area he was entering was still in the developmental stages with

25

less traffic and even fewer buildings. Then rising out of the horizon there it was. Sawyer wasn't sure what to make of the structure which loomed closer as he drove. It did remind him of a scene from one of his favorite movies… Star Wars when Obi-wan Kenobi saw the death star from a distance and stated "that's no moon" that's what this moment felt like. He passed the structure and turned right on to the opposite side of the road where another construction site looked like a strip mall of some sort he pulled his car in. Sawyer got out of his car, shut the door then leaned up against it. "And Mohammad came to the mountain" he said as he lit a cigarette. The mountain he was referring to was the car dealership, if one could call it that. The building itself looked more like a palace than a dealership. A dealership, at least the ones Sawyer had come to know, were crowded with pushy people in nice suits with more bullshit than brains but this had style, class, it was organized… too organized Sawyer thought. The building was overwhelming with a front parking lot and a circular driveway and a fountain in the middle. The bottom floor had all glass exteriors showing off the vehicles inside very high-end vehicles. The second floor was the same as the first, all glass very revealing. Sawyer took a drag off his cigarette and blew the smoke skyward as he observed the next two floors. An eyebrow raised as Sawyer found it very odd that the next two floors had very small windows and solid walls but even more odd then that was the fact that there were two armed guards patrolling the top of the building which also had a helicopter on it. Sawyer dropped his cigarette to the ground and crushed it "what kind of car dealer needs guards and a helicopter? Tell me that" he was talking to the building, which across the front had a giant picture of his mark bearing a huge smile and the quote "an exceptional, extraordinary experience that's what I'm talking about". Sawyer with one last look, got in his car and headed across the road into the massive parking lot. The parking lot itself could have qualified as a car lot in itself; he viewed the parking lot as he exited his car. It was a virtual who's who of very exotic and very expensive cars: Bentley, Jaguar, and Mercedes. They were all here "so much money, so little brains"

Sawyer thought as he walked to the main entrance. Walking into the building he immediately noticed it catered to the well off the climate was perfectly controlled the air was clean without a hint of any foreign odor just "that new car smell" and the stench of money ego and greed all this and ol' blue eyes crooning in the background as only he could Sawyer gave the showroom the quick once over the concentrated on a bright orange McClaren so that he wouldn't appear to be gawking. Looking at the interior of the car he noticed the reflection of a man behind him and Sawyer slowly turned around. "Yes," Sawyer said with a smile. He noticed the man was wearing a red coat and holding a platter with orange colored beverages in long crystal glasses. "Sir, would you care for champagne and orange juice". Sawyer pondered for a moment and replied, "What kind of person drinks champagne and orange juice in a car dealership?" The man holding the platter looked a bit confused for a moment "the kind of person that's thirsty I suppose". Sawyer looked at him and shrugged his shoulders and sighed as he removed a glass from the platter "oh well when in Rome" he turned back towards the car as he sipped his drink. A few minutes had passed as Sawyer walked around the showroom observing the automobiles and drinking the last of his tasty beverage. He looked around the room for the man with the platter the drink was so refreshing he wanted a refill just then as he looked around he saw something he dreaded anywhere he had traveled in his life... a car salesman.

The salesman approached and Sawyer took in details as he usually did. "Admiring our wide selection are you?" Sawyer nodded "yes you have quite a selection indeed" A broad smile came across the face of the salesman. Sawyer continued "and if someone wished to purchase more than one of these vehicles who would they make their inquiry to?" The salesman looked a bit puzzled and scratched his head. While he was contemplating the question Sawyer looked the representative over. He was of average height, slightly balding about forty-five with a nice tan suit, white shirt, tan tie and shiny black shoes but the one feature that stood out to Sawyer was the shiny tag under his nametag which stated boldly "top sales representative 1997-2007" He finally answered Sawyer his voice a little shaky "how many vehicles are we talking about sir?" Sawyer reached in his coat and showed the list. Then he looked at the nametag "about this many Thomas"and held up three fingers "I like variety" The salesman stared and after composing himself "you can talk to me I would be more than gracious to help" Sawyer sighed "I kind of wanted to talk to the owner you know the that's what I'm talking about guy?" The salesman paused for a moment then putting his finger beside the sales rep tag he said "I think I have more than adequate expertise to handle this little endeavor "and with that he extended his hand to Sawyer. Sawyer put the list back into his jacket and shook the salesman's hand. The salesman was relieved that his little spiel had worked and shook Sawyer's hand but the smile soon disappeared when the handshake was overshadowed by an amazing amount of pressure. Sawyer looked into his eyes as he continued to put the pressure on his grip with a calm, cool demeanor "I really would like to talk to your boss… please" The salesman in an obvious amount of pain slowly nodded his head as a bead of sweat rolled down the center of his face he started to stutter as he spoke "I'll see if he's in, I mean I'll see if he's busy just let go of my fucking hand please and I'll see what I can do"he said with as much elequince as he could muster. Sawyer loosened his grip. The salesman started to shake his hand to get some circulation going as he walked across the showroom to the other side and around the corner out of sight Sawyer just continued to look at the cars so as not to draw attention to himself. Ten minutes had passed as Sawyer stood beside a Porsche 911 Turbo, the beautiful slick black finish did not deter his stare, which was locked on the corner where the salesman had gone. Sawyer started to wonder if he had blown the whole deal when suddenly the salesman emerged from around the corner with a large figure following close behind. Sawyer watched as they advanced towards him trying to come with a plan. As they got closer Sawyer noticed the man behind the salesman was much larger then he anticipated he was black wearing a white shirt with a black tie and the rest of the suit was black. The large man walked up to Sawyer and smiled then

The Silencer

in a smooth tone of voice spoke "my name is Griffin" and he shook Sawyer's hand and continued "You showed a rather large list of automobiles to one of my sales representatives and requested to speak with the owner of this business establishment. Is this correct?" Sawyer nodded "more or less" Griffin looked at Sawyer for a moment "well then let's go see the boss". Sawyer nodded his head approvingly "don't you even want to see the list?" Griffin looked back at him because he already started back to the far corner of the building "no need, you wouldn't have been so insistent to meet him if you had nothing to offer, now follow me please". Sawyer followed behind the large man his back was big enough to watch a movie on… at a drive-in. When they got around the corner Sawyer noticed an elevator. The large man pressed the button and he and Sawyer entered. The doors closed and the man removed a card and swiped it across the panel with the buttons. Sawyer looked at him "kind of a V.I.P thing huh?" The big man looked at him and replied "something like that". Sawyer looked up above the door they were coming up on the third floor. "Ding" the elevator came to a halt. The door opened and the big man motioned for him to exit the elevator. When Sawyer exited he was impressed with what he saw. A big open area with two giant oak doors at the end and a small desk with numerous filing cabinets behind it off to the left. The two made their way over to the desk. The secretary looked up. "Good morning Kate" said the big man "this fine gentleman here would like to talk to Mr. Mackinnon, he has a business proposition could you make it happen?" The secretary looked at him for a moment then looked into a small book on her desk "well… I could squeeze him in right now, let me check" she opened the doors behind her a crack and looked in, then closed the doors and turned towards them "he can go in now but be extremely quiet when you enter and take a seat near the door." Sawyer slowly walked towards the doors and before opening them looked at the secretary one more time, she in turn looked at him and put a finger to her lips "remember shhhh!" Sawyer opened the doors silently and entered then closed them with equal silence and took his chair by the door. Sawyer looked around it was more a playroom then an office.

29

It did have a desk and quite a big one but that notwithstanding the room was filled with many amusements: a giant pool table, a card table, and a foosball table. The one side of the room was lined with nineteen eighties style video game cabinets, everything from Pacman to Donkey Kong and several others ten from what Sawyer could count. The other wall had a large screen plasma television surrounded by couches, recliners etc. Sawyer then looked to the far side of the office where he saw a white canvas screen hanging down and on the screen it bore the image of the eighteenth tee at Augusta and upon listening to the commentary which rang through the room it was the masters. In front of the screen was his mark Terrence Phillip Mackinnon clad in throwback golfing attire from the nineteen twenties. He looked over at Sawyer and nodded, Sawyer nodded back then his concentration returned slowly to the little white dimpled ball resting on a small patch of fake grass. He drew back the club slightly and tapped his ball hard enough for it to tap the screen. On the screen the ball rolled slowly on the green until the clunk of the ball hit the bottom of the cup in the hole. The commentators went wild over the putt. People on the screen applauded, as did Sawyer. T- Mac looked back at Sawyer and gave a small grin "thank- you" he then turned toward the screen and reached for a remote which he had on a small table next to him. He pointed to the remote and in an instant Augusta was gone. T-Mac walked over and sat behind the large and expensive looking desk "so they tell me downstairs you have a pretty big order to fill". Sawyer nodded "yes "and he pulled the list from the inside pocket of his jacket and slid it across the desk. T-Mac picked up the piece of paper, sat back and stared at it for a few minutes. Then looking at Sawyer "is this for real?" he stated, "Do you really expect me to believe what is written on this paper because I hate being played for a fool!" Sawyer immediately sat up "yes it is a real list, I'm not playing games." He knew the ball was in his court so Sawyer gave a big smile "but… if you can't handle an order that size I'll have to find someone who can." T-Mac got up from his desk and walked over to a bar in the corner of the office. He pulled out a bottle of scotch from a cabinet and pulled out two small glasses then returned to his desk placing the bottle and two glasses in the middle. He then proceeded to pour the glasses half full of scotch and slid one across the desk to Sawyer and then T-Mac sat forward and pulled out a eighty-eight magnum the kind Clint Eastwood used in "Dirty Harry" and pulled the trigger a small click and a flame came out of the end which T-Mac used to light a cigar which he pulled from his shirt pocket. Sawyer was impressed "that's pretty cool" said Sawyer. T-Mac smiled and blew a large puff of smoke in the air. "Thank-you. I have a real one in my desk just like it and to answer your question yes I can handle an order that size when you need it? Sawyer opened his cell phone and acted like he was checking his date book when in reality he knew what was going on." In one week "Sawyer stated with a grin. T-Mac stared a Sawyer for a moment then laughed, "a week, man I can have that order in a couple of days". Sawyer sipped his and nodded his head "that's fast, how do you do it? Do you have a warehouse full of cars or something?". The smile that was once prevalent on T-Mac's face was now disappearing as he took the last swallow of scotch and put his glass down slowly and took a much more serious tone. "What concern is it of yours? I mean I get the goods, what do you care where or how I get it?". Sawyer looked at the slightly pissed off T-Mac "I'm sorry if I have offended you, I'm just so impressed with your speed, other places I've dealt with just talk but you're… a man of action I like that". T-Mac's smile returned as his already swollen ego had grown another size "it's cool man I can't say as I blame you for being impressed I'm good at what I do, another scotch?" Sawyer looked at his watch as if he were in a rush "no I'll take a rain check but it was so great to meet you as well keep in touch" and Sawyer stood up as did T-Mac and they shook hands "indeed we will" and having said that Sawyer left the room, the first move was made. As Sawyer got into his car he pondered how he was going to find out where this warehouse was; he knew there had to be one because why would his mark get so defensive when he inquired. Sawyer knew there was only one option to finding out what he needed to know about an old-fashioned stakeout.

CHAPTER 7

RECON AND RESEARCH

Sawyer drove to a fast-food restaurant and bought food and drinks, enough to sustain him for a long while, then he drove back to the location of his endeavor and parked across the road amidst raw building materials for another project yet to be underway. He made sure he was parked so that he was hidden but his line of sight would be impeccable. He eased the seat back, opened the windows and dug in. It was going to be a long wait. Hours had gone by but Sawyer's vigil remained unwavering. He had eaten all his food, smoked a few cigarettes, remembered where he put the key for the storage locker in the store in Sweetwater. He even peed in a water bottle so as not to lose a minute of time, but all the waiting was about to pay off. It was ten o'clock when Sawyer checked his watch, he was about to light another cigarette he saw a nineteen fifty-seven Chevy pulling up to the road from the dealership he grabbed his binoculars and took a closer look the front license plate read "T-Mac" this was what he had been waiting for or was it? Sawyer started his car when he noticed something was wrong, the plate might have said "T-Mac" but the window on the driver's side was open enough for him to see… Thomas the salesman Sawyer had encountered in the dealership. Sawyer figured to himself that his mark was worried about his safety, after all money can spawn strange

32

bedfellows. He lit the cigarette still dangling in his mouth; he now had a dilemma to follow or not to follow. This whole situation reminded him of the books he liked to read as a kid, the ones that gave him the choice of following the brave knight into the cave after the dragon or waiting until the dragon came out so he could be slain... Sawyer hated those books he always chose wrong, he watched the car pull into the street, he would wait for his dragon. An hour later a black hummer was pulling out of the dealership parking lot, it was him it had to be. Sawyer started his car and waited for the hummer to be about five car lengths ahead of him then he slowly pulled out into the street "now that's what I'm talking about." Sawyer kept his distance during this somewhat slow pursuit, this was his chance and if he blew it he might as well go home. Twenty minutes later the scenery had changed dramatically, it had gone from a bright shiny outlook for the future to a look back into the past. The buildings that surrounded Sawyer while he was following the mark were old and worn and shrouded in values from the past. Then Sawyer saw ahead of him the hummer signaling to turn left Sawyer immediately pulled to the side of the street just behind a dumpster and shut the engine off. He grabbed his binoculars and got out. He peered around the dumpster but he couldn't see very much so he decided to try a different vantage point. Walking slowly Sawyer went into an alley directly across from where the Hummer made the left turn. The binoculars gave a clear view of goings on across the street. The Hummer had disappeared into a shipping yard of a very big warehouse. Sawyer looked at the giant structure. The whole setup looked less like a shipping yard than a military compound. Bright lights everywhere, men with mean looking dogs patrolling the grounds and all wrapped in a ten-foot chain link fence. "It's secured like Fort Knox but why? He definitely has something to hide but how the hell do I get in?" Sawyer pondered quietly scratching his head. Standing in an alley wouldn't get it done, he needed to know the entire layout, there was always tomorrow. It was late and Sawyer was tired so he went back to his car with new questions in his head, he knew the where but the how and why were still a mystery but they would have to wait until morning. It had been a long day. The next day Sawyer decided he needed a better look at the warehouse so he went for some air support. Posing as a real-estate agent he hired a helicopter to see the buildings in the vicinity of last night's reconnaissance mission. It was on the waterfront. Then he finally saw it, he asked the pilot to circle once or twice so he could get a good look at it and take some photos then he inquired "what's the building down there?" The pilot looked for a moment then replied, "that's the old Thorn fisheries building. It was built in nineteen-thirty eight and ran for sixty years, it used to be just another rental on the waterfront, it's been rented out a few times… but it was purchased about five years ago, I think that they leased it out as well." The pilot then asked Sawyer "You seen enough?" Sawyer nodded and they returned to the helicopter hanger. That night Sawyer sat in front of his laptop and reviewed his pictures, "that place is like a bloody fortress, a guard on the roof, on the ground a big fence, dogs it 's impenetrable" Sawyer walked in the bathroom and started his shower running so it was hot when he got in but the thought of the warehouse and how to enter it consumed him. He stepped in the shower. The water was almost scalding but after a minute or so it felt good it relaxed him, he needed this. He hung his head down as the water ran down his body and down the drain he watched the water go down and suddenly a smile came over his face "the drain that's it. It's a fishery that must have drains". After this thought had come to pass Sawyer felt a lot more positive and knew his next step would need the blueprints of the building. Tomorrow he would obtain them. He would take a tour down to city hall and check building records, the trail was a little warmer. The next day Sawyer went to city hall to check for schematics for Thorn Fisheries. When Sawyer arrived he walked over to a giant black info board on the wall next to the entrance. It had the listings for the entire building floor for floor and he quickly sighted the floor he needed and got on the elevator. "Ding Ding" the elevator arrived on the floor on which records were kept, it wasn't very lively. He walked over to the main counter and behind it was a young girl with about as much enthusiasm as a wet blanket. She was wearing baggy black pants, a baggy white shirt and an oversized black tie hanging loosely from her neck. She saw Sawyer and walked over. She looked pale with dark black mascara which gave her a rather gothic look and a small stud in her nose and Sawyer shuddered when he thought of where else she may be pierced. "May I help you sir?" she said as she chewed her gum. Sawyer was never good with the younger generation; he always saw them as weird but he had to be a professional "yes you may, I'm looking for the schematics to Thorn Fisheries or the building that used to house it... whatever you got" The girl stared at him for a moment "do you have authorization? I just can't hand out that kind of stuff without knowing who you work for?" Sawyer paused for a minute; this girl wasn't as slow as he first anticipated "I don't really work for anyone per say but I really would like the information" as he spied her name tag "Shay". She repeated her statement in a slightly higher tone. Sawyer knew he would have to switch tactics so he reached in his right front pocket and took out a small wad of money, mostly hundreds and twenty dollar bills, the girl's eyes lit up immediately. Sawyer looked down at the small wad and opened it up flipping the bills precariously in front of her then looking up at her with a devilish grin. The girl was looking at the money almost in a trance "now" Sawyer said while maintaining the devilish grin "it would really make my day a little more worthwhile if I could get the item I need and it would make yours a little more profitable" he said with a raised eyebrow as he slid a hundred dollar bill across the counter. The girl placed her hand over the bill and slid it off the counter out of sight "Wait here I think I know where it is' ' she turned to a computer and quickly tapped a few keys she then turned back to Sawyer "well, I have good and bad news". Sawyer nodded his head "ok lay it on me". Shay took a breath "the bad news is the original prints are locked in the archives but the good news is that I might be able to access the plans and download them on a flash drive for you." she said, rolling her eyes down to the wad of money still in Sawyer's hand. A befuddled look came across Sawyer's face "I just gave you a hundred dollars what am I? A bank?"

Shay looked at him the same way he looked at her from the outset with a devilish grin. He looked at her for another moment and signed "touché" he pulled another hundred from the wad. She smiled and waited for him to lay it on the counter but he held the hundred tight between his index and middle finger and taunted her with it "not until I get what I want, love". She looked at him with a bit of a sneer "tease" she turned back to the computer screen and tapped the keys then she loaded in a disk and with a press of the key downloaded the information. A few minutes passed and the disk ejected Shay, put it in a disk case and waved it in front of Sawyer. He cocked his head to one side and ran his hand over his head. Shay seemed confident, even cocky "you want this? Give me that" as she pointed to the money. Sawyer shook his head "ok look I don't have all day, I'll hand you the cash and you hand me the flash thingy we will exchange them at the same time ok?" Shay nodded little did she know she was about to be taken to school "Interpol 101." Sawyer and Shay locked eyes "ok on three" Shay looked tense. "One.Two.Three" Sawyer grabbed the flash drive and flipped back the hundred Shay grabbed in the air. Sawyer stuck the cash back in his pocket and the flash drive in his coat needless to say Shay was pissed "you bastard, you cheat, give me my money I've earned it!" Sawyer looked at her with his cool demeanor "your money? I gave you two hundred and you want more? Yeah right you earned jackshit you're just lucky you're a woman" Shay looked at him with contempt "and why am I so lucky?" Sawyer started walking to the elevator then he pressed the button and the doors opened he turned as he entered "your lucky because if you were a guy I would have tossed your ass out the window for asking for more money you greedy bitch, have a nice day" he said with a smile and the doors shut.

After leaving the building with the information he had been looking for Sawyer headed for the famed "Kensington Market". When he arrived he parked his car at a pay and park and decided to hang out in the market for a while and find a nice quiet place to look over the information he had acquired. After wandering the market watching the activity of vendors selling their wares Sawyer spied a café with a small patio and three tables, a nice quiet place. After finishing a piece of pie and a coffee he got down to work first ordering another cup of coffee then opening his laptop which he carried in a leather bag. The briefcase would have been way too conspicuous. Sawyer inserted the flash drive hoping in the back of his mind that he hadn't been duped by the girl in the office. Sawyer's fears were unwarranted once the information started to present itself. The sun started to shift as Sawyer went through the schematics of the building. It was a lot to take in. After three cups of coffee he finally came to what he was looking for in the plumbing layout. He watched intently at the images on the screen and he noticed that all the drain pipes lead to one major drain that ran under the plant and out underneath the pier but looking closer if that were true then it would be close to the water. Sawyer sat puzzled for a moment then moved on with the schematics and noticed something, that the plant was updated two years previous to it's closing and not only was the drain relocated it was shut down due to an updated drainage system but that wasn't what caught his attention it was the fact that the whole plant had gotten gas pipes fitted, they were probably trying to up their game. Sawyer sat back and drank the last of his coffee and pondered the information. He spoke to himself quietly and unnoticed, "If the drain was moved and shut down where would they put it?" Sawyer looked through the remainder of the schematics but their was no information, so he used the information he had and discovered that if they moved the old drain it would have to be attached so it was just a matter of finding the lowest point were the drain used to be and following the pipe he nodded and shut the laptop placed it in his bag and left. He drove out to where the warehouse was located and keeping his distance he looked with his binoculars at where the drain would go, then it dawned on him there was a launching ramp down the road and to the right he might get a better vantage point from there so he drove down the street and parked. He walked to the ramp and looked to his left, there was an under belly to the whole thing. He looked at it for a moment; he of course would need a better look and a suit and dress shoes wouldn't cut it if he wanted to seem part of the local scenery. Sawyer walked back to his car and drove away. He found his best ideas came to him while driving, today was no exception. As Sawyer was stopped at a red light he noticed a lot of the store window displays with Halloween themes after all it was October. The lights changed and Sawyer drove on until he had a revelation "Halloween of course" Sawyer knew what he needed… a disguise. He drove until he saw a costume shop and parked. After twenty minutes and advice from the make-up experts Sawyer left the store and then drove to a thrift store and bought some old clothes. As he drove back to the hotel he smiled as the plan was starting to take shape. Hours later after a couple of drinks and a nap Sawyer was ready to move forward with his plan. He laid out an old suit on the bed and the make-up which consisted of a fake beard, hair and an old fedora. Sawyer wasn't really a fan of makeup mainly because he had never been seen by his marks but nonetheless this particular situation called for it. Sawyer put the makeup in a small bag and then put on the suit. He then put on his black overcoat and dress shoes he had the others by his bed but he had to make sure people wouldn't see anything out of the ordinary. He got in the elevator and descended to the main floor. He looked around as he walked to the door but everything seemed business as usual. Little did the staff know that underneath the long black cashmere coat was a suit that was probably stylish when President Nixon was in the Whitehouse. Sawyer went outside and got in his car and left for the destination. As he drove he applied the adhesive to his face, he needed to think on his feet. As he approached the launching point he parked his car between two boats that were dry-docked so as to not attract attention. He opened the bag and put on the beard, wig, hat and lastly the old pair of sneakers. As he took off his coat he saw a bottle of scotch in the backseat he left it in the brown paper bag for effect. Sawyer walked with a stagger over to the launch and then under the pier so far, so good. He looked around as he walked, the light from the street illuminated the most disgusting array of filth he had witnessed in recent memory. Soiled diapers, syringes, liquor bottles and a bra or two. He concentrated on walking to the drain and kept his eyes forward. Sawyer finally reached the drain, it was bigger than it looked from a distance, the letters overtop were barely legible and the pipe itself was loaded with garbage. Sawyer looked at the pile and sighed then pulled out his black leather gloves "it's a dirty job but someone's gotta… oh who am I kidding this sucks". Sawyer started to move the garbage, the stench was overpowering. He threw the bags aside, some held together some fell apart. Sawyer was making good progress. As he bent down to pick up another bag he felt the barrel of a gun against his forehead. Sawyer slowly stood up to see a scruffy man dressed in old clothes pointing a handgun directly at him. The scruffy man asked in a rough voice "what do you want?" Sawyer just looked at him. The man cocked back the hammer of the pistol "I said what do you w…?" Sawyer's bristly adversary then started into a medley of coughing that made Sawyer think that he would be dead in a minute. While coughing the man raised one finger to signal Sawyer it would be another moment before he would finish and was playing on Sawyer honor not to try anything. Sawyer just watched sympathetically and knew he was in no real danger. When the scruffy man finished coughing he pointed the gun at Sawyer. Sawyer looked at the man "what's your bug anyway?" he said. "This here's my apartment," he said, pointing to the large pipe he was standing in. With that he pointed the gun skyward and pulled the trigger, the gun fell apart and all that was left was the handle and trigger in his hand. Sawyer folded his arms and shook his head. The gruff old man looked at Sawyer "please don't kill me, this old pipe is all I have, I got no place to go, I don't want to leave" he said with sadness in his voice. Sawyer, still with arms folded, gave a small smile "I' m not gonna kill you pop, but I would like to look inside that pipe… with your permission of course.The old man rubbed his chin "I don't know, what's in it for me?" Sawyer tried to think of something, if he pulled out his cash it would expose him, after all what kind of homeless guy carries hundreds in his pocket, Sawyer would have to find something else. Sawyer then noticed the old man had his eyes fixated on the paper bag containing his bottle of scotch. Sawyer pulled the bottle out of his pocket "how bout…" before he could even get the words out the gruff old man said "sold" and snatched the bottle out of his hand with the speed of a ninja. "You mean that's it?" Sawyer said in amazement. "Yep" the old man said as he began to unscrew the top of the bottle "it's all yours… it wasn't mine to begin with ya gullible asshole". The old man walked away, stopping only once to take a sip and turning to Sawyer, raising his bottle and nodding his head in thanks. "Yeah it's tough there" Sawyer said and stepped over the pile of garbage and started his walk in the drain. Sawyer looked back once and turned on his small halogen flashlight as he proceeded onward. For the first thirty to forty feet more broken bottles and other debris litter the ground but Sawyer saw something even more interesting and it was right over his very head. As he walked into the unknown he noticed on the drain walls and above him graffiti that spoke volumes. Slowly he walks looking at all the graffiti, which in his opinion represented the generations like clothing, and music never could. The drain had a contribution from each generation from the fifties right up to the late nineties. From unlegible at the opening to real works of art just above and beside him but soon it was gone and all that remained was the corroded, ribbed inside of the drain. Sawyer kept walking when off in the distance he saw that the pipe was closed off with a massive barred plate. When he arrived at that point he stopped and looked at his current situation and noticed that in the center was a gate with a chain and a lock. Sawyer looked down at the lock; it had seen better days and was covered with rust as was the chain. He decided not to touch anything, on his return it would be dealt with. Sawyer, still observing the drain lit up a cigar and stood as close as he could to the bars, he then blew a puff of smoke through the bars to see if there were any laser alarm systems but there were none to be found. Sawyer then looked at his watch and it was time to carry on. Walking backward from the barred barrier Sawyer shifted his foot side to side to wipe out any of his tracks, which may have been in the old sand and would be a give away but on the other side of this he could see if anyone was here. Sawyer walked down to the end of the drain and as he did the stench of garbage became more predominant. As he approached the end and stepped over the garbage bags he took a whole new stance on the homeless and oppressed, putting the shoe on the other foot changes one's perception quite emphatically. Sawyer slowly walked to his car and realized in a strange way he was a very lucky individual indeed as he removed the beard and hair. He opened the trunk and put the disguise in the bag and put on his long cashmere coat and headed for the hotel and a hot shower.

October 26 2007.

Sawyer awoke to the delightful sounds of the Old' Blue Eyes crooning a song that oddly enough described one of the qualities he would need to accomplish tonight's endeavor "Luck be a Lady Tonight". Sawyer always knew skill could only take you so far and the rest was blind, shot in the dark luck. As the hot water and suds ran down Sawyer's body he felt like a student before a big exam or a football player getting ready for the big game. He had butterflies and they were flapping at full speed. Sawyer was going to stay in his room all day and study the layout of the entire building because as his father once said" knowing is half the battle but not knowing leads to a quick defeat." Sawyer started up the small coffee maker in his room, looked through the small fridge and found two chocolate bars and a bag of peanuts this combined with coffee would be a well-balanced breakfast even if it was just a lot of caffeine and sugar it would keep him up and focused to much food always made Sawyer tired. He devoured everything and washed it down with a can of ginger ale, then he poured the coffee and started looking at the laptop screen. Aside from a one-hour catnap he studied the maps and went over every scenario all day until it was time to get ready, and by that time he knew the layout cold.

CHAPTER 8

THE SLOW RISE

9pm October 15

Sawyer clad in his black fatigues once again donned the long cashmere coat and left the room. As he drove his car through the illuminated Toronto streets he went over his plan again and again. Failure was not an option. He finally arrived once again a block from the launch ramp, he decided a block opposed to a block and a half in case the plan went sideways. As he walked down the ramp and under the pier he was tightly coiled ready for anything or anyone that got in his way. As he approached the drain he noticed a figure rising from behind the garbage. It was the homeless guy he had seen yesterday and in his hand the gun, this time it was wrapped in duct tape. Sawyer walked towards him with purpose. As the homeless man started to walk towards him he pointed the gun and yelled "hold it right there". Sawyer kept walking towards him at a deliberate pace. Then when he was close to his gun-toting adversary he stopped and said "sorry pop". The old man still pointing the taped up gun said "sorry for what?" Sawyer drew back his fist and punched him as hard as he could, knocking the man on his back cold "For that". After dragging the man back in the drain behind the garbage he pulled out a small roll of duct tape and taped the man's hands, feet and mouth. Sawyer knew that guy would be found just hopefully not anytime soon. He continued down the drain flashlight in hand, the anticipation slightly overpowering him. Sawyer finally reached the point he stopped at yesterday, but that was yesterday and today it was go time. He held the rusty old lock in his left hand and pulled out his lock pick set. As Sawyer held the lock he could feel it was old so before he actually used the pick and pulled on the lock it cracked apart with ease he then opened up the gate and it made a dry creaking sound. Sawyer then walked inside and shut the gate slowly behind him putting the rusty chains back in it's place and then he pulled from his pocket a shiny new padlock and locked the chains together to prevent an ambush or anyone wandering too far. He made sure the lock was on the inside as to not arouse curiosity... by anyone. Sawyer saw a ladder up ahead leading up to the main floor. Sawyer leaned against the side of the pipe and did a small weapons inventory and made sure he was ready. He then walked over to the ladder and looked up. It was dark. He hung his head and took a deep breath then ascended the ladder. When he reached the top he tried as quietly as he could to lift the cover then suddenly it began to move slowly he lifted and slid it not far he wanted to see what he was up against be it was hard to see only nightlights lit the massive building so the building was dimly lit, Sawyer couldn't see he needed a better vantage point. He lifted the lid completely and slid it over to the side and slid up. He noticed he was under some kind of truck above him hence the drive shaft but it was more than a truck it was a fuel truck he could tell by his reflection under the truck. Sawyer carefully slid the lid of the drain back on. Sawyer breathed slowly and silently as he tried to stay in the shadow of the truck, he heard footsteps coming his direction and judging from the sound they were made by combat boots. Closer and closer they came until they were right in front of him. Sawyer slowly looked around if anyone else was around; there was no one else in sight. Sawyer patiently waited for the precise moment to attack. The guard turned his back to the truck and Sawyer was now observing the back of his boots. He drew a breath and with the speed of a viper he grabbed the guard's ankles and pulled fast and hard, the guard never knew what hit him; infact Sawyer's offensive was so quick the guard had little time to stop himself from falling and hit his head against the concrete so hard he was instantly knocked out. Sawyer dragged him under quickly and taped his wrists, ankles and mouth just in case the guard came before his job was done. Sawyer waited a few minutes then stuck his head out again and looked around and listened, dead silence, Sawyer pondered "a big warehouse and one guard... bullshit". He slid around under the truck checking all vantage points but then he noticed a steel staircase about fifty feet from him and at the top an office and at the bottom an armed guard, this place was looking more like an army base then a warehouse. Sawyer needed a way to get in the office, his mark was probably in there but the guard at the bottom of the stairs was facing out he needed a distraction he needed a... nut? Sawyer reached behind the front rear wheel and found a wheel nut, it was only a half-inch nut but it would have to do. He threw the nut as far as he could and from his current position it would go too far but maybe far enough. The nut flew through the air and hit the bottom part of the railing right behind the guard and when the guard turned to look, Sawyer ran over as fast as he could and caught the guard from behind as he was just getting up from picking up the nut. Sawyer grabbed his head and turned it so fast it was like a whiplash effect and it broke the guard's neck in an instant. He quickly pulled the body under the steps in the shadows invisible to anyone. Sawyer slowly ascended the staircase and withdrew his gun from the holster and took the safety off. Sawyer had reached the door and he kicked it in and there was... no mark... nothing. Sawyer lowered his gun and sighed then suddenly from behind he heard a voice speak to him in a pronounced and familiar tone "may I help you sir?" and the next moment he felt a pain in his neck and saw white flash along with the carpet coming up fast to greet him.

Sawyer's eyes flicker as he starts to come to, he felt like he had been run over by a bus. "Headache?" Sawyer slowly raised his head and looked around to find the source of the voice, his search would be short. A large man with a very dark tan got up from a chair and walked over to Sawyer who was handcuffed and sitting in a leather office chair behind a big desk. As he approached Sawyer recognized him "hey Griffin long time no see". Griffin looked at Sawyer, smiled then laughed "Sawyer Briggs I had a bad feeling about you the moment I saw you, so do you like the warehouse?" he said with an air of sarcasm while maintaining his smile. Sawyer smiled, "I don't know, are you going to give me the tour?" Griffin's smile soon disappeared "no you've seen enough" he said. Sawyer is still smiling "awww too bad, so where's the big kahuna?" Griffin crouched down slightly so he could be a eye level with Sawyer his smile returning "I called him and he has another engagement but he will be here in the morning so I wouldn't worry my head about it cue ball because when he does show up tomorrow I have a feeling your gonna go for a nice refreshing swim the only problem will be you won't float on the count of your going to be so full of lead you'll probably just sink to the bottom." Sawyer looked at him "so will you due to the amount of all the bullshit you're full of Griff." Griffin just laughed and told the one man to stay in the room and he wanted the other one at the bottom of the stairs. Griffin started to walk towards the door when he turned back "good-night Sawyer see you in the morning" then he turned back towards the door. Sawyer quickly responded "goodnight you big prick you'll be dead in the morning, now come over and give me a kiss" Sawyer puckered him as Griffin turned and started walking back toward Sawyer. As he walked towards him he clenched his fist and punched Sawyer in the mouth so hard the chair he was sitting on rolled into the wall. Griffin then walked out the door and slammed it behind him. Fifteen minutes had passed since Griffin left the room. Sawyer sat quietly as his guard sat on the leather couch and watched a basketball game on the big screen television hanging on the wall. Sawyer looked around the room and the pictures that hung on the wall of T-Mac and various celebrities and dignitaries, he then studied the whole room. It looked almost like the room at the dealership, only not as big but still full and plush. He then turned his attention to the television, as long as it kept the guard busy it bought time to think of a plan. Sawyer realized he had until morning, but he wasn't going to wait that long because he wanted to deal with his mark one on one. The washroom was the perfect place to formulate a plan of some kind, just then Sawyer had a crazy thought but he needed access to the washroom to prove his theory. "Hey, guard, I have to use the washroom," Sawyer said. The guard reluctantly got off the couch and helped him off the chair and took him to the washroom door, opened it and shoved him in. The guard stood in the washroom door and folded his arms watching Sawyer. Sawyer looked back at the guard "do you think I can have some privacy?" The guard stared at him stone-faced and didn't answer. Sawyer smiled "look buddy I have to have a shit right now take off these cuffs please" The guard without changing his expression answered Sawyer "I have orders not to take off your cuffs for any reason." Sawyer raised an eyebrow "ok man if you want to wipe my ass be my guest" he said as he tried to unbutton his pants. The guard changed his mind "alright I'll shut the door" he said. Sawyer shook his head "not good enough" he raised his wrists "I need to lose the cuffs." The guard scratched his head and knew he shouldn't but under the circumstances it shouldn't be much of a problem. Sawyer could tell the guard was weighing his options and decided to add a little more pressure "c'mon make up your mind already!" The guard took a breath and unlocked the handcuffs "no tricks or you'll be getting wiped up with toilet paper... fool" pointing his weapon at his chest. Sawyer looked directly at the guard "no tricks, what the hell do you think? I'm part of the A-Team? I'm going to build a tank in there. It's a washroom, go watch your game and I'll knock when I'm done" Sawyer then proceeded to walk in and shut the door behind him, the guard returned to the couch to watch the game. Sawyer put the lid down on the toilet and sat for a moment to contemplate his next move. He looked around the washroom for something, but he wasn't sure what. Then it came to him, he stood up and walked to the door "well I'll be damned" he said as he looked through a small peephole in the door "this guy has some serious paranoia problems". Sawyer rubbed his head and thought to himself "if a guy is paranoid enough to have an employee drive a decoy vehicle out of the lot and have a peephole in the shithouse door then he is paranoid enough to…" and Sawyer walked to the toilet, slowly he took the lid off the tank and propped it against the wall, inside he saw a black box attached to the inside of the tank with suction cups. Sawyer reached in and detached the box and put it on the lid of the toilet. Sawyer opened the lid and found a small pistol with a silencer and two loaded clips. He took out the weapon and loaded it while finishing his sentence "keep a gun and the tank of the toilet". Sawyer put the extra clip in his pocket then put the lid back on the box he then returned it to the side of the tank and put the lid back into place. Looking through the peephole Sawyer knew he would have to be quick. The last thing he wanted was more guys coming into the equation, he had to be subtle. He then backed up a step from the door and shrugged his shoulders a few times and moved his head from side to side like a prize fighter listening to the sickening clicking coming from his neck. One more deep breath and he was ready "ok man, I'm done opening the door with my wet hands" he said as he took his position. Sawyer could hear the steps coming towards the door then it opened. As it was being opened his guard started making an off color comment, "how long does it take you white boys to take a s…" When the door was fully opened the guard never finished his sentence. The action was so fast he never knew what hit him. Sawyer stood there with the gun aimed directly at the guard and squeezed the trigger. The gun fired quietly but accurately at the guard. The bullet penetrated his head in a matter of seconds with a sick thud and the guard fell backwards on the floor. Sawyer without hesitation dragged the body into the washroom and shut the door, then he walked over to the office door and looked through the peephole on the door but all he could see was one guard at the bottom of the stairs. Sawyer walked over to the desk and retrieved his pistols, holstered them and sat down on the couch to gather his thoughts and access the situation. He knew Griffin must have more men in this warehouse but where were they? And if so how many of them would he have to contend with? Thoughts went through his mind but nothing he could use to his advantage so he sat back and looked at the television and maybe something would come to him. Suddenly Sawyer noticed in the upper right hand corner a picture, small but a picture nonetheless and it was sectioned. Immediately Sawyer checked the table in front of him for the remote. Once he found the remote he looked for the picture in picture command and then he reversed it and what he found made him breathe a bit easier. The image that revealed itself was an entire view of the warehouse divided into sections; this was the advantage Sawyer was looking for. As he studied the screen he noticed at least thirty men spread out over the span of the building, this could prove to be a bit of a challenge. Sawyer found himself looking for an exit rather than a way to destroy the building; he just wanted out, his plan had obviously gone sideways. Sawyer examined the screen further and noticed the best way out would be the back of the building through a man door next to a big steel garage type door. Sawyer then turned from the screen and pulled his guns out from his shoulder holsters one at a time and checked the clips then reupholstered them, he then tucked the walther in the front of his pants. Reaching down where he took down the guard he picked up the Uzi 9mm and checked the clip then slung it over his shoulder. Sawyer looked back at the screen if any changes had developed, none were apparent. He was about to walk towards the door when he spotted something on the wall that caught his attention. Sawyer walked up to the wall behind the desk and stared. Behind the desk in a frame was a cheque and above it in the same frame was a picture of T-Mac shaking hands with the Vice President of the United States Bob Bradley and behind them was a silver and black Mercedes. Sawyer looked at the top of the frame "06/21/15 my first sale" Sawyer pondered for a moment "Bradley was just a senator back then" he then turned his entire attention to the door, he would try to be quiet when he made his exit; no use to get all the bad guys to come out at once. He pulled the UZI forward, took a deep cleansing breath, then with the weapon clinched in his hand he squatted down and slowly turned the latch on the door. He would have to be silent, stealthily and above all… "hey look up there he's trying to escape!" invisible. Sawyer rolled his eyes "well so much for invisibility" he thought and in an instant he jumped up and straddled the one railing and began to slide down. The guard at the end of the stairs, now aware of what was going on, turned and pointed his weapon at Sawyer who was already sliding down towards the guard at a fast pace. The guard was about to pull the trigger when Sawyer pointed the weapon at him and fired. A hail of bullets saturated the guard's chest and he almost seemed to be swaying side to side. Sawyer slid down to the end and landed on the guard who was dead before he hit the floor. Upon that impact he somersaulted and ended up on one knee firing at on coming guards only to discover he was out of ammunition. He stood up and dropped his weapon. He was surrounded by five men and knew soon there would be more if he didn't act fast. There was an uneasy silence for a moment and then one guard lunged from behind and caught Sawyer in a bearhug. Sawyer faked struggling to escape to draw in the rest of the men who had already slung their weapons over their shoulders and were preparing to give Sawyer a major beating. The one guard in front went to throw a punch and Sawyer jumped up using the guard who was holding him as a base pushed both his legs into the chest of the guard in front catapulting him backwards onto the cement. Then Sawyer threw his head back and broke the nose of the guard holding him from behind, his grip immediately loosened as he reached for his nose, Sawyer then jumped in the air and delivered a flying roundhouse kick to the jaw of the guard with the broken nose and he fell to the ground almost lifeless. That left Sawyer with three more guards to deal with. They circled for a moment and then suddenly they attacked all at once in an effort to surprise Sawyer, but Sawyer was ready. What ensued next was a melee of kicks and punches all too fast for a normal person to comprehend and as fast and furiously as it began it was over. Sawyer stood alone as the last three guards lay at his feet but the victory was short lived as a bullet went whizzing over Sawyer's head. Guards it seemed were coming after him so Sawyer ran down the long corridor to the end where there was a door next to a big steel door. Sawyer pulled on the latch but the door would not open then Sawyer realized that there was a keypad on the door so that it was controlled access only. He could hear the other guards on their way, he needed to open the door. Time was a factor as Sawyer entered code after code but was with met with "access denied" after "access denied" Sawyer was running out of time so he cleared his mind and pondered the question "what was the code"

For opening this door the answer came to him the "first sale" he thought he thought quickly back to the office at the dealership. 06/21/15 the door unlocked and Sawyer rushed in and shut the door and punched in the code again the door once again was locked, but then he thought "someone else must know the code" so Sawyer pulled out his gun from his shoulder holster and shot the keypad twice it sparked and smoked and went dead but the door remained locked. Sawyer saw a large door next to a small door exactly like the one he had just come through on the other side he ran over as fast as he could. Once Sawyer got to the door he grabbed the handle, it didn't turn he pushed and pulled but... nothing. Laying his back against the door Sawyer wiped his forehead with the back of his hand and took a deep breath. Turning and looking at the door he noticed a pipe coming out of the brick. It ran across the room and down to the keypad, which was still billowing smoke. Sawyer hung his head and walked back to the other side of the room. When he got back he sat down in an old chair next to a beat-up desk with a small television on it. The television turned out to be a monitor and Sawyer looked at the screen and saw Griffin. Griffin looked into the camera, which was broadcasted on to the screen "Sawyer you're a dead man! You hear me? A dead man!!!" Sawyer looked at the screen "can you hear me Griff?" and he could thanks to a monitor outside the door. Griffin replied sarcastically "yeah". "Can you see me pal?" Sawyer said. Griffin grinding his teeth "yes you white son of a bitch!" Sawyer then stood up and picked up his one gun from the desk and pointed it at the monitor "Well well look at this" Sawyer said as he pulled the trigger and the television burst open and smoke coming from it bought Sawyer some time. Griffin looked back at his men at the sight of the blank monitor and laughter. One of his men said, "What's so funny sir?" Griffin put his hand on his shoulder and responded, "what's so funny? I'll tell you what's so funny my boy" as he pointed to the keypad on the wall "he just trapped his sorry ass in that room, he's not going anywhere" Griffin then composed himself "guys get the blowtorch we will cut our way in and I will make that cocky bastard my bitch!" Sawyer took his ear away from the door, he had heard the entire conversation and as much as he hated to admit it Griffin was right. Sawyer looked at the big door, it was thick and it would take them time to cut and that would possibly give him the edge. The lights were very dim in the room so Sawyer decided to see where exactly he was and why it was the most secure room in the entire warehouse. Sawyer went over to the panel and switched on the light. The panel had several buttons so he started to push them one at a time. One by one the massive lights came on. A banging noise accompanied each on until they were all on, then a very light humming noise. Sawyer turned around and got weak in the knees when he discovered what was in the room. Sawyer walked forward a few steps then stopped and stared in awe at the sight before him, almost hearing a heavenly choir. The entire room was loaded with military equipment of every kind. Sawyer, still standing in the same place, looked over a king's ransom in paraphernalia. There were light armored vehicles, portable missile launchers, tanks, hummers, helicopters and boxes upon boxes of weaponry all stacked neatly on skids against the far wall; he had indeed found the mother load. Then something caught Sawyer's eye, which caused a sense of disbelief. In the back behind everything ten feet in front of the far door, which more than likely was not working, a scorpion f-21 predator fighter jet "my God I've found a unicorn" he said in total disbelief. On the outside Griffin's men had brought back the torch with a forklift when one of his men asked a question "should we put some men on the roof just as a precaution" Griffin scratched his head as he watched the blowtorch being unloaded then he stared back at the guard. Griffin responds sharply "what do you think he's fuckin' Superman, you think he's going to fly out there? The only flying' he's going to do is when I toss his sorry ass around when we get in there now get back to work you asshole!" Griffin turned his back at such an asinine question "put men on the roof" he muttered "why do I have to be surrounded by such dumb assholes" Sawyer walked over to the sleek, black fighter jet and just stared. Then he put his hand on it gently and slid it along the smooth fuselage; he just couldn't believe his eyes. The reason Sawyer was so intrigued with this fighter jet was there were only three ever made. One of them was destroyed during a test flight, the other was sent to an aviation museum somewhere in Florida and the third had simply vanished on route from the facility in Houston to Washington. Sawyer recalled that every organization was looking for it, the F.B.I, C.I.A and even in his formative years with Interpol they were investigating its disappearance. The intrigue with this jet was it's development was ahead of it's time and it was a fighter that could be flown by a seasoned pilot or a teenager with a love for video games, it was as easy as driving a car. Sawyer stood for a moment almost dumbfounded then gave his head a shake and returned to reality… he needed a way out. Looking over the room for a way out he looked up at the skylight and then at the jet… a plan was brewing. Suddenly Sawyer heard a hissing sound and looked over at the big steel door and saw a small orange spot about six feet up. It was turning red and then it started to spark, the cutting had begun. Sawyer walked over to the crates until he found one marked "M-60" he opened it up with a crowbar, which was hooked on the wall. Sawyer pried the lid off and took out the weapon then close by he found the ammunition he grabbed a coil and walked close to the location of the skylight. He loads the beginning of the belt of ammo and pulls the action back. The bullets flew at the skylight as the M-60 pulled the belt through; it felt like a jackhammer in Sawyer's hand. The last of the belt went through and when Sawyer stopped all that remained of the skylight was the frame. Step one of the plan was complete, now it was time for step two. Putting the gun on the ground Sawyer walked to the fighter. As Sawyer walked over chards of glass crunched under his feet. Sawyer climbed the ladder to the cockpit, all the while the blowtorch was half through it's first cut. Sawyer slid into the cockpit and almost instantly a computer screen revealed itself from the left side of the control panel and lit up with the words "Scorpion program begin" and at the bottom of the screen it also stated "voice or keypad control" Sawyer touched the option "voice" then he asked for the menu and in an instant it appeared. The menu had more options than even he could imagine. Sawyer looked at the list and asked for a weapons list that in seconds was listed on the screen. He looked over the list the scorpion had every weapon imaginable. Sawyer rubbed his hands together in anticipation of what he could do until he checked the ammunition list. The list scrolled down on the screen and the most frequent word on the list was "empty" Sawyer slumped back and as he scrolled further a ray of hope appeared. Listed in front of him a weapon, the only weapon for that matter was a single short range missile. This particular weapon could lock on a target and depending on the size of the obstacle the missile would crash through anything to destroy it's target and if something too thick was in it's path it would make contact and crash to the ground to be collected. Sawyer said, "activate" and the rocket was armed and ready for launch. The blowtorch was cutting at an alarmingly fast rate; Sawyer knew time was of the essence. He first walked over to the crates he needed a few things. While looking for the crate with the supplies he needed he hummed "jingle bells" because for a brief moment Sawyer felt like he was Christmas shopping. He finally came upon a crate marked "plastique" and took three twelve inch pieces and put them in a canvas bag then he walked to the next crate over and took twelve digital detonators then he slung the bag on his shoulder and walked over to the light panel. Pushing the buttons he shut off the lights so only the night lights remained and he proceeded to shoot the light box and also the power box so now there was total darkness all except the orange glow and sparks coming from the almost cut door. Sawyer could barely see his way to the fighter but once there he climbed up the ladder into the cockpit and put the bag on his neck and strapped himself in. The next few minutes would be crucial and a bit rough.The blowtorch had reached the bottom of the door the cut was complete all was quiet for a few brief moments and then the giant section which had just been cut fell forward into the room like a drawbridge and landed with a mighty thud on the ground and light smoke rose from the smoldering edges and once again all was quiet. Slowly the men from outside started coming in quietly and cautiously it was dark and they were using it to their advantage. Some got down on one knee, others took up positions behind the light armored vehicles there were at least ten men in total. The last man through the door was Griffin. His big frame came through the opening and he was brandishing an automatic assault rifle. Clearing his voice he gave Sawyer an ultimatum "Now Sawyer I know you're in here and you're outmanned and outgunned" he said with a real air of confidence "and if you give up right now I promise that you'll be killed quick, wrap your head around that for a minute". The ultimatum as it fell on deaf ears Sawyer was getting ready for his escape. Sawyer quietly instructed the jet to find the closest fuel source and lock on target, which it did to the fuel transport under which Sawyer entered. Then he instructed the fighter to put on its main headlights and wing lights. "Now" the bright lights shone on all the men including Griffin temporarily blinding everyone. Griffin squinted through the light and pointed to the fighter and yelled, "get him, shoot that son of a bitch" Immediately all guns were firing on the fighter. Sawyer didn't worry the entire jet was bulletproof. He had never been a holy man but just to be on the safe side he said a small prayer and made the sign of the crucifix, then commanded the jet to self-destruct in two minutes and eject his seat now. A small puff of dust and the seat started to go skyward toward the skylight he then yelled out his second command "fire!!!" A hail of bullets tried to take down Sawyer but to no avail he had already cleared the skylight and was headed for the safety of the night sky. The men in the warehouse would not be so lucky. The missile fired moments after it was ordered. In an instant the missile flew across the room through the big steel door and crashed through a concrete wall until it had found its target. Target. The missile itself hit the fuel truck with such velocity that the truck exploded on contact and the entire frame of the truck did a three hundred and sixty degree turn in the air wiping out lights and two massive beams before coming back down and landing on several exotic cars in a big ball of flame. The gas pipes on the wall started to burst under the extreme heat. Flames shot out as well as shattered pipe shrapnel flew everywhere. The whole one side of the warehouse was totally engulfed in flames. Griffin and his men heard the giant explosions and could see the bright flames. Suddenly the scorpion exploded sending flames and debris everywhere and because of this explosion all the missiles activated and fired. The missiles flew straight out and destroyed the remains of the steel door which came crashing down and a giant ball of flame came from down the corridor like a tidal wave. Gas pipes in the hall started to explode one after another until it arrived in the section where the light armored vehicles and crates upon cretes containing explosives and munitions were completely destroyed. The entire warehouse was nothing more than a giant bonfire raging out of control. Sawyer was observing the destruction from high in the air and then started to slowly ascend. After falling a few feet the bottom of the seat separated from under him and fell straight down to the water below. A parachute then ejected from the top of the seat which he was harnessed to. As soon as the parachute was fully open two strings with handles fell on each side of Sawyer, he put each of his hands through the handles he was now in total control of the direction he would take. Sawyer floated through the air with the grace of a feather caught in a breeze. Watching the warehouse explode impressed even him but he now had to find a good out of the way place to land before rescue crews converged on the site. He took one last look at the sheer chaos he had caused and then tugged hard left. Sawyer then spotted an old building two blocks over, no wires and a nice wide, flat roof. It was perfect. He slowly advanced on the prospective landing site by pulling down on the cords, first right then left. In mere moments he landed in the center of the roof with pinpoint accuracy. Upon landing he quickly undid his rigging and discarded the parachute gear in between two old air conditioning units. After climbing down off the roof using a service ladder, Sawyer walked out to a main road and signaled for a taxi to pull over. The taxi pulled over. Sawyer told the driver "Sheraton Hotel please" the driver nodded and they were off. Along the way the snow began to fall slowly as Sawyer sat back almost dozing off; at least he would have if it weren't for all the sirens going off. He looked out the window and watched an entire convoy of fire, ambulance and police vehicles rushed by at top speed and not to far behind two camera crews for the city's local news station Sawyer just sat back and enjoyed the ride he knew that the job was not accomplished "The fat lady hasn't taken the stage, not yet".

CHAPTER 9

STORMING THE FORTRESS

9:00am T-Mac Exotic Auto Sales Incorporated

The next morning as the sun rose and reflected off the tall buildings and the frost covered grass started to regain its somewhat greenish brown colors, T-Mac awoke in his oversized bed. He sat up placing pillows behind him so he could remain erect, then he reached for the television remote and turned on the seventy-inch screen across the bedroom. Aside from the normal weather, sports news is what caught his eye, especially the report about the exploding warehouse last night. The reporter was standing in front of what used to be T-Mac's warehouse now; however it was nothing more than a smoldering pile of rubble still casting a dark shadow of smoke into the crisp clear morning air. T-Mac watched the broadcast for a few minutes, then shut it off and climbed out of bed to get ready for the day. Thirty minutes later clad in a yellow, green and black tracksuit with the words "Jamaican Track and Field team" embroidered on the back and wearing flip-flops he arrived on the office floor with a cup of coffee in his hand… a typical sunday morning. He walked over to the double doors leading to his office and only opened the left side. There was no need to open both and there wasn't anyone around to impress.

57

T-Mac walked in the office, he was almost to his desk when the door that he opened slowly shut. He kept walking towards his desk then sat down behind it, knowing full well whom it was. He sipped his coffee slowly then put down the mug "Sawyer Briggs you really made a mess of my warehouse" he said calmly. Sawyer sat down on the other side of the desk pointing an eighty-eight magnum at T-Mac. He was totally relaxed except for the fact that his mark didn't sound very concerned about the events of last night. T-Mac looked across at Sawyer. "You're probably wondering why I don't seem to give a shit about losing the warehouse aren't you?" he said with a very laid back demeanor. Sawyer replied, "The thought crossed my mind". His mark would now put all the wondering to rest "well you see the warehouse is owned by a numbered company which is located somewhere in Africa it's leased to me and by the time the authorities get done chasing that paper trail they will hit a wall and probably give up if they even get that far" Sawyer was quite impressed at the creativity displayed by the mark but as he contemplated T-Mac had something else in mind. Suddenly T-Mac pulled out an eighty-eight magnum of his own and pointed it at Sawyer "look who's got a gun asshole, now the game has changed!" Instead of being shaken Sawyer sat in his chair very relaxed, a little too relaxed for T-Mac's comfort. He looked at Sawyer with a little bewilderment but resolved to take the lead. "Now I'm gonna kill ya" as he pulled the hammer back on the weapon "you got anything to say before you die?" Sawyer gave a small smile "yes I do, before you kill me can you do me one tiny favor let's call it a last request shall we?" T-Mac gave a smile of his own "sure whatever you want." Sawyer nodded and put the gun down on the desk, which T-Mac considered a bold move, he put a cigarette between his lips then he picked up the gun and sat back again totally at ease. T-Mac stared at him for a moment "well what the hell do you want?" he yelled, his voice with a slight hesitation. Sawyer answered, "Could you light my cigarette please?" T-Mac looked confused and answered as such "light your cigarette? What kind of a dumbass last request is that?" Sawyer gave a slight laugh and explained "well seeing as you have a lighter in your hand you have a better chance then me doing it." T-Mac stood up and pointed the at him "you have it all wrong I got the gun you have the lighter I'm not stupid man" Sawyer looked at him, the smile fading "that may be so but when you pull the trigger and a small flame comes out the end that's the time I turn you into a colander and say I told you so". T-Mac looked very uneasy at this point and a bead of sweat rolled down his face "bullshit! You've got the wrong gun," he said in a shaky tone as if he didn't want to believe it. Sawyer started to get pissed off and raised his voice while pointing the gun deliberately and decisively at T-Mac. "What kind of stupid shit are you? Do you honestly think that I would bust in here two hours before you get up to rig this shithole with explosives and then grab the wrong gun? My god you are the dumbest son of bitch I have ever met" T-Mac' confidence faltered and he reluctantly put the gun on the desk and shoved it forward then he sat down. Sawyer with cigarette dangling from his mouth and a sheepish smile asked a question "do you play poker?" T-Mac looked at Sawyer with contempt "no I don't and what does that have to do with anything?" Sawyer then pointed the eighty-eight magnum's barrel at the tip of his cigarette and pulled the trigger a small flame came out the end and lit his cigarette "well you see you just been bluffed stupid" T-Mac expressions ranged from surprise to rage "why you dirty son of a bitch" he said while lunging at the gun. T-Mac had barely had a chance to grab the gun let alone pointing it. Sawyer pulled a smaller gun from his left pocket and shot T-Mac three times in the chest. T-Mac froze for a moment then fell backwards into his chair and then slid onto the floor. Sawyer placed the smaller gun and the magnum on the desk and left slowly, closing the door behind him. A few moments later one hand came up on the top of the desk then another hand, it was T-Mac he was still alive. He sat in his office chair still grimacing in pain holding his chest gazing down at the three bullet wounds. He reached down and unzipped the track jacket to reveal a very thin but obviously effective bulletproof vest. T-Mac stared down at the three indentations in the vest and breathed a sigh of relief. The gun laid in front of him on the desk and he picked it up with his right hand and stared at it for a moment and pulled the hammer back with his thumb. T-Mac pointed the gun at the chair where Sawyer had been previously sitting and started talking to it as if Sawyer was still there. "Who's the big man now? Bitch" he said, as the pain wasn't a factor now. His finger pulled the trigger and fired a round at the chair across from him, foam flew in the air as the headrest was penetrated. T-Mac smiled and fired five more rounds into the chair as the foam flew in everywhere. The gun was empty and he threw it on the desk and stared at the chair "that's right bitch no one messes with the Mac, you can't kill me I'm indestructible, I'm Superman asshole" With that he got up and walked over to his bar to have a drink. The scotch was in a crystal decanter, he drank right from it. After a good long drink he muttered to himself as he sat down on a stool in front of the bar "who doe's this guy think he's messing with?" then mocking Sawyer "I've wired explosives to blow this place up, what a liar, if I ever get a hold of that motherfucker I'll chop him up, I'll crush him, I'll destroy him, I will lay a serious smackdown on his ass" he sat down once again "that's what "I'm talking about bitch" Meanwhile outside Sawyer was already sitting in his car looking at his watch then he looked at the building "I may have lied about the gun" he said looking down at his watch. Sawyer started his vehicle and slowly pulled out of the construction site across the street. Staring down at his watch as the small red hand was almost to the twelve, "but I wouldn't about the explosive, that's how a roll". Then he looked at his rear view mirror, as the small red hand was right over the twelve. A few of the exotic cars on the bottom floor exploded this sent them crashing on to the other cars which in turn engulfed in flames also exploded and not before long the entire bottom floor was engulfed in flames. The same thing happened on the second floor. The third floor where T-Mac was, weaker underneath from the explosions and came crashing down as did the top floor. Sawyer watched his rearview mirror as the big beautiful building was transformed into a pile of flame, glass, twisted metal and blocks "plastique and detonators, now that's what I'm talking about, told you so asshole" he said with great satisfaction as he made the call into Fuller to tell him the first.

MARK ELIMINATED.

CHAPTER 10

ONE MOUNTAIN TO ANOTHER

6:00pm Sheraton Hotel

Sawyer was laying facedown on the bed, his suit still on and guns still in their holsters. He had laid down at almost eleven o'clock in the morning for a catnap, which turned into a serious siesta. Then his cell phone rang and Sawyer strained to pull the phone from his jacket pocket and looked at the piercing red digits on the alarm clock then he sat up to talk on the phone. The voice on the other side was Fuller's. "Sawyer this is Fuller" he said. "I know" Sawyer tried to say something but Fuller stole the conversation and didn't let him get a word in edgewise. "I saw your progress on television, outstanding." He then asked Sawyer a question: the only one he was really going to ask him. "How in the blue hell did you get out of that warehouse alive and that dealership alive boyo" Sawyer fired back in a gentle tone "a good magician never reveals his tricks" Fuller was silent for a moment then started his conversation. "Touché, anyway we have a little snafu with the next two marks but not to worry you will still receive the three million as agreed but tomorrow night myself and my employer would like you to meet us in Los Angeles

61

at The Golden Fox restaurant so wear a tie and look sharp I've already arranged your ticket for L.A for old time sake so get some rest and I'll see you in L.A" Sawyer snapped the phone shut and threw it on the floor then removed his shoulder holsters and put them on the ground as well. Turning over on his back he fell fast asleep tomorrow without a doubt was going to be a busy day.

8:00pm The Golden Fox Los Angeles California

Sawyer arrived right on time at the restaurant and was led to Fuller's table right away. "Sawyer, good to see you please sit." Fuller said as he motioned for him to sit down. Sawyer looked around at the restaurant and it was absolutely exquisite. A waiter came over and filled Sawyer's glass from a bottle that was in a silver bucket loaded with ice. He caught the label on the bottle before it was put back in the bucket, it was a rare brand of very expensive champagne. Fuller took a sip from his glass and started to say "if you're wondering where my employer is, he couldn't make it tonight, however he sends his apologies and will try to meet you at a later date". Sawyer nodded and sipped his drink "well at least I have you" he said giving a small smile and a laugh. Fuller started to laugh "I may not be a prom date, but here I'am". Then they both raised their glass to one another and drank. Sawyer put down the glass and put on a slightly serious face "I don't mean to sound ungrateful for this wonderful evening we are about to have, but…" Fuller stopped him in mid sentence "I know what you're going to say, look under the table what do you see?" Sawyer looked under the table and saw a black briefcase then looked back at Fuller. He continued "you see there it is, now let's not talk shop we will have plenty of time for that after dinner ok?" Sawyer nodded "ok Ron sorry if I seem overeager". Fuller responded "not at all Sawyer now get ready for your senses to be blown away" Sawyer raised his glass once again and was ready to lose himself in the moment. Two hours, three bottles of champagne and a gourmet meal later the two retired to a very special exclusive room in the establishment known as "The Study". Sawyer entered the room and was awestruck. The room itself was a refurbished turn of the century study complete with authentic leather armchairs and couches each with a beautiful oak table just big enough for a pair of drinks and a small ashtray for cigars. The walls were rich dark oak and the ceiling was also made of the same rich material. A giant fireplace opposite the door crackled briskly with a warm glow of an artificial flame while wall lights and select tables with lamps lit up the room. The room was half full when Sawyer and Fuller entered the room. A blue plume of smoke hung high in the air as they were escorted to their place. Sitting down another waiter came over and brought two glasses of cognac and two Cuban cigars, he put down the drinks on the table after he placed a coaster under each then clipped the tips off the cigars and offered them to Sawyer and Fuller and then lit them and informed them if they needed anything just ask. Sawyer and Fuller sat in their comfortable armchairs like a couple of aristocrats puffing on cigars, drinking cognac and taking in the ambiance of a long past era. Fuller placed his cigar in the ashtray and picked up his briefcase and placed it in his lap. "Well Sawyer" he said as he opened up the case "here's three million dollars" and he turned the case towards Sawyer. Sawyer nearly swallowed his cigar. "What the hell are you doing Ron?" he snapped, keeping his tone of voice low and almost talking through his teeth. Ron slowly closed the case "what do you mean Sawyer? I'm just showing you the money you earned." Sawyer swallowed the remainder of his drink and breathed a sigh of relief as he saw him close the briefcase and return it to the floor. Sawyer puffed his cigar then leaned over to Ron. "You just don't go flashing that kind of cash around people you know." Ron looked at Sawyer like a sympathetic father "don't let it make you nervous just look around" So Sawyer looked around the room people seemed to keep to themselves drinking and talking and smoking. Ron continued, "You see all the people here? They couldn't give a shit if you had twenty million in the case they are the elite, rich and powerful." Ron then signals the waiter to bring two more drinks. "They are all lawyers, producers, politicians etcetera, powerful people with no regard for money. They are a bunch of greedy little bastards all bringing potential clients here to dazzle them, butter 'em up and close a deal." Sawyer smirked "kind of like you?" Ron looked at Sawyer and laughed, "that's funny real witty and I see you brought back my case as well" he said looking down on the floor next to Sawyer's foot. Sawyer slid it over. "Don't worry I went easy on the credit card" Ron looked over nodding his head "and we thank-you" The waiter brought the drinks to the table. Sawyer and Fuller clinked glasses much like they had been doing most of the evening. Fuller was about to sip when his cell phone started to ring to the tone of "Raiders of the lost ark" he took it out and opened it. Sawyer looked at him as he finished a sip "Indiana Jones?" he said with a raised eyebrow. Ron grinned at Sawyer "I like a good adventure" he said as he pulled out his phone, pressed the answer button and winked at Sawyer. Looking around the room Sawyer couldn't help but wonder who was talking to Ron. He tried not to look conspicuous as he watched Fuller's range of emotions going from happy to dismay. Ron 's last words that Sawyer could make out were "yes sir I understand" then returned it to the pocket inside his jacket. Ron sipped his cognac ignoring Sawyer, he appeared to be deep in thought. Sawyer cleared his throat to get Ron's attention "ahem, remember me?" Ron turned to Sawyer "sorry, just bad news" he said. "What's wrong?" Sawyer inquired. Ron looked at him and was about to say something, and then he shook his head "no nothing it's alright". Sawyer looked at Ron and took a long drag off his cigar "no it's not alright, what's the problem?" Ron looked at Sawyer; he almost looked like a dog about to be shot. "Ok fine I'll tell you" he said as he finished the last of his drink he then ordered two more. "My employer informed us that our shooter left with half the money he had paid up front and now we have a mark that's still standing and time that is running out, that's my problem" he said as he reached for another drink off the table, which had just arrived. Sawyer had a small smile on his face "how much?" Sawyer asked. Ron just stared at him and said "oh no you don't I know where this is heading and forget it you did the job requested of you and you were compensated so that 's it" he said sounding

The Silencer

solid on his decision. Sawyer asked again "how much?" Ron shook his head and gave the amount "three times as much as you got" Sawyer gulped his drink "three times as much, that must be a hell of a mark" Ron puffed his cigar "it's not the mark it's the rarity of it, one week a year it's left vulnerable and then that's it getting near it again is just impossible" Sawyer scratched his head "impossible" he said. "Yep, way too much security," Ron assured Sawyer. He asked Ron "how much time is left?" Ron replied "day after tomorrow he flies out at five in the afternoon, but Sawyer I' am not even asking you to do it" Sawyer looked back at Ron with a crooked smile "you're not asking me Ron I'm telling you I'll do it" Ron ran his fingers through his hair "give me one good reason you want to risk a sure thing for something that could be detrimental to your health as well as finances" Sawyer sat back a blew smoke in the air as he explained "you see man in my entire career there wasn't really a defining moment when I could put the period on the end of the sentence and when I went to Texas after Sicily I still pondered the question is that the best I could do? Is that as good as it ever would be? What I'm trying to say is I want one last… big… score, a defining moment and this is it, one and done". Ron smiled as he raised his glass to Sawyer "ok you made your sale, I'll make the necessary arrangements and inform my employer." Sawyer raised his glass and then swallowed the last of his drink just as two fresh ones were being put on the table. After closing Sawyer and Ron stood outside for a while making small talk waiting for Sawyer's taxi to arrive. Finally Sawyer's cab pulled up "well I guess I'll see you tomorrow Ron" Sawyer said as he began to open the taxi door. "Ron looked at him with a semi drunk look "I'll see you tomorrow at the airport at one o'clock I'll get you on the Three o'clock flight if I can". Sawyer nodded and stumbled into the cab. He then shut the door and rolled down the window "till tomorrow then" he said to Ron as the taxi slowly rolled out of sight. Ron watched the taxi disappear just as the valet pulled up with his car "till tomorrow Sawyer till tomorrow "he said in a low voice as he got in his car and drove away.

1:00 pm Los Angeles International Airport (LAX)

Ron sat at a table in the airport lounge affectionately known as "The Hanger". He was drinking a scotch on the rocks and just about to check his watch when he saw a familiar face coming towards his table. "Sawyer, good to see you, did you get much sleep?" Ron asked. Sawyer sat down and looked at Ron with a small smile and bloodshot eyes and answered "yes Ron can't you tell by my up and at em' complexion". Ron laughed and sipped his drink and ordered one for Sawyer as well, but Sawyer raised his hand and told Ron he just wanted a coffee and he wanted it black and strong. The coffee came and Sawyer took a sip, put down the mug and let out a satisfying "aaaaaahhhhhhhh" now he was ready to talk. Fuller opened his briefcase, pulled out a folder and opened it on the table. Ron remembered something "here is a cell phone and a credit card. We wouldn't want you spending your own money" he said as he handed the items over. "Ok here is a layout of the property where your mark is located" he said as he pointed at the photo on the table. Sawyer observed Fuller; he was the picture of concentration. Fuller downed his scotch and then got into a detailed description and rundown of the mission. "Now you will pick-up your boat here. It has a water jet engine, it runs silent, your weapon is here in this old fishing shack just open the floor panel and it will be there in a hard case along with six rounds you will probably only need one but what the hell." Sawyer pointed at the map "where is the starting point?" he asked. Fuller was quick to point it out "this starting point is a bay five miles from your hotel; it's about fifty yards from the road it's abandoned." Sawyer nodded and Fuller continued "you take the boat to this side of the island where the mark is, there you will walk through a bush, it used to be a tree farm, experimental land actually." He ordered another drink and continued in great detail "there's a lot of different trees oak, ash, etcetera when you get close to the house you will notice a rod iron fence and a big backyard with a large garden and bee boxes find a tree about one hundred yards and get set up so you have a clear shot" Fuller's drink came and he offered to ordered another coffee for Sawyer. For the last part Fuller looked directly at Sawyer "He will come out at eight o'clock and tend to his bees then he will work on his garden, the whole thing takes two hours but the important thing to remember or should I say the important things to remember is during this time he sends all his bodyguards away and his garden ends at the fence which gives you an open shot." Fuller then turned his attention once again to his drink taking a big gulp. Sawyer asked "and once I'm done?" Fuller smiled broadly "then you move out fast take back the boat, return the rifle to where you found it and go back to the hotel, take a couple of weeks on us and when we meet again you will collect the cash and that will be as they say that" Sawyer needed to know one more thing "Fuller, how do you know all this stuff you know times locations stuff like that?" Fuller finished his drink and placed the glass down slowly "This is one of the biggest marks that we have ever attempted to take down Sawyer. I researched every angle. Failure is not an option besides I'd hate to send anyone in blind." Sawyer nodded. He and Fuller talked a little bit longer and the announcement came over the speaker for the flight to Honolulu. "That's me," Sawyer said. Ron gave Sawyer his tickets and a confirmation number for the hotel in Hawaii. So he grabbed his carry on and a wardrobe bag as Fuller walked him to security. "Well I'll be seeing you" Sawyer said as they shook hands "You bet," answered Fuller and with that Sawyer was checked by security as his bags went through the X-ray. He collected them and turned once more and waved at Fuller and disappeared behind a white wall. Fuller then sauntered back to the bar and sat up on a bar stool and placed his bag on the floor and ordered another scotch. Pulling out his film phone he pressed one digit "the ball is in play" he said and put his phone away, then he picked up his drink and started to sip it as he muttered to himself "Judas".

CHAPTER 11

SUNSET SNIPER

Honolulu, Hawaii, U.S.A

The engines powered up as Sawyer's flight was preparing to land. Smoke trailed the tires of the plane as they all touched down on the runway as the voice of the captain echoed from throughout the plane "aloha and welcome to Honolulu Hawaii" and from there passengers basically ignored the rest of the announcement as they were anxious to get their carry on from the overhead compartments and wondering if there were cabs available or not. Sawyer was quite relaxed not just from the good meal, the two bottles of Merlot, plush pillow and blanket provided but the fact that he was in first-class and would exit the plane first was the clincher. Sawyer exited the plane with his bags in tow and surveyed the facility. There were women and men in grass skirts doing the hula and playing ukuleles. Sawyer felt like he was on the set of "Blue Hawaii" with Elvis. After he escaped the culture shock of the airport he hailed a cab. While Sawyer was waiting he could feel the fresh cool evening breeze of the island surrounding and permeating him. It gave him a second wind even though he had a case of jet lag and he was really fatigued. The breeze seemed to be the cure-all at this particular time. After a twenty minute cab ride with a driver who gave all the information about the island, hotspots etc Sawyer finally arrived at his hotel the "King Maivia" he almost felt he should pay more for the education he received. Sawyer checked in at the front desk and went to his room. Sliding the card in the door and entering the room he noticed it was less of a room and more of a suite complete with a generous sized hot tub, big bathroom, a wet bar, fifty-two inch television and a king-size bed. Sawyer was overwhelmed to say the least. He walked over to the bed and laid down and within minutes he was fast asleep. The next morning Sawyer awoke at ten o'clock it was the first time in a while he had slept in. Sawyer slowly got out of bed to the sound of his bones cracking and snapping, "you can't beat the clock" he thought. The cold water running from the tap was just what he needed to come to life; he splashed his face, turned off the tap and let the water run down his face, neck and chest. While walking from the bathroom he noticed he was only clad in his boxer-briefs at some point during the night he had removed his clothes but was dumbfounded to remember when. Sawyer went over and opened the balcony doors. He was immediately greeted with a warm breeze, which made the water running down his chest almost relaxing. Standing at the edge of the balcony he wrapped his hands slowly around the railing and looked around. The pool boys were setting up chairs and cleaning the pool in preparation for the coming guests. As Sawyer looked down he figured tomorrow is the assignment but he had today, the whole day and it had been a long time since he had a vacation, granted this one would be short but a vacation was a vacation "what the hell". Sawyer walked over to his closet and found two Hawaiian style shirts and shorts along with a wetsuit the kind the Jet Ski guys wear. He quickly dawned his new Hawaiian garb and proceeded to go on vacation. Sawyer spent the early part of the day drinking Mai Tai's and tanning by the pool as he did this he observed the people around him. He saw every walk of life, newly weds, families, retirees and of course pale business people who were at a "conference" at the expense of their company, "yeah it takes all kinds". After relaxing in the sun for a few hours Sawyer rented a scooter for a couple of days this would give him transportation to and from his assignment launch point but for now he was more interested in soaking in the local culture so he took a ride around the island stopping at a café for lunch and then moving on. After returning to the hotel taking a power nap and showering, Sawyer decided on one last thing to cap off the day, which had been simply glorious in every aspect of the word; he walked out to the beach to watch the sunset. The sand still had some heat in it as Sawyer slowly walked along the water, as the sun began it's descent into the horizon. A great feeling of peace came over him almost zen-like as a light breeze added to the whole experience. Thoughts filled Sawyer's mind, but mostly thoughts of his beloved Gwen. The sky started to turn a brilliant shade red as Sawyer stopped and turned toward the ocean folding his arms as the tide pushed the water between his toes. All Sawyer could do was stare out into the horizon and think of how he promised Gwen that someday they would come to this enchanted paradise and with that he sighed as the sky's brilliant shade of red started to fade. The sunset did however remind him of their honeymoon in Cuba. It was the greatest week of his life, dancing till dawn, making love on the beach not to mention the long walks along it. Arm in arm they would walk every night and there was one thing she said that stuck with him and would always until the end of his days, she looked into his eyes and said, "don't ever let the sun set on us". A last glimmer of light was the only remnant of the beautiful sunset that once was. The tiny glimmer reflected off of single tear that ran down Sawyer's cheek as the thoughts and memories of his beloved flowed through his mind's eye... cuts can be stitched, bones mend over time... ... but it's the wounds you don't see especially the ones of the heart that never heal.

4:00am October 30

Sawyer awoke to the buzzing of the alarm clock although he was already awake waiting for it to go off, it was mission day he was ready. Being meticulous was Sawyer's strength when he got out of bed his clothes were laid out across the desk along with his gear so all he would have to do was get ready and not search for anything, time was always of the essence. Within ten minutes he was dressed and ready to go. Sawyer put the surf suit under his shirt and shorts so that the staff on duty wouldn't suspect anything, they would just figure he was going out for a scooter ride. Sawyer checked his watch at five o'clock and he arrived at the starting point. Sawyer put the scooter in some shrubs and placed his shirt and shorts inside the seat he wouldn't need for now. With the shack in sight Sawyer proceeded over to it, walking slowly and cautiously not knowing what to expect. Sawyer opened the door which wasn't locked and made a slight creaking sound. He entered the shack, which was small, and in disrepair there was one table, two chairs and an old wood stove. This place was just as Fuller said… abandoned. Walking further into the shack he was suddenly startled by a set of wooden wind chimes, which made a noise when he touched it with his head unknowingly. A broad smile came across his face. Not only was he realizing he was a little paranoid but he heard a hollow sound below his feet. Without hesitating Sawyer dropped to his knees and looked at the floor he could clearly see the edges. As he followed the edges he then saw a cast iron ring attached to the door where underneath he would find his weapon and a box or two of ammunition… he hoped. Sawyer pulled a small penlight from a leather bag, which resembled a purse; it also contained binoculars and several other pieces of gear he would need for this sort of mission. Placing the penlight in between his teeth illuminated the ring and pulled the hatch open. Inside he saw a hard gun case and nothing else so he grabbed the case by the handle and pulled it up, and then getting to his feet he placed the case on the old table. Sawyer with the penlight still in his mouth pulled on the latches and opened the case. Inside the case was a twenty-two two fifty caliber broken down to two pieces; the barrel and the stock and triggering mechanism also six rounds of ammo. Closing the case Sawyer was satisfied the firepower was adequate; his meticulous nature was coming to the forefront, he had only two rules when it came to working in this profession. 1. Know your weapon. 2 Know your mark. Sawyer picked up the case and proceeded. A short time later Sawyer arrived on the small beach at the rear of the island where his mark was only a walk away. After hiding his boat in thick brush, well off the beach he proceeded on foot through the dense woods. Sawyer was walking at a good pace when he saw bright lights up ahead. Slowing down his pace he walked up to a big old oak tree that was about one hundred yards from the target area… perfect. Carefully Sawyer climbed the tree to a point where he had a clear view of the backyard. He stood on a thick branch and set his rifle in the crotch of the tree then he quietly pulled the bolt back and loaded three rounds put the safety on, he couldn't afford a misfire. Sawyer pulled out his binoculars and glassed the yard. There was a lot to see, a guard on the roof, two patrolling the yard and there were probably more in front whoever this mark was; he must be extremely important having been surrounded by so much security Sawyer thought. Looking at his watch he noticed it was five minutes to six. This gave him two hours before he had to be at the ready so he decided to take advantage of his slightly early arrival. Silently Sawyer climbed down the tree and then set his watch alarm to seven thirty and on vibrate. He then sat at the base of the tree and rested his head and closed his eyes. He was going to take a power nap, he had no fears of being spotted because of the importance of their assignment they wouldn't leave their posts for nothing less than an earthquake and with that he closed eyes and rested. A slight vibration awoke Sawyer from his speedy slumber and he quietly yawned and stretched. Stealthily Sawyer climbed back up into position it would be only a short time now before he put the exclamation point on his career.

8:00am

The sun gave a beautiful pink hue to the sky as off in the distance seagulls could be heard echoing in the start of a new day. The guards that loyally and with great consistency patrolled the grounds and the roof slowly dispersed. Sawyer stood at the ready. His mark opened one of the double doors at the back of the house and proceeded outside to a small garden shed. Sawyer looked into the scope but some low lying branches obstructed his view he would have to wait. The mark emerged from the shed wearing a beekeeper's mask and holding a smudge pot went over to the four stacks of boxes containing the bees. With his mark in the clear Sawyer could have made the shot but Sawyer was a traditionalist he preferred to see his target when making a hit it was just the way he rolled. A half an hour went by and finally to Sawyer's delight the beekeeping part was over and it was time for Sawyer to get down to business. The mark went back into the garden shed for a few moments then returned to the garden with a gardening hoe in hand. Sawyer set up for the shot but branches once again blocked his view. Sawyer shook his head and muttered to himself under his breath "doesn't anyone know how to prune?" With a small rag Sawyer cleaned his scope and then picked the cleanest area in the garden for the shot. His mark went into the garden and got on his hands and knees and started pulling weeds, all Sawyer could see was the top of his head in his crosshairs but kept dead aim on his head. All his mark had to do was look up or sit back on his knees and he would be just another statistic. The mark sat up on his knees to whip the sweat from his brow now was Sawyer's chance. Sawyer clicked off the safety with his thumb, put his finger on the trigger, took a deep breath and closed his eyes tight then opened his left eye and looked into the scope. For the first time in his life Sawyer froze with his finger still on the trigger and his mark still in the crosshairs he froze completely. The image on the other side of the scope was not only overwhelming but also totally unexpected. The mark he was sent to eliminate, the mark that would be the exclamation point on his career, the mark that was of the utmost importance to Fuller and his employer was Edward Clark Doyle the president of the United States. Sawyer, for a moment, couldn't move a muscle; it was an extremely uncomfortable position he was in. He felt like he had a devil on one shoulder and an angel on the other, each trying to pull Sawyer to their side in a tug of war of the soul. A full two minutes went by and Sawyer started to relax and he eased off the trigger, flicked on the safety with his thumb and pulled away from the scope he then rested his forehead against the scope for a moment, he then took one more look at the president "screw this "he said silently to himself as he slung the rifle over his shoulder and prepared to descend from the tree. The sun filtered through the trees and a gentle breeze blew as Sawyer slowly walked back to the landing point trying to comprehend the surreal moment he had just experienced and one word kept repeating itself over and over again "why?" An hour later after returning the boat and the rifle to their rightful places Sawyer arrived back in his hotel room, he was very tired and retired to his bed, he would call Fuller when he woke up and find out what the hell was going on. Several hours had passed and Sawyer slowly began to wake up. He sat up on the edge of the bed; one eye open one eye shut trying to focus on the clock radio. The red digits revealed the time was ten past three Sawyer rubbed his eyes and then reached for the cell phone on top of the clock radio he needed to make a call, an important one. He pressed the digits and then the send button and waited for a response. The ring tone was only heard twice then a woman's voice came on and stated that the other party was not available. Figuring that Fuller was talking to someone else Sawyer hung up and placed it back on top of the clock radio. The cold water from the sink instantly revived Sawyer; he then dried his face and walked over to the balcony after grabbing a cigarette on the way and a lighter. He walked out onto the balcony and lit his cigarette then stared over the balcony and what he witnessed was very odd indeed. All the guests were standing near the bar or sitting on bar stools watching something on television. It was a rather large crowd. Sawyer looked down for a moment, finished his cigarette and walked back in; the reason for everyone gathered round was probably a sporting event. "I 'm not going to bother flicking on the television. The only sport that matters is futbol" Sawyer then called room service to send up his late lunch. He returned to the balcony and looked over once more, the small crowd was still gathered around the television in the bar. Sawyer scratched his head and figured "if you can't beat them join them". So Sawyer picked up the remote on the night table just then there was a knock at the door and a voice on the other side declared "room service". Sawyer opened the door, his lunch was wheeled in on a cart close to the balcony doors he tipped the man and then shut the door behind him. Loading up almost everything he could on a silver platter. He always kept his meals simple. Lunch was mostly cold cuts, a few different cheeses, assorted vegetables and fresh crusty bread. Water was his drink of choice with lunch, he never liked a drink that overpowered the flavor of his meal. Sawyer made his way out to the balcony to eat his lunch out in the fresh air, he found all foods taste better outside... As Sawyer started to eat he felt like he was being watched. He needed a quick vigil of the area so he casually knocked his newspaper on the floor. He slowly bent over to pick it up and gave his surroundings a quick glance. Sawyer noticed he was indeed being watched from atop the other building then saw that he was also being watched from the other two buildings on either side from the rooftops as well. Lastly he noticed two men watching from the pool area as he slowly got up something was going to go down he needed a plan before the shit hit the fan. Being the ever great strategist he was, he ate his meal, read his paper, stood up and stretched, faked a yawn and went inside, closing the doors behind him. Sawyer then pulled the blinds, he wasn't sure why he was being observed but he was about to find out. Sawyer maybe wasn't being observed, maybe it was just security and he was being paranoid. Sawyer flicked on the television and his paranoia would soon be dismissed as fact.

CHAPTER 12

EAGLE DOWN

A picture of the president was behind a news anchor and with a sad tone of voice he gave the grim news. "Now to recap our top story, the president of the United States has been shot. President Edward Clark Doyle was assassinated this morning while tending garden at his once thought secret retreat just off the coast on the island of Tutu, he was shot in the head by an unknown assassin from the dense brush surrounding the back of his cottage and…" The reporter stopped for a moment and then looked horrified "We have just been informed that the president has passed away we have also been informed that the entire island of Hawaii was been locked down no flights in or out will be permitted until the assassin has been found more details as they become available." Sawyer didn't know what to make of it, he didn't kill the president but someone did, he then walked over to the balcony doors and looked through the blinds as best he could the man on the roof was gone, he then stepped out onto the balcony and noticed they had all left their positions so Sawyer shook it off as coincidence and returned to the room. Within twenty minutes of the President's death Vice President Robert "Bob" Sutton Bradley was sworn in as the acting commander and chief. Clearing his throat he then approached the podium and gave a statement "I take this

76

position with a heavy heart and swear to do everything in my power to do justice to and for the office that I have sworn to uphold, I will have a full address later this evening and God Bless America" Sawyer watched the sequence of events from his television in fact he never left his room… not yet. At six o'clock precisely the new president came on the television from the oval office and addressed the nation "my fellow Americans today is a dark day in the annals of American history, today we lost a president". Bradley took a sip of water and continued "America didn't just lose a leader of a country it lost much more than that it lost a man who was a son, a brother, a husband, a father, a grandfather, a teacher and a friend… he will sadly be missed" Bradley then wiped his eyes and kept speaking "friends I promise that the monster, the coward that carried out this horrifying act of violence will be brought to justice and will be punished with extreme prejudice and the individual who will carry out this domineering task has already started to put together the pieces of this inhuman termination of a human life and will be giving a status report following this address, so in closing, America lower your heads and in memory of a fallen hero, a fallen friend". Sawyer poured himself a cup of coffee and sat up on his bed in anticipation to see if they had an idea who rubbed out Doyle. No sooner did the president finish then did the setting move from the oval office to an empty podium in the Whitehouse with reporters from all over and the next image to appear shook Sawyer to the core. As he sipped his coffee the empty podium on the television was now occupied by Ron Fuller, Sawyer spilled some coffee on the floor in disbelief. Fuller adjusted the microphone and spoke decisively "good evening my name is Ronald Abernathy Fuller and I'am in charge of this investigation I represent a small department of the government which deals strictly with assassinations and attempts, now the U.S army, marine corps and local law enforcement as you know have sealed off the entire island of Hawaii and the air force is patrolling the rest of the islands in case our assassin got off the island before the lockdown." Sawyer's disbelief wore off and turned to praise because if anyone could catch this killer it was Ron, at least it explained the reason he wasn't picking up the phone. Ron cleared his throat "I will take no questions at this time however I can report with the utmost confidence that with our resources the assassin will be captured in the very near future." Then looking directly at the camera he stated very coldly "whoever you are or wherever organization you are affiliated with remember this fact you are no longer the hunter you are the hunted" he said with no expression. Sawyer looked at the television and remembered hearing the exact same quote from Ron in the park back in New York, Sawyer never did the dirty work but still something didn't feel right. Slowly Sawyer put down his coffee on the floor, walked over to the blind and looked through until he could see the figure back on top of the building which meant that he was being watched again. This was no coincidence, Sawyer needed to get out and find new accommodations post haste. In his rush from the blind to the closet he kicked the cup of coffee over and reached down to pick it up. The lukewarm coffee got on his hand, he put the mug on the desk and reached for the cell phone next to it. Sawyer grabbed hold of the phone but his hand still being wet from the coffee couldn't quite grip it properly and the phone slipped out of his hand and fell to the ground. The impact with which it fell was enough to open the back up and that is when Sawyer made the astonishing discovery that there was a small light inside blinking. The light was hard to miss, it was small but the light was red and was very prominent. Sawyer reached down and picked up the phone, "I'll be damned" he said looking at the small blinking light. A thought crossed his mind at that moment. Sawyer took out the credit card from his wallet and proceeded into the bathroom, closing the door behind him. Sawyer stood in the dark for a moment so his eyes could adjust, then he looked at the credit card. Slowly he started to notice the outline of the holographic symbol was pulsating red. Sawyer looked at the card for another moment then walked out of the bathroom over to the bed and sat down. Looking at the card in disbelief "fiber optics I can't believe it this is C.I.A shit and that being the case I'm being tracked" Sawyer could have simply destroyed the tracking devices but instead he kept them intacted and placed them on the top shelf of the closet and shut the door he then took off his shorts and shirt and hung them back in the closet right next to his garment bag containing the wardrobe he had received during his first job in Toronto "what a shame" he thought as he closed the closet door., Sawyer grabbed his bag it was time to leave but suddenly he saw something on television that grabbed his attention. The news anchor had some new information "We have just been informed by the president's press secretary that president Bob Bradley and the head of assassinations division Ron Fuller will be flying to Hawaii. The president will be on hand to attend a small memorial tomorrow before the deceased president's body will be flown back to Washington to lie in state before being laid to rest in his home state of North Carolina, Ron Fuller will be coming along not only to attend the service but to oversee the investigation personally". The anchorman stopped and put his finger on the small plug in his ear, nodded and continued "We have also been informed by the Hawaiian Airport Authority that Air force One and a small air force envoy will be the only aircraft landing and taking off from island pending the investigation, more details as we receive them." Sawyer put on a pair of green military looking shorts, black t-shirt, a plain blue ball cap and his sandals. He kept the clothes and sandals in the bottom of his handbag just in case his luggage didn't make it through, shook his head, picked up his bag and walked out into the hall. Taking a good long look at the hallway, first up one side and down the other, but there was no one a clear field so to speak. So Sawyer proceeded down the hallway to the elevators trying his best to be cautious and casual at the same time. When he arrived at the elevators he pushed the button down and waited. A few moments passed a small ding and the doors opened. There was one other person in the elevator, an older man with a big white mustache, blue jacket and pants. Sawyer entered the elevator and gave a small nod to the old man and looked at the numbers which gave the floor number. Sawyer noticed the old man's jacket stated he was in maintenance and this gave Sawyer an idea. Sawyer struck up a conversation and before he knew it he was in the basement, "must have missed my floor," he said. The maintenance man asked, "Where is it you wanted to go?" Sawyer replied "the parking lot". The old gentleman told Sawyer "go down the corridor, past the recycling and garbage trucks turn left and there is a door, go through it and up seven or eight stairs and there's the parking lot". Sawyer shook the old man's hand and proceeded down the corridor. At the end he opened the door and crouched down, then went up the stairs to the lot. Stopping three stairs away from the top Sawyer saw three men in the parking lot just standing around. They were waiting for him and he knew it, a new plan was definitely in order. Sawyer walked back past the trucks when he got an idea. Looking both ways for no witnesses he climbed over the back of the truck, it was more of an old truck with wooden sides but it was what was inside that piqued Sawyer's interest. Recycled plastic bottles, hundreds of them. Sawyer assessed the situation and came up with a plan. He jumped up on the truck and shimmed himself into the massive truck load of bottles until he was hidden entirely by the bottles. He patiently waited, bag in hand covered with plastic bottles he felt safe. Suddenly the truck door slammed and started to move. Up the ramp to the street the truck went. Sawyer had done it; he had slipped out undetected and now he had to concentrate on which direction he was heading, but one thing was for sure the farther the better. The truck traveled for nearly a half an hour all the while Sawyer couldn't really do anything but lay amidst the plastic bottles and wait until an opportunity to leave presented itself. Meanwhile in Washington, Air Force One was preparing for take off. A convoy of three black SUV's and a black limousine made their way to the air force base. Inside the black limousine president Bradley and Ron Fuller were alone together as Bradley spoke "are you sure that this will be wrapped up by tomorrow morning? because I want it to be quick, clean and done... understood" he said as he pulled a small flask out of his jacket and took a sip. Ron responded "yes sir, he's been under surveillance for the day and hasn't left the hotel, tomorrow morning we move in early, take down the mark and take him back to the U.S with us along with the body of president Doyle following the memorial on the runway, did I miss anything?" The limousine pulled into the air force base and was making it's way to where the plane was, "no that's about it, but top marks for staying on the ball, you're getting more innovative... I like that". The limousine came to a stop right beside the plane where a red carpet was laid leading the passengers and the president to the stairs, which leads up to the door. The driver got out and opened the door for the president first. The president exited the limousine followed by Fuller. They boarded the plane not stopping for pictures or statements about anything for the press. After everyone on the plane was strapped Bradley leaned over to Fuller who was sitting next to him and looking him straight in the eye said in a low voice "Ron I'll do my part you do yours and we will get through this... ok?" Ron nodded "yes sir" and he sat back in a thick leather seat and nodded off, he needed the rest of the business to pick up.

The recycling truck's engine started to power down and the truck slowly pulled off the road after what Sawyer estimated was about an hour drive from the starting point of the hotel. He slowly sat up and looked through the slats, it appeared the driver was in need of refreshment as he saw him enter a small side of the road rest stop. This was the opportunity Sawyer needed and he was going to capitalize on it. As quietly as he could he got up and climbed over the side of the truck not visible to anyone in the rest stop. At this point in time Sawyer started to recall his survival training. He knew he needed two things at the present time a good place to dig in and a clear escape route out incase he needed a hasty retreat he would get food later because as his trainer would emphatically state "what's the point of having food if you don't have a mouth to put it in." Sawyer walked down the roughly paved road for a short while until he came upon a beautiful beach and just up the road from that was an older style motel it was called "The Starfish Motel". Sawyer walked up to the motel and into the front door. He first noticed there was no one behind the counter but then looking to his left he saw a rather large woman sitting in a chair with her feet up on a stool watching the television that was up on a shelf on the wall. Sawyer approached the woman who was wearing a red moo moo with palm trees on it. "Excuse me, I would like a room please" Sawyer inquired. The woman answered "put fifty dollars on the desk and take any room you like," without even looking away from her program. So he did what she asked and took a key off of a hook behind the front desk and proceeded down the hallway. Sawyer chose room five for the simple reason that it was the furthest down the hall and if he needed to make a hasty retreat the location would buy him a little time. As it turned out his assumption of what the room would look like was partially right and partially wrong. He entered the room and shut the door standing in the doorway. He did a brief scan of the room then he walked around slowly looking closer at what it had in store. The room was simple and clean with a single bed and nightstand with a lamp, one small closet and a beautiful thirty-eight inch high definition television "they know what works" he said. He entered the bathroom and washed his face and looked at himself in the mirror trying to make sense of what was going on but no answer came to mind. Feeling a little depressed and confused he opened the long wooden slatted doors on the other side of the room, which led to something that took his breath away. The back of his room led out onto a private, undeveloped beach he was stunned by the unsurpassed beauty of it all. Sawyer slid the screen door open and walked out onto the soft golden sand and watched the sky over the course of what seemed like a few minutes turn red then pink. Sawyer walked back in the room and shut the screen and the two doors then turned the television to see the developments of the day. At that moment Air Force One touched down at U.S military base Hula. The plane taxied then came to a stop at a designated area with military men, local authorities and reporters. After security exited the plane the President came out and made his way down the steps with Ron close behind they both waved at the cameras and then entered a long limousine and were whisked away to the "King Kotuku hotel where the it would Serve as Housing for the president and a main base operations for Fuller. Sawyer sat on the edge of the bed drinking a bottle of water, which he found in a mini bar. Watching the developments and listening to the interviews Sawyer tried to gather all the information he could and try to figure out how he fit into this complex web of deception. The darkness had settled in and Sawyer grew tired and pulled back the covers and laid in bed, he propped his head up and watched the screen for a few more minutes then he fell asleep due to sheer exhaustion but with the confidence of knowing he was safe at least for tonight. The next morning just as the sun started to peer over the horizon five federal agents stood outside the front doors of the "King Maivia" Hotel. A black jeep pulled up and Ron Fuller got out and addressed one of the agents then with great haste they entered the front doors. Ron and the agents ascended to the level where all the suites were located. When the elevator arrived and the doors opened Ron laid down the game plan "ok here's the way it's going to go down I want two men on both sides of the door the fifth man will kick open the door and take the lead the other four will follow him in I'll come last and remember take him alive got it?" he said looking at the agents they nodded "alright quickly and quietly let's go". Stealthily Ron and the agents advanced down the hall then putting the plan into action the agents took their assumed positions. They all withdrew their weapons. Ron held up three fingers and then slowly lowered them one by one, three… two… one. The door to the suite then swung open as a result of a good hard boot to it and then the agents all rushed in to take down the assassin. Ron waited a few moments then slowly walked in. "The room is secure sir" one agent told him. Ron looked at him "I can see that but where is he?" Ron said with a confused and bewildered look on his face. He got on his small hand radio and consulted with the agents on the far rooftops and then by the pool but no one saw the target leave Ron took a deep breath and spoke to the agent closest to him "alright" he said in a calm tone "I want this whole floor shut down, I want an agent posted at the door twenty four seven and no one is to come on this floor or in this room without my authorization is that clear?" The agent nodded. Then Ron motioned for the agents to and shut the door behind them; he wanted to examine the room himself. Fuller looked around the room there and didn't really seem to be anything out of place. The bed was made, the towels in the bathroom were folded, and even the complimentary mints weren't opened. Not a spec, not a hair… nothing. Fuller walked over to the closet and opened it and found the garment bag hanging and on top of the shelf the credit card and the cell phone. He laid the garment bag on the bed and unzipped it and then laid the suits on the bed along with shirts etc. Looking over the clothing carefully he noticed that they were clean, not only were the suits clean but pressed along with the shirts, the ties and the shoes were buffed to a high shine. Turning his attention away from the clothes he sat down on the edge of the bed and looked at the credit card in one hand and the cell phone in the other gave a small smile, shook his head and at that moment he gained somewhat of a respect for Sawyer he was as good, very good. Fuller slipped the cell phone and card into his coat pocket and then proceeded out the door into the hallway. All of a sudden the familiar ring tone of "Raiders of the Lost Ark or Indiana Jones Theme" Fuller pulled out the phone and opened it, the voice on the other side sounded inquisitive to say the least. The voice on the other side of the conversation was the employer demanding a status report. Fuller calmly described the situation "he got a way I don't know how but we will find him sir everything with the exception of Air force One has been grounded indefinitely and there's no way out he is trapped". For a few moments he listened to his employer's disappointment and advice and then the call ended and he put the phone away. He would need a different strategy to catch this prey; it might take longer then he would anticipate "I like a good adventure" he muttered to himself.

Sawyer awoke slowly after a good night's rest. The sleep had done him well; he was also happy with the fact that nothing had happened during the night; his advance planning had paid off. He sat up and reached for a half bottle of water that was sitting on the night table next to the bed he then grabbed the remote which was also laying there and turned on the television to catch up on what was going on. The television came to life and he flipped to the news channel. They were live and waiting for a statement from a government official. Then at exactly nine o'clock a single man walked out and took the podium, it was Fuller. He looked a bit haggard and dismayed as he stood behind it with its big seal of the United States Government. Fuller took a deep breath and cleared his throat as cameras were flashing. He looked directly at the cameras and delivered his statement. "Good morning everyone, this morning an attempt was made to capture the assassin who terminated our beloved president". The reporters who were in the room sat up a little more and turned on their recording devices, pulled out notepads and any other means they had to record all the facts as they were announced... to get the story as it was actually unfolding. Fuller took a sip of his water and then continued. "Now whether or not we had bad Intel, we acted too soon or this assassin has great instincts I don't know but I do know that he escaped capture, but rest assured he will be caught". Sawyer sat at the edge of his bed watching what was going on and at the same time trying to come up with a plan, but then something happened that changed everything. Fuller spoke into the microphone again "I have the name of the culprit. He is a twenty year veteran of Interpol, he will be hard to find but he will be found and with the help of the public we will find him, and if anyone sees him do not try to capture or confront him he is trained in combat and tactics" Fuller then stared straight into the

CHAPTER 13

REMEMBRANCE AND EXODUS

Camera..."His name is... Sawyer Joshua Briggs". Fuller then took another sip of water and did not break his stare at the camera... For the first time Sawyer's name had been made public. Sawyer didn't know what to do so he stayed on the edge of the bed and then the bomb dropped. Fuller added they also had a couple of pictures from the security camera and they were then broadcasted for all to see. Sawyer hung on every word and image that was presented. Fuller decided to bring the press conference to a close but not before there was mention about today's tarmac memorial at the air force base for president Doyle at three o'clock. Fuller walked off and Jason Cobb the president's press secretary took the podium "as everyone knows today at three o'clock the late president Edward Clark Doyle will be given a brief memorial and speech by president Bob Bradley then his casket will be lead a short distance and finally loaded on Air Force One to be flown back to Washington and..." Sawyer stared at the screen for a moment as Cobb's words lost all meaning. At that moment Sawyer came up with a plan "Air Force One, that's it" the president's plane, it would be the only aircraft allowed to leave the island in the near future, he had to get on it. First he needed to get to the air force base and then he would come up with a boarding plan. A complimentary

86

map of the island was provided in his room. It gave the lowdown of the island Sawyer grabbed it and put it in his bag for future reference. He checked his watch. It was ten minutes past nine he would have to be on the plane by three if he had any hope of getting off the island because he knew at three the plane would still be on the ground, if he was late and the plane left he would be caught. He grabbed his bag and walked out of the room sliding the breezeway door behind him. A mode of transportation to the air force base was going to be the first order of business but a quick look around the motel and he discovered there was nothing to jack. He sighed and was going to have to hoof it. Sawyer found a path which would be ideal for him to travel on. It was located fifty feet from the road and was all covered with dense bush, palm trees, shrubs, vines etc. This would provide excellent cover. Sawyer walked a good five miles and then sat down on a fallen palm tree. He pulled out a bottle of water he scammed from the room. He looked out onto the road and he saw something that put a smile on his face. Across the road he noticed a truck pull over but it wasn't any ordinary truck, it was a military fuel truck and there was only one place that needed a truck of that persuasion and that would be the air force base. Now whether it was luck, fate or karma he didn't know, it may just have been the lord saying, "let's give that poor bastard a chance". Sawyer watched as the driver stepped down from the truck and sprinted around to the other side of the vehicle. No doubt he really needed to relieve some pressure. Sawyer quickly guzzled the water down and grabbed his bag, then ran as fast as he could through the scrub to the road. He stopped for a moment to look both ways for other vehicles then ran over to the truck. Carefully and quietly Sawyer opened the door, slipped his bag up into the cab and then got in. He slid across the bench seat to the other side and then slowly looked out the window where the driver was still "draining the lizard." Sawyer was a gentleman and waited for the driver to finish. Just as the driver pulled up his fly Sawyer pushed the door open and hit the driver in the face and knocked him on his back out cold. He then slipped out and dragged the driver into the scrub out of sight and stripped him of his uniform which was just about Sawyer's size, maybe a touch larger. Sawyer walked back to the truck and grabbed a roll of duct tape, then he returned to the driver who was only clad in a green t-shirt, boxer shorts and combat boots. Sawyer decided to leave the boots they weren't his size anyway. He wore his sandals and hoped he wouldn't have to get out. The driver's wrists and ankles were taped along with a piece over his mouth, someone would find him eventually and Sawyer wanted to be a long way away... Camera crews were setting up for what would be a brief ceremony but a sad one as well. Soldiers were gathered around the president's plane, as well as snipers and other means of security, the base was locked up tight. Sawyer pulled up to the main gates with the fuel truck. The officer at the gate approached Sawyer "good morning may I see your paperwork please?" Sawyer handed them to him. The officer looked it over and handed it back to him. "Ok you're clear to drive to the other end, fuel up eagle then park it in spot 221, have a coffee and after the ceremony you can go, now move on" and with that the gates opened and Sawyer drove in. As the fuel truck made it's way to eagle (slang for Air Force One) Sawyer watched as barricades and chairs were set up next to a podium on a small stage which is where the president, dignitaries, the late president's wife and family would sit. Another thing he noticed was the amount of security that seemed to be everywhere. Finally Sawyer pulled up to the plane. He had no idea how to fuel a plane up, no problem he would improvise. A small skinny soldier was waiting by the fuel port of the plane for Sawyer to get out. Sawyer got out holding his stomach "awww man I don't feel so good where's the infirmary?" The soldier answered, "right behind you buddy, you must be new" Sawyer nodded." Could you do me a favor and fill it up? The soldier looked at Sawyer "you want me to fill up the president's plane?... Oh hell yeah, you just take all the time you need to feel better and thanks... I'll even park the truck for you" Sawyer smiled holding his stomach "thank you my friend the spot is 221." as he walked into the infirmary. Sawyer ducked into the men's room, walked over to the window and looked out. The security was tight, too tight. He needed a way in. Then Sawyer's troubles went from bad to worse. A jeep pulled up and inside were two military police but Sawyer really got nervous when he saw sitting in the back of the jeep was the fuel truck driver. Sawyer noticed the young skinny soldier pointing the M.P's in the direction of the fuel truck, it was time to move. Sawyer walked down the hall and grabbed a doctor's coat from a laundry bin he would try to blend in. Sawyer tried to walk at a fast pace but not too fast so as not to attract attention. He could hear the faint pounding of military boots on the ground as he ducked down a hallway and walked all the way to the end. He then paused, the sound had not only gotten louder but had quickened. In his head Sawyer went through different scenarios but they all ended the same way he was dead meat. Sawyer then looked at where he'd ended up. The sign above the door read "Chapel". Pausing for a moment Sawyer made the crucifix sign and slowly opened one of the double doors in front of him "I suppose in light of what's happened he owes me" he muttered to himself and he entered the chapel closing the door behind him and then sprinting to the front and hiding behind the altar. Moments later the doors opened slowly and quietly. Sawyer could see two pairs of combat boots entering the chapel from underneath the altar. As the boots drew nearer to his position a plan had already formed and he would take them out quickly with maximum stealth, he didn't want to harm them, just slow them down. Suddenly the men stopped, turned and stood at attention or so Sawyer could tell from the boots. "What in the name of Sam Hill are you men doing here?" The two men jumbled their words. The one soldier spoke up with a rather uneven tone "Sir we were in pursuit of an intruder who hijacked a fuel truck and got on the base, possibly the assassin who assassinated president Doyle sir" and he finished with a snappy salute. The man who had them in such disarray was General Herbert Justice, a forty –year veteran of the army and at seventy-five was still looking spry and ready for action and was in charge of the American forces anywhere he was, a journeyman general so to speak. The general rubbed his chin "ok boys do a final sweep and get out" The two men approached the altar from opposite sides and then quickly went behind and pulled their sidearms. After a moment they discovered there was no one. The one soldier looked back "all clear sir" and the general responded, "ok then, dismissed… double time!" and the two soldiers quickly left the chapel. As soon as the two soldiers were out of sight the general signaled four higher-ranking soldiers "bring him in boys." The four soldiers, two on each side, wheeled in a casket, which was mounted, on a wood structure with wheels. They brought it to the front of the chapel in front of the altar so that the opening was facing the pews. The four soldiers walked back down the aisle, turned and snapped to attention. The general opened a small wood box that was sitting on a small table at the foot of the casket. Inside the box was an American flag neatly folded. The general removed the flag, handling it as if it were a newborn child, and unfurled it. Slowly he draped it over the casket and then took two steps back and saluted, the soldiers behind him did the same. The general then turned to the soldiers "at ease gentlemen, could you please wait outside. I need a moment and close the door, thank-you" Following orders the soldiers left and closed the door. The general turned to the casket and started to speak to it "you know I carried that flag in my pack all through the jungles of Vietnam saving it in case I was killed so they could put it on the casket and then give it to my wife, yep I never thought…" wiping a few tears from his eyes, "that it would be draped over your pine box, but don't worry old buddy whoever did this to you will pay… I promise, see ya' little brother" and the general walked out of the chapel closing the doors. As he started to make his way down the hall he assigned two soldiers to stand guard "I don't want anyone in or out without my ok, I'll be back in time for the service, is that clear?" The two soldiers answered in unison "yes sir "and saluted. The general saluted back to then and walked away with the two other soldiers in tow. The chapel was silent once again. Slowly, cautiously Sawyer came out from behind a long red curtain which covered the wall all along the back of the chapel behind the altar. Sawyer knew he was lucky that the general came in when he did and provided a distraction so he could change his hiding place. He walked past the altar and down to the pews and sat down quietly.

The Silencer

Sawyer was safe for the moment; after all he had guards outside instructed not to let anyone in until at least the service and with that he looked up at the clock on the wall and knew that his time was limited and he needed to find a way out of this room and off the island. Sitting for nearly ten minutes he racked his brain and nothing came to him. He then took a mental break trying to think of something else. He thought about General Justice. Sawyer knew him, not personally, actually every troop in the army, navy and air force along with government officials knew him; he was a legend. The general kept his family secretive but Sawyer did know he had an adopted brother who was involved in the government as did the rest of the country but that was all the general told everyone. Sawyer sat for a few moments but then curiosity got the best of him and he got up and walked over to the casket. Looking down at the casket he muttered to himself "it must be tough to lose a brother". Sawyer never had to endure the death of a brother, but if it was as half as painful as losing both of his parents he was glad he was an only child. After a few deep breaths he carefully and quietly pulled back the flag half way down. Then he opened the top front of the casket. Lying before him was the deceased President of the United States Edward Clarke Doyle. Sawyer looked at him, here before him was the most powerful man in the world and yet he looked like an ordinary old man. Sawyer took the president's arm and gently squeezed, he was already embalmed for the flight home. Sawyer released the president's arm and put his hand on his chest and said a small prayer. Sawyer was not a religious person, but he knew someone or something created this whole "you only go around once" world and if indeed there was a place where good, pure souls went then the soul from this gentle old man who lied before him would make it there. Sawyer then removed his hand and slowly, silently he closed the casket and covered it once again with the flag. Then taking two steps back he stood at attention, saluted and returned to the pew and tried to figure out how to escape with the assurance that if he couldn't then his fate would be the same as the flag draped coffin. Two o'clock and Sawyer was still at a loss for an idea. Several thoughts entertained his mind, all resulted in failure. Sitting and staring at the flag draped coffin Sawyer was fixated on it. In his head he wished he was in the casket. It was a sure way off the island. At that exact moment Sawyer's eyes lit up and he stared at the casket this time not as a mourner but as an architect. He looked closely below the casket at the stand under it and he grinned with renewed optimism.

It was ten minutes to three when the general and four servicemen returned to the chapel. They were all dressed in full uniform, but none so pronounced as the general who was dressed in his black uniform with several medals adorning his chest with five stars on each shoulder, his hat under his arm and his black shoes with a high shine. Solemnly the casket was wheeled out of the chapel and down the hall, two men a side with the general leading them. They proceeded to the infirmary doors and stopped just inside. It was two fifty – eight not three o'clock the general told them to wait, the one thing the general prided himself on was punctuality, they wanted to start at three o'clock then that's when they would go out. The moment finally arrived and the casket of the deceased was slowly brought out of the infirmary and began its final journey down the runway. The general turned to a lone piper clad in traditional Scottish garb and holding a bagpipe and signaled him to start to play. The lone piper played "amazing grace". The runway was full of army, navy and air force personnel as well as major news broadcasting companies set up high atop scaffolding. The general public was also in attendance crowded behind barricades to catch a glimpse of the casket containing the former president. At the end of the long procession of onlookers was Air Force One with the cargo bay open ready to accept the vessel which would return North Carolina's son to Washington and then back home. As the casket moved down the runway the men and women of the U.S military bowed their heads in silence. The casket stopped halfway to the president's aircraft as the four men and the general turned to the small stage in front of them and stood at attention. The recently sworn in president Bob Bradley put a reassuring hand on Doyle's widow's shoulder, then stood up and approached the podium.

Clearing his voice he started to speak. "Once in a while someone comes along who defies the odds, who makes the impossible seem possible, who sees the glass half full not half empty and who does it with such vigor, resolve and conviction that failure is not even remotely an option that was who Edward Clarke Doyle was". He stopped to clear his throat and wipe his eyes. He regained his composure and continued "He now lies before us at rest, at peace and at ease, he was embraced by a nation and loved by all". Bradley then stared down at the casket "may god welcome you into his kingdom and may you rest in peace, you will be missed god bless you old friend" and with that president Bradley went back and sat down whipping tears from his eyes. The piper started playing and the casket moved on. It finally reached the base of the ramp and stopped. The general and the four soldiers turned their backs to the plane and stood at attention as all the servicemen and women turned to the direction of the plane in unison and gave a loud stomp. In the air three F- 14's flew over the base and each released colored smoke. One was red, one white and one blue as a symbol of America. Then at the order of the general twenty-one soldiers marched into the center of the runway and gave a twenty one gun salute as a sign of respect. After the last round was fired to make twenty-one and the soldiers had exited the middle of the runway the piper played one more chorus of "amazing grace" as the four soldiers and the general turned toward the big, empty cargo hold which only contained the presidential limousine and made their way up the ramp. After loading the casket up and locking the wheels in place to the floor they exited the plane and then the humming sound of the loading ramp sounded as it was raised up and then closed with a loud metallic clang. After a few moments the crowd slowly dispersed, the small stage was taken down and president Bradley, Fuller, the press secretary, four news reporters and five secret service agents boarded the plane. The wife of the deceased president would remain in Hawaii for another day to relax before heading home for burial proceedings and such. The mighty engines roared as the aircraft headed upward against the late afternoon sky.

CHAPTER 14

DECEIT AND DECENT

Meanwhile on the well to do side of Honolulu a well-dressed man with a long black overcoat entered the front door of a penthouse suite "hello? Is anybody here? Hello?" he called out, but there was no response. He walked through the living room and noticed that a sliding door leading to the back was open. Walking through he suddenly was in a lush green environment and just ahead of him was an in ground hot tub with someone in it. Once again the man called out "pardon me I' am looking for…". He stopped in mid sentence noticing the body in the hot tub was not moving, he advanced closer and noticed that it was a man with his head resting on a cushion on the side of the hot tub. Then without warning the man in the hot tub sprang to life like a steel trap grabbing a gun from the side of the hot tub and pointing it directly at the well-dressed man standing between the sliding door and the hot tub. "Who are you and how did you get in here?" the man with the gun abruptly asked. The well-dressed man knowing full well that he should answer right away or run the risk of being perforated answered quickly and decisively while still keeping a cool air about him. "I'm James Mass and I have a key to this particular penthouse suite," he said, dangling a key from his right hand. The man in the hot tub kept the gun on Mass. "How did

94

you get it, did you steal it?" he said in a direct tone. Mass looked back at him "no, nothing like that, I work for your employer and I have something you will be interested in, that is if you're Eli Rose." The man in the hot tub put the gun down on the side of the tub and put his back on the cushion completely at ease "payday is it?" Mass smiled and answered with a laugh in his reply "you got it fella I'll just put it on this patio table" he said as he pulled a large white envelope from the inside of his overcoat and placed it down. After placing the envelope down he walked over to a fully loaded bar just on the inside of the room "mind if I have a drink?" he asked. Eli answered in relaxed manners "why not? it's free". Mass poured a drink for himself then went back out and walked to roughly where he stood a few moments ago. Eli then inquired in a rather serious tone "so how much is there?" Mass paused for a moment "the amount you were quoted is the amount you are being paid plus a bonus fee you earned for being such a pro." He swallowed his drink and started walking to the door. He stopped just short of the door and walked back to the sliding door. He gazed at the envelope on the patio table then switched his focus to the hot tub "I'm sorry Mr. Rose, I almost forgot, my employer on top of making you a wealthy man and you in turn providing him with what he just wanted me to relay a message to you". Eli, not even moving a muscle, replied "can you move it along, I've got plans for tonight!" Mass smiled uncomfortably "oh sure, no problem" and then reached inside his overcoat and pulled out a .88 magnum and proceeded to pull back on the hammer. Eli's one eye opened at the sound and then he sat up. Mass with the .88 magnum pointed at Eli relayed the message "my employer's message is simply... fuck you". Eli went for his gun at the same time Mass fired. The first shot was right in the chest, Eli fell back and then went for the gun again this time he was successful and he managed to fire a shot which shattered the sliding door right next to Mass. Mass fired another shot, Eli's right shoulder looked like it was going to explode as the bullet slammed into it with extreme force and Eli screamed in pain. Again, amidst all the pain Eli stood up and fired another shot, this one had an impact. The shot hit Mass right in the arm but he didn't flinch, Eli, too weak to stand, fell back in the hot tub as Mass pulled the hammer back slowly and the next cartridge loaded into the chamber. Blood was running from Mass's arm, as it was from Eli's shoulder and chest as Mass walked closer towards Eli. He looked at the bleeding heap in front of him and said "I'm surprised you never heard of me, of course the name James Mass wouldn't be familiar to a person of your persuasion and intelligence for that matter" At that moment Eli's eyes opened wide and he recognized the assailant' s face as he stepped into the lights. Mass saw this reaction and continued "you'd probably know me as The Messiah" and with that he pulled the trigger. Eli's head whipped back as the shot found it's target and cracked through his skull. Eli slowly slid below the water. Mass very casually put his gun away, walked over to the patio table and picked up the envelope. On his way to the door he poured himself another drink, then he left shutting the door behind him. He then got into the elevator and it stopped on the main floor. Mass stepped out, he walked through the lobby and out to the street. Summoning a cab he instructed the driver to take him to the airport, the job was done and now it was time to return home and enjoy the spoils of the job.

Meanwhile high over the Pacific Ocean the president's plane was at cruising altitude and everyone aboard was settled in for the flight home. The secret service men were sitting around a table playing Texas Hold'em, the press secretary was on his laptop as well as the news reporters all trying to stay on top of the news as well as sending correspondence to the home office. Ron was reading a newspaper and drinking a screwdriver trying to relax knowing full well that when they touched down in Washington the media circus would reach it's apex. As for the relatively newly appointed president he was sitting near a window starting at his third highball, eyes closed with a headset on listening to ol' blue eyes croon as only he could, the scene was relaxed. The silence in the cargo bay was broken by the sound of small screws hitting the metal floor with tapping sound, until once again silence. Then the side of the stand with the President's casket resting upon it slid over to the side and out came slowly and cautiously Sawyer's head. Looking one way then the other making sure it was safe to come out. The area seemed safe and with that he came out of hiding. stretching and loosened up after being crammed in a tight space for a while, joints were sore and locked up. While stretching Sawyer looked around at the cargo hold "so this is where our tax dollars go" he said to himself. The cargo hold itself was empty with the exception of the casket, which was set further back in the hold, and the president's limousine which was sleek black and rugged looking. Sawyer was happy to be out of his wooden gulag. There was little space, and no ventilation with the exception of the side of the stand being a quarter of an inch over so there was a slim slit. Sawyer reached in the stand for his bag and put it on the trunk of the limo and then felt the sweat on his body start to evaporate. Unbeknown to him a tiny sensor was triggered the moment he came out from underneath the casket and a small red light started to blink on the console in the cockpit. The pilot noticed the tiny red light and left the cockpit to see the agents. He walked over to the table where the agents were playing cards, he cleared his throat "sorry to break up your game gentlemen but the motion sensor for the cargo hold is flashing, now I know it must be a glitch in the system but I have to tell you security measures, you know." The agent closest to him nodded in acknowledgement and the pilot returned to the cockpit. Gene Horowitz, who was the head agent looked at the men at the table "any volunteers" he asked, one of the agents responded "you're the boss man" Horowitz looked at the men who were looking at the ground or fidgeting with the poker chips "ok, fine I'll go, deal me out I'll be back in a minute" he said leaving the table. Horowitz started to walk to the rear of the plane when he ran into Fuller going back to his seat with a cup of coffee. "Where are you going Horowitz?" He enquired. "The pilot said the motion sensor in the cargo hold had gone off, I know it might be nothing but you know..." Horowitz was cut off by Fuller "yeah policy, well let me know what you find... if anything" and with that the agent nodded and made his way to the back of the plane where an elevator was that would take him down to the luggage compartment and then a set of stairs to the cargo hold. Fuller sipped his coffee as he watched Horowitz walk towards the rear of the plane and the elevator. As Fuller watched a strange thought entered his mind, "what if, just what if Sawyer had somehow managed to get on the plane? but that was too impossible to contemplate because everyone was monitored coming on and the plane had a complete sweep while it was on the ground" Fuller took another sip of his coffee and began to second guess himself "and yet... he infiltrated the base in a fuel truck" Fuller put down his coffee on an open tray table "I'd better check it out myself" he said to himself. Fuller walked toward the elevator as it was coming back up. Horowitz walked down the stairs to the cargo hold and then keyed in the special code and entered. The next sight he saw baffled him beyond all reasonable doubt. Ahead of the agent was someone trying to jack the president's limousine. The agent, still not being able to comprehend what was going on, withdrew his gun from his shoulder holster "hold it right there". The agent, a little nervous, then started to say "ok now slowly stand up". Sawyer slowly stood up holding two wrenches in each hand that he was using to try to pry off the cover which housed the wires to hotwire the limo. Slowly Sawyer started to turn towards the agent, as he did he threw one of the wrenches at him. At the last second the agent moved his head to the side and avoided the wrench completely. He looked at Sawyer and stated quite sarcastically "you missed" as he smirked. Sawyer on the other hand simply raised an eyebrow and answered with "oh did I" The agent looked towards the back of the cargo hold and noticed that the keypad which assessed the door was smoking and slightly sparking with a wrench protruding from its center. The agent looked back at Sawyer "what did you do that for?" he asked. Sawyer squeezed the three remaining wrenches in his left hand, then without warning Sawyer threw another wrench at the agent, this time the wrench knocked the agent's radio right off his belt and sent it smashing into the solid metal floor. The agent looked at Sawyer "stop that already you're pissing me off!" Sawyer, with a wrench in each hand, put his index fingers through the ends and began to twirl them almost resembling an old time gunslinger. A few moments passed and another wrench was hurled at the agent, this time it knocked the gun out of his hand and onto the floor. The agent looked at Sawyer "so ya' wanna play rough huh?" he said with a smile. Sawyer dropped the last wrench on the ground "why not." Sawyer said, answering the challenge. Much to Sawyer's surprise the agent, who was close enough to pick up the gun, instead opted to kick it away, sending it skidding across the floor to the side of the plane. The agent then rolled up his sleeves and started to jump side to side doing pre fight warm-ups. As the agent was "warming up" he talked to Sawyer listing his accolades in the boxing ring. Sawyer was impressed and replied" yeah, ok I've watched the Rocky movies I think I get the jist of it" The agent came at Sawyer like he was standing still and planted three right jabs and a left hook and while Sawyer was shaking his head trying to figure out what happened the agent caught Sawyer with a crushing blow to the ribs and the a huge upper cut which knocked Sawyer backwards into the back of the president's limousine. Sawyer placed his hands on the bumper and slowly pulled himself up, leaned on the trunk, reassessed the situation and went back on the attack. He unloaded three big right hands directly to the agent's head, the agent in turn smiled as his head snapped back from every blow as if it were spring loaded. Sawyer was then greeted with three big right hands that rocked him down to his soul and a left uppercut, which sent Sawyer sprawling backward into the limo's bumper. Sawyer had to give the agent credit after giving out the beating to him the agent always backed up and obeyed the rules. "That's it" Sawyer thought the Achilles heel of the agent was the rules, Sawyer now had his second wind and a plan. Sawyer stood up, his feet steady and his eyes focused on the agent "round two assholes!" Sawyer stated to the agent. The agent, while still bouncing around motioned with his hands and replied "bring it on bitch!" Sawyer came at the agent like a man possessed, hitting him with left and right combinations but the agent covered up and the blows had little effect. The agent in turn delivered a right hook which staggered Sawyer for a moment and then out of nowhere Sawyer connected with a left jab right to the bridge of the agent's nose which dazed him. Sawyer could feel the momentum start to shift as he unloaded with another left jab which hit the target and then Sawyer decided it was time to switch strategies so he drew back with his right hand and faked a right punch the agent raised his hands and blocked the punch. At that same moment Sawyer buried his right foot into the agent's crotch and raised him off the ground a few inches then as the agent crouched clutching his pride Sawyer came up with a knee, which hit him in the face and shattered his nose. The agent's head flew back as a wad of blood and snot was launched at the ceiling. It was time for Sawyer to wrap it up, as the agent teetered, almost falling down Sawyer took a few steps back then ran, leaped into the air and delivered a roundhouse kick which connected with his target's chin spinning him around once and then falling back onto the shiny steel floor with a thud. Sawyer walked over to the bumper of the limo and sat down to rest a moment and catch his breath, "two... four... six... eight... ten... you're out". A few moments later Sawyer dragged the agent across the floor to the side of the aircraft where he handcuffed him to the side railing all the while wondering which was harder, dragging the agent to the side or knocking him out. The task was finally completed and Sawyer walked over to the driver side door, which was still open and knelt down hoping to finish the job. He finally opened the panel but didn't touch anything because he felt the cool touch of a gun barrel against the back of his head. A voice behind him instructed him to get up and walk slowly back to the rear of the car, Sawyer complied. The voice then told him to turn around and to keep his hands where he could see them. Sawyer turned around and kept his hands in full view. Sawyer then saw who was holding the gun and it shocked him for a moment. "You" he said with an air of disgust as he stood by the trunk. There stood Ron Fuller with a gun pointed no more than three feet from Sawyer's face. Ron then pulled a small radio from a pouch on his belt. With the gun still pointed he spoke into the radio, but spoke in quiet tones, Sawyer couldn't quite make out what he was saying all he knew was it was about him. A few minutes passed and Ron put the radio back in the pouch on his belt and gave a small smile

The Silencer

to Sawyer. He then spoke to Sawyer in an almost upbeat tone "well Sawyer I just spoke to the pilot and in twenty minutes we will begin our descent to Las Vegas, there will be a small welcoming party there and you will be taken to a maximum security prison for holding until it's time to take you to one in Washington where you will stand trial we on the other hand will proceed to Washington so as not to attract too much attention." Sawyer stood silent for a moment then jokingly said, "You mean no buffets?" Ron raised an eyebrow and shook his head. Sawyer knew he had at least twenty minutes to formulate a plan because once on the ground he was toast. Sawyer started to pace back and forth while Ron kept the gun on him. Sawyer stopped and turned to Ron "well seeing as it's just you me and sleepy over there let's try and pass the time." Ron looked at Sawyer "what did you have in mind?" Sawyer, seeing Ron was on board, made his pitch "How about twenty questions" Ron nodded. A sheepish look came over Sawyer's face. "I really only have four but they are really good ones." he cleared his throat "ok question number one how does it feel to set someone up and then screw them over?" Ron calmly answered the question "I didn't screw you over, it's complicated." Sawyer nodded his head indicating the answer was adequate. "Ok question number two, why did your employer and you want the president rubbed out and who is this all mighty employer?" Ron stared at Sawyer with a look that could cut lead and didn't answer the question, instead he pulled the hammer back on the gun. Sawyer had struck a nerve "ok no need to get hostile, question number three how long do you think you can hold that gun on me until your arm gets tired?" Ron smiled "that's easy I'm not going to, as soon as we begin our descent I'm gonna cuff your ass to that higher railing on the side until we land." Sawyer's eyebrows rose "good enough, now here's the final question: are you ready?" Ron answered "lay it on me" Sawyer took a deep breath "alright what kind of vehicle keeps guns underneath the steering?" Before Ron could even comprehend the question Sawyer reached behind himself and produced a gun and held it on Ron. Ron looked surprised and answered" the president's limo do I win?" he said sarcastically Sawyer gave a small laugh "yes you do but now here is the bonus question, do you know what kind of situation we are involved in right here right now?" Ron shook his head side to side. Sawyer piped up "it's a Mexican standoff but in Mexico it's just called a standoff, thanks for playing." For several minutes both men stood facing each other, guns pointed not a sound not a movement, a total test of stamina. Beads of sweat started to form on both men's foreheads, but neither would give the other the satisfaction of showing fatigue. Sawyer stood poised and knew time was ticking by and they would start their descent soon he needed to gain the advantage and get moving. Sawyer finally decided it was time to get something in motion "Ron this is stupid we are gonna be standing here until one of us gets weak then the other will gain the advantage, I have a better plan, would you like to hear it?" Ron just stared at Sawyer. Sawyer kept on coaxing "c'mon Ron how long do you think you can last? Because the moment I see weakness I'm on you like flies on shit, believe it!" Ron finally spoke, much to Sawyer's delight, "ok I'll listen but if I don't like your idea then screw you". Sawyer nodded in agreement then laid it out for Ron. "Ok I'll count down from three to one and at the same time we lower our weapons and at one they will be pointed at the floor so we can have a civilized flight into Las Vegas, sound alright?" Ron contemplated the proposal and voiced his opinion "fine, under one condition, you don't try to escape". Sawyer looked into Ron's eyes "on my honor, you have my word." Ron then nodded with an apprehensive look on his face. Both men locked eyes more intensely as Sawyer started the count. "Three" the guns started lower, "two" they lowered even more, "one" the guns were pointed at the floor, and the tension was broken for a moment. The eyes were still locked but there was a slight look of relief on both their faces as the numbness that started to overtake their extremities was slowly beginning to disappear. Suddenly Sawyer twirled the gun on his finger and the barrel rested in his hand and with the handle of the gun exposed he swung it catching Ron in the face before he could contemplate what happened. Covering his face Ron dropped his gun and Sawyer caught it before it hit the ground. Now

Sawyer was pointing two guns in Ron's face and all Ron could do was hold his nose and stare in disbelief as Sawyer motioned him over to the side of the plane. He looked at Ron holding his nose "ok now cuff yourself to the rail next to Tyson over here and let go of your nose it's not that bad." Ron cuffed himself to the rail and sat down. Sawyer then went over to a storage locker and took out a parachute and just as he passed Ron he heard a statement being made. Ron spoke up "you've got no honor you bastard!" Sawyer sprung around and walked back a few steps and squatted down so he was face to face with Fuller. "What did you say?" he said calmly. Ron stared into Sawyer's eyes "you heard me you asshole, you've no honor, integrity, not a fucking thing!" With his head hung for a moment Sawyer then addressed the statement "you're upset at me because I promised not to try to escape if you lowered your gun when I did… right, am I in the ballpark?" Ron lip started to quiver, not only because he was irate and Sawyer was calm, but also because he was stating the obvious and making Ron feel like a child. He finally snapped, "My God you're a fucking genius asshole, that's absolutely right ya' jerk off!" he shouted stating to turn red. Taking a deep breath Sawyer gave his defense "Yes I did promise to try not to escape" he said then he raised his index finger "but as you can see I'm not trying I' am escaping". Ron's red face started to lighten but the scowl remained. Sawyer added insult to injury "so who's the jerk off now?" he said, giving two fast, light slaps to the side of Ron's face, then stood up and walked around to the open door on the driver's side of the limo and knelt down. Ron sat quietly for a moment, and then came up with an idea he decided to heckle the unflappable Sawyer and throw him off his game; if he did that he might buy some time until the descent into Las Vegas. Sawyer twisted a black wire and a red wire together and the interior light and a small screen came up out of the dashboard and asked for the password in order to start the vehicle. Ron could hear the password screen and a few choice adjectives from Sawyer as well, now was the time. Ron cupped his mouth "can't start the car without the password? Huh genius?" Sawyer stood up, folded his arms and laid them on the top of the car followed by his head "and I suppose you do?" Ron smiled back at him "yep, but it doesn't matter what I know because I won't tell you, you're screwed" Ron said laughing. Sawyer started laughing along with Ron and that's when he stopped. Sawyer, still slightly laughing told Ron why he was laughing, "Ron I don't need you to tell me shit because this is Doyle's limo and he was a strong believer in tradition so it stands to reason that he has the same code as his predecessors which I think hasn't been changed since the early nineties, so unless I'm wrong the password is…" and with that he sat in the driver's seat. As Ron watched, Sawyer punched in the five-letter password and all of a sudden the limousines engine started. Ron's mouth hung open for a moment then he waited until Sawyer emerged before he spoke "how the hell do you know the password and don't give me any of your brain baffling bullshit either". Sawyer shrugged his shoulders "driver went on vacation and I got time and a half". Ron just shook his head. Sawyer put on the parachute and once it was secure he walked over to the ramp controls on the side fifty feet from the tail of the plane. One panel read, "boot control" and underneath were three buttons "on" "off" "lock" and "unlock". Sawyer pressed "unlock" and "off" and in an instant the boots on all four tires dropped off with a "clang" on the steel floor. The panel next to it had numbers and letters on it; Sawyer knew where this was going. Looking over his shoulder at Ron who was smiling "now I know you don't know that code, smartass". Sawyer cracked a small smile "on the contrary Ron I do it's "trigger" do you want me to prove it?" Ron nodded, so Sawyer withdrew his gun, took a few steps back and fired a single shot at the panel, which busted open in a puff of smoke. Sawyer looked back at Ron and winked "you see it was "trigger" and you thought I didn't know it… silly boy" Ron snickered "how do you intend to open the door you just blew the controls". Sawyer walked over to a big lever next to the smoldering panel, and pulled it half way down which would release the ramp halfway down so that it was horizontal with the plane. No sooner was the lever pulled then the ramp started to come down and a cool breeze came over Sawyer. The ramp's descent was steady and when it reached the position required it stopped with a hiss and a bang. Sawyer then walked over to the limo and grabbed his bag from the back seat and put it in the front seat. With the driver's door open Sawyer placed one foot inside the door and looked back at Ron one last time and spoke "ask yourself why and you might be surprised, your better than this, your just a puppet, control your actions don't let someone else just keep pulling the strings" and with that Sawyer got in the limo and slammed the door. He was sitting in the driver's seat and revving the engine. Looking in the rearview mirror he saw Ron fidgeting in his coat pocket looking for the key to cuffs and Sawyer could bet he also had a gun strapped to his ankle. Putting the limo in drive with his foot on the brake as well as the gas.Using all the strength he had to hold them down, waiting until the time was right to release the brake. Ron was finally uncuffed and reached for his gun which was strapped to his ankle just as Sawyer thought. Sawyer had seen enough and took one last look at the horizon ahead of him, he took one last deep breath, closed his eyes and released the brake. The limo's wheels smoked and slid on the smooth metal floor and then sped out straight across the ramp and out of the plane. The limo went a full five feet then started it decent to the ground. Ron with one hand on the railing and one hand on his gun rushed as fast as he could to the ramp just in time to see the limo disappear into the clouds. Dropping his head Ron knew no one could survive a big drop like the one he just had witnessed. He went over and pushed the lever back up and the ramp slowly closed back up. Ron took his radio out and told the pilot to keep on course to Washington and then he radioed one of his men to inform the president and keep the reporters at bay. Meanwhile as the limo sped towards the ground Sawyer couldn't help telling himself "this was a bad idea".

November 11 Veterans Day Arlington, Texas.

CHAPTER 15

HUNTING FOR A UNICORN

The sky was gray as the cool November wind blew the last of the colorful leaves from a tree in Arlington Cemetery. The president stood alongside governors, senators and other government officials as well as onlookers who were all there to honor America's veterans and war dead. Speeches were read, wreaths were laid and "taps" was played, all the standard protocol and traditions that were a part of Veteran's day. Afterwards all the officials went their separate ways and back to work. The president opted to take the private jet from Washington because he hated the media always traveling with him on Air Force One. On the jet were only the pilot, one stewardess, the president, Fuller and four secret servicemen and no reporters, much to the president's delight. The president sat next to Fuller. "So Fuller, anything on Briggs?" Bradley asked. Ron answered with a dismayed look on his face "no sir, not since two days ago when the limo was found". Bradley rubbed his chin "hmmm do you have all the proper measures in place?" Ron answered decisively "yes, we have a five hundred mile radius being swept and so far nothing, it's like he vanished". Bradley smiled. Ron raised an eyebrow "is there something I should know about... sir?" Just then the stewardess brought beverages for them, a scotch on the rocks for Bradley and a coffee for Ron. Bradley took

The Silencer

a sip of his scotch and let Ron in on his smile "well truth be told Ron I posted a ten million dollar reward for anyone who brings in Briggs dead or alive, now I know he must be dead after that hellacious fall so I might get the carcass and if he survived be may be headed deep underground so big deal at least he's gone but I would like you to hop on out to the crash site and look the car over, you know for clues and such" Ron was stirring his coffee and answered without even looking at Bradley "I'm way ahead of you sir, I've already called and advised the crew there to take pictures, look around but leave the limo until I have had a chance to look it over" he said while taking a sip of coffee. Bradley's smile grew even more intense "Outstanding. That's the reason I am putting you at the head of the class very slowly my boy because you've got integrity, loyalty and desire to do your job and do it right" he said as the jet made it's way back to Washington. No sooner did the jet touch down in Washington then it took off with Ron for the crash site just near the California and Nevada state line. Ron landed at a military training facility where a helicopter had been arranged to transport him to the crash site. Ron got off the jet, walked fifty feet and got into a military helicopter which already had its props spinning in anticipation of the flight. The helicopter came over a mountain range as Ron got his first view of the crash site, from what he gathered about a mile and a half was closed off around the site and it looked heavily guarded. Ron's helicopter landed five miles outside the site so dust wouldn't compromise the investigation. A black S.U.V picked him up and drove him in. The sight of the limo as he got closer chilled him to the bone; it was nothing but a twisted mass of metal; in fact it almost didn't resemble a limousine at all. Once Ron arrived he walked over to the site, which looked more like a command center that he had seen in Vietnam some years ago. A man dressed in military fatigues and sporting a gray crew cut came over to greet Ron. The man saluted then shook Ron's hand "Captain Ric Fox, I run this chaotic mess Mr. Fuller, anything you want or need just ask". Ron nodded "thank-you Captain and for starters call me Ron". They both started walking towards the limo and when they were standing no less than five feet from it Fox stood in front of Ron "with all due respect... Ron I have never covered anything like this I have done plane crashes, train wrecks, helicopter mishaps but nothing like this," he said with a smile shaking his head in disbelief as he looked at the limo. Ron gave a small smile as well and slapped Fox's back "there's a first time for everything, do you mind if I spend some time with the car, I want to give it the once over or even a twice over, if that's alright?" Fuller inquired "Sure, I can't see a problem with taking all the time you need, but if you find anything please tell me I sure could use some help on this one" Fox said. Ron agreed and with that Captain Fox left Ron to investigate the wreckage. Ron looked at the wreckage closely trying to first figure out where the back and front were located. Ron closed his eyes for a moment and visualized the car without all the damage and then opened his eyes and immediately he could recognize where everything was supposed to be. He first pulled out a pair of latex gloves that he was handed in the S.U.V on the way to the scene. Opening the driver's side door with the utmost care and looking in, the realization of Sawyer's demise was starting to look more realistic. Then Ron noticed a detail that was probably overlooked due to the shape of the vehicle in question. The panel between the front of the limo and the back, which contained a small window was pushed in and had come out and it wasn't due to the impact of the fall, if that were the case there would be chards of glass and plastic all around but this was right out of the frame. After making a mental note of the first observation he walked over to what used to be the door to the back of the limousine which even still bore the presidential seal or what was left of it. Once again opening the back door he used the utmost care and started looking around. Starting his search at the divider panel he looked on the floor and saw the panel then he looked around the once luxurious back section of the limo but nothing. Looking over the whole section, another detail struck him as odd: the sunroof was open. For a moment Ron stood dumb founded and scratched his head and muttered to himself "a pushed out divider panel and an open sunroof" Ron tried to make a connection but came up empty. Suddenly he made a connection, a small one but at least he had something. Ron looked into the back again; he only needed to find one more piece of the puzzle. His anticipation was growing as he looked at every detail he knew it would present itself, it had to. The sun slowly started to sink into the horizon and the sky took on a light pick color as Ron still searched the back of the limo for something, which links everything together. Ron was about to give up after looking closely at the back when something miraculous happened. As Ron watched, the sun shone through the broken glass of the window and cast a shadow on a pair of footprints, which were on the backseat. Ron smiled, that was the piece of the puzzle that was the connection. He took a deep breath and walked to the back of the limo to piece everything together. Closing his eyes once again he saw what had transpired. Sawyer somehow pushed the divider panel out, slid through to the back, got up on the seat, opened the sunroof and propelled himself out like a rocket by pushing up and letting the natural force of the fall pull him out. Everything fit, Ron withdrew a cigarette and lit it as he stared out into the desert as the sun started to set and a light breeze blew. One question still remained "where did he land?" Ron walked over to the command tent and looked at a map of the surrounding area, now depending on the wind Sawyer could have landed anywhere it was going to be a very long search and even longer if Sawyer could find a good place to land and he could hightail it out to somewhere safe and he probably he would. Ron walked over to the wreckage once again still smoking his cigarette and couldn't believe Sawyer was alive, he didn't know where but the son of a bitch was alive. Ron was finishing his cigarette when Fox came over and startled Ron from behind. "So Mr. Fuller… er I mean Ron did you find anything?" Fox inquired. For the first time in Ron's life let alone his career he found himself at a crossroad. On the one hand he should tell Fox everything he knows and keep the investigation going and on the other he should just keep the information to himself. Sawyer's words were still echoing in his mind. It was a moment, right vs. wrong, good vs. evil, light vs. dark. It was as if there was an angel on his one shoulder saying, "Do the right thing" and on the other a devil saying "fuck'em". Finally he told Fox what he had found "I found nothing absolutely nothing, wrap it and ship it to Washington the lab boys will figure it out, I'm going to grab a coffee and get out of here, thanks for your help Fox" Fox shook Ron's hand "thank you Ron it's been a pleasure and if you want coffee there's a tent over there" Fox then walked back to the command tent. Ron walked over to the mess tent, all the while thinking, "if this is a case of conscience, I don't want it but it's not as bad as I thought". Ron entered the tent and immediately was greeted by the smell of fresh brewed coffee permeating not only the tent but his senses as well. He walked up to the coffeemaker and poured two cups, one for himself and one for his driver. Ron thought to himself, "after all the poor guy waited in the vehicle all this time" and headed for his ride back to the helicopter. Ron opened the door to the S.U.V and took one last look at the wreckage, although it was twisted mass Ron had a small smile on his face having renewed faith that Sawyer might still be alive but he didn't understand why he lied to Fox or why he cared if Sawyer had survived it puzzled him and he shook his head, got in the vehicle and shut the door. The S.U.V made it's way down the road on the rather short trip back to the waiting helicopter. Ron put a cup of coffee in the cup holder for the driver, the driver turned to Ron "thank-you sir" he said as he picked it up and took a sip. Ron nodded his head and sipped his coffee. While looking out the window at the darkness as it started to blanket the desert. The driver put his coffee back in the holder and spoke "did you find what you were looking for sir?" he asked. Ron looked over at the driver and wanted to say something positive but he knew he couldn't "no, not really just doing my official thing" he said with a rather awkward look on his face. "Oh ok, by the way my name is James" he said. Ron put out his hand "Ron Fuller" and shook James' hand. "Do you think he could have survived?" he asked. Ron looked at the driver with a small grin "no, not really". James, now concentrating more on the road"trying to get off the subject. "That's too bad," he said with a disappointed tone. "Oh yeah and why is that?" he queried. James with a broad smile on his face looked over at Ron "because that would have been one hell of a trick, for a simple assassin don't you think?" Ron was silent for a few moments then addressed the question "yeah it would have been a hell of a trick indeed." The miles drifted by as Ron finally arrived at the helicopter, he shook the driver's hand "thanks for the ride James" Ron said. James smiled back "it was my pleasure Mr. Fuller see you around" then Ron got out and shut the door and no sooner did he get on the helicopter then the S.U.V disappeared into the darkness in a cloud of dust. Ron sat back and closed his eyes for the trip back to the base and the jet home. He could hardly wait. It had been a long day.

CHAPTER 16

THE KEY

The days and weeks seemed to melt together as winter was coming at a rapid pace. The period of lying in state for the former president had come and gone with all the family, friends, heads of state, media and onlookers getting their last glimpse at the best loved president of the modern era. After all the ceremonies and documentaries the assassinated commander and chief was flown via a military escort back to his home state of North Carolina where after a small humble service Edward Clarke Doyle was laid to rest in a family plot which spanned back five generations, no cameras were allowed near the service. Agent Fuller and Agent Horowitz were awarded medals of bravery for their courageous efforts on board Air Force One, trying and failing to apprehend the killer of the deceased president but protecting the current president in the process Fuller also was promoted to the president's head of security and special operations which included a substantial bump in pay and an office in the Pentagon. Thanksgiving was fast approaching and it was also time for the former president Doyle's cabinet to get together for their annual turkey dinner at the White House a tradition he maintained like his predecessors when he first came into office for everyone to get together eat and sneak in a quick meeting with his cabinet, although the figure at the head of the

112

table may have changed the tradition remained the same and the cabinet could hardly wait. The president's cabinet came together at the white house two days before the actual Thanksgiving Day so as to give the cabinet the chance to celebrate the day with their families. The entire cabinet was sitting around a long table, which had been set up in the white house's dining room. The table was decorated in the pomp and circumstance of the day. Napkins, wine glasses, plates and cutlery adorned the table with pinpoint accuracy, in short the table was about as near perfection as it could get. The only two items that were missing from the whole thanksgiving ensemble were the turkey and the president. Suddenly the large set of double doors at the end of the room opened and the president entered the room. Quickly the cabinet rose to it's feet as the president made his way to the head of the table. He picked up the sterling silver butter knife to his left and tapping the crystal wine glass to his right spoke "welcome friends it is truly an honor to be among all of you breaking bread and sharing in this enduring tradition which brings together a cabinet of colleagues and turns them into a table full of friends, once again welcome, good appetite and may god bless and keep you, thank you very much". Then the president sat down, two succulent turkeys were brought out and the meal commenced. After the meal concluded, coffee and a traditional dessert of hot apple pie was brought out and distributed to the cabinet as well as the president and as everyone was enjoying the pieas well as the coffee, the president stood up. He took a sip of water and began "first off. I hope everyone enjoyed the meal" and he looked up and down the full length of the table, noticing a vast array of smiles. The president continued "I had an ulterior motive for inviting you here tonight, I want to make an announcement of sorts if you will indulge me for a few moments while you finish your dessert". Everyone's attention was now solely on the president as they ate and drank slowly and quietly. The president took a big gulp of coffee and began, "friends... on December twenty second I will give a state of the union address, now I know it is highly irregular to do this being so close to Christmas and all" he said as he peered at the table which was hanging on his every word. He left his seat at the head of the table and started to walk down the one side of the table while talking, "That evening while I have everyone's attention I will outline an idea I have, not just an idea but a groundbreaking historical concept that will not only strengthen America as we know it but will make this country better and safer for the future generations to come". The president started coming up the other side of the table with a enthusiasm that was building as he spoke "I call it "The land of the free and the home of the brave initiative, this plan alone will eliminate casualties of war, crime in this great nation, terrorism which plagues this country day in and day out while bringing back jobs and a sense of pride and confidence to what I personally consider the greatest country in the world." The cabinet was speechless. The president continued, "now I know there will be some naysayers and I know there will be people who will hate me for what I' am going to do and I' am damn sure this concept will be a tough pill to swallow and it might infuriate the entire world for that matter, but the end will justify the means and that's why it's so imperative that I have your unwavering support, the cabinet's support in this my time of need and I guarantee all of you will bear witness to the greatest transformation of a nation in the history, thank you for listening everyone." Then the president sat back down and finished his coffee. The cabinet was silent, everyone trying to find the words for such an awe-inspiring speech. Ron drank his coffee and while his cup was up near his mouth he surveyed the table and needed to do something so he put down his coffee and began to clap his hands. Slowly but surely everyone at the table started to clap and after a moment or two the room was immersed in applause and the president nodded in approval. As the night lingered on all the members of the cabinet slowly started to leave but not before going up to the president shaking his hand and wishing him a "happy thanksgiving". Soon the room was empty except for Ron, the president and the kitchen staff who were cleaning up the leftovers of what was a wonderful meal. Ron rubbed his eyes and looked at his watch. It was almost ten o'clock when he got up from his chair and stretched. He yawned

The Silencer

as he walked over to the president "well I guess I'd better hit the trail, have a happy thanksgiving Mr. president" he said shaking president Bradley's hand. President Bradley held on to Ron's hand for a moment "do you have a minute Ron?" Ron nodded and the two sat down. Bradley poured Ron a glass of wine and then poured one for himself. Bradley held his glass up "to progress" he said and then took a drink, Ron did the same. Then Bradley reached into his inside coat pocket and removed a black case with the presidential seal on it similar to the cigarette case that was used back in the sixties and put it down in front of Ron. Ron looked at the case and then jokingly said "Mr. President are you proposing?" Bradley laughed for a moment "just open it". So Ron did just that, opened the lid but what he saw inside was no laughing matter in fact the smile that was on his face had completely disappeared. Inside the case was a white card with a series of numbers and letters on it encased in a hard plastic cover with a line going across the center with a blue cord and on the end of the cord was a plug and a chain with a hole through the top. Ron looked at the card in the case "is that what I think it is?" he asked. The president nodded. Ron quickly swallowed the rest of his wine "I can't accept this. I'm not even supposed to see this, this is not supposed to leave your possession by no means, I… I can't accept this I'm sorry sir" and Ron slid the case in front of the president. Bradley sipped his wine "now wait minute I'm the president and I want you to hold on to it, heaven forbid you're not going to use it, I'm only doing this because if something happens to me the code can't fall into the wrong hands, do you understand what I'm saying Ron?" and he slid the case back in front of Fuller. Putting his finger through the chain Ron lifted the card out of the case and dangled it in the light. The president put his hand on Ron's shoulder "Ron I trust you and that's why I've decided before the next year is out and my concept is in full swing I would like to make you my Vice President, that is if you'll accept the call when it is given". Ron looked at Bradley and put one hand on his chest and took a deep breath "this is a real sudden sir of course I will answer the call if it is given". Bradley patted Ron's shoulder and stood up taking the last swallow of his wine "ok then Ron it's past my bedtime and I'm sure the cleaning crew wants to start finishing up here too, I'll see you Monday". Ron had already finished his wine when the mention of him becoming vice president came up. Ron grabbed the president's hand with both of his hands and shook it "Thank- you once again and have a happy thanksgiving Mr. President". Ron put the card inside his inner coat pocket and started walking towards the door. "Excuse me Ron," the president said as Ron had his hand on the doorknob. Ron turned back to the president "yes sir?" The president smiled at Ron "try not to lose it… ok?" Ron smiled back "I'll try not to" he said then opened the door and left.

December, 22, 2009 Oval Office, The White House 7:45pm

CHAPTER 17

THE ADDRESS HEARD AROUND THE WORLD

The cameras were set up in the oval office for the president's "State of the Union address". Security was extremely tight, no one was allowed in the room except for people wearing a special holographic pass on their neck. The night itself had been hyped as if the Pope were coming for a visit or a heavyweight title fight either way America if not the world would be watching. A young blond woman was applying the last touches of make-up on the president who looked a little nervous until Ron entered the room. Ron immediately made his way over to the president amidst the confusion. "Sorry sir I just made the last security check, it's tight," Ron said with the utmost confidence. President Bradley looked more at ease and then asked the make-up girl if she was done which she was and left. The president had last minute concerns about security and related them to Ron "I don't mean to be a pain but tell me about the precautions taken tonight." Ron looked at Bradley with a warm smile "ok, I have snipers on all the rooftops, a two block radius has been sectioned off around the building, the building itself has military in front of the entrance six highly skilled agents will be in the room for the entire duration of the address and..." he said pointing at a red telephone on the desk next to his regular one "the red phone which only you can access has direct contact with the military incase of a crisis, any more questions sir?" The president scratched his head "tell me about it after the speech". Ron explained "When you finish the address, I will personally take you to your helicopter on the South lawn where you will be taken to the air force base and depart to an undisclosed location at least to everyone in general, for a little rest and relaxation". President Bradley smiled knowing he was covered. Then the president had a somber look "Ron after I do this I want you to still respect me I know what I'm about to do could have dire consequences but I'd rather swallow this horse pill then down the line have everything fall apart" The director walked over to where Ron and The President were talking "three minutes till Showtime" Ron shook the president's hand and wished him good luck then took a seat on the couch and waited to see how this would all turn out. The clock on the wall was the focal point for everyone and as the time ticked down the director got in position, the president smoothed out his gray hair and straightened his tie. The director got the president's attention and then started the countdown "five... four... three..." and then he went silent and motioned with his two fingers, two and finally one then he pointed at the president who in turn saw all the cameras red lights light up... It was go time. The president looked straight into the camera "Good evening my fellow Americans, my name is Robert "Bob" Sutton Bradley and I' am the president of the United States of America a position I was thrust into by the sudden assassination of my beloved predecessor and friend if you will, a position I will not take lightly". Then in an unorthodox move the president got up from behind his desk, walked over to the front of his desk and leaned on the front like a high school teacher lecturing his class. The director nearly had a stroke when the president went off the script by changing position, but motioned the cameras to stay with him. The president then loosened his tie and continued "I' am supposed to give a state of the union address and I will give one soon enough but first allow me to tell you a little about myself, in nineteen thirty-eight I was born an only child in Iowa, my mother was a seamstress and my father was a sergeant in the US army and fought in world war two, in fact my grandfather fought in world war one and eventually I enlisted in the military in nineteen fifty six and saw action in Korea, and did three tours of duty in Vietnam, became senator, a vice president and now I stand before you the weight of this great nation on my shoulders" The entire room was wondering why in the hell president Bradley was rambling on and not getting to the address, they were about to find out. The president took a sip of water and continued "the reason I' am mentioning all of this is because back in their day and when I was a child, products in this country said made in the U.S.A." now they say assembled in the U.S.A, made in China or India or Mexico or some other third world country and, hell more Americans are driving Asian vehicles than ever before and we invented the damn automobile as I recall didn't we? That's right friends, they may be produced here and assembled here but it sure as hell isn't built here but the profits go across the pond out of the pockets of Americans and into the pockets Asian business higher ups and why is that because of what? Price? And another term which gets used way too much is melting pot. I still want to see old glory on my flagpole years from now, don't you? Now I know I may be coming off as a bit of a racist to a great many people right about now but it's not racism it's patriotism I' am proud of this country and what it stands for or what it stood for but I think slowly but surely we will lose our identity and become the minority unless we do something now, you want to know the state of the union? It's weak, has no backbone and if it is not addressed soon will lead to America's demise." The president then stood up and went back behind his desk and sat down. After a brief pause spoke calmly and eloquently "On January sixth in an emergency meeting of congress I will try to pass my plan, my vision, the Land of the Free and Home of the Brave concept it will not only be a concept but a way of life that will give quality of life back to Americans". President Bradley then opened up a black hard binder and started to describe his concept "If my concept… vision passes it will close the borders and allow no more immigrants into this country and for those who are here five years or less they will be sent back to their country of origin, this sudden move will give Americans back jobs that they desperately need and create new opportunities for our next generation and this will go for all foreign imports such as food, toys, etc and in the process decrease the population which in turn will lower crime, unemployment and welfare fraud which has been putting a strain on our law enforcement and justice system for years." Turning the pages in his binder, the entire room was stunned at the statement they had heard, but none more so than Ron who could tell the president was getting more fired up as time passed. The president took another sip of water and spoke in a slightly louder and more volatile tone "We send the military to countries to help a cause and we are spat upon by the very people we are trying to protect or has the Vietnam conflict faded from memory. America will let the countries fend for themselves and work out their own problems if they don't want our help they shall not receive it, instead America will pull it's troops and defend the only country that matters… America!" The president, his face now slightly red, drank the last bit of his water and slammed the binder shut and got up from behind his desk again but this time he did not go in front and lean on his desk he simply walked in front of his desk and stood there looking directly at the camera "and last but certainly not least… terrorism." The president started pacing slowly back and forth as he spoke "now my predecessors said they would never negotiate with terrorists and yet they negotiated and when that didn't work they sent in the military and yes they used big words like "deadline" "ultimatum" and "final option" I however, don't believe in smoke, mirrors and fooling all the good people of this country and giving them a false sense of security and I definitely don't believe in sending our men and women in the service as lambs to a slaughter, if so much as a threat is made to the security or the people of this great nation by whatever country or faction the threat will be dealt with swiftly and with extreme prejudice, no big words or negotiations will be applied just action!" and he slammed his fist into his hand. Ron looked around the room inconspicuously and saw the shock on the people's faces. He himself was a little uncomfortable with the content and tone of the address, which started sounding more and more like the sales pitch of a dictator and opening his eyes to the real person the nation's president really was. The president calmed down and returned to his seat behind his desk and folded his hands placing them in front of him "I realize this is a lot to process and I know that people, a lot of people hate me right now not just here but around the world as well for what I have said this evening" he stopped to wipe a tear from his eye and continued "but I need your support, the American people's support, it will be rough there's no denying that, but if we the people stand together this country, this land, this great nation can salvage it's pride, it's dignity and recapture the spirit that made this country the greatest on God's green earth so in closing may everyone from the heartlands to the coast and all points in between have a Merry Christmas and a happy, bright and prosperous new year, God bless everyone and god bless America, good night... friends" The president sat at his desk and watched the camera lights shut off one by one then twiddling his thumbs he looked around the room which was absolutely silent and as the old saying goes you could hear a pin drop and all around the world the proverbial pin had dropped and it could be heard loud and clear. Ron, noticing the silence sighed and clapped his hands and slowly but surely everyone started to applaud, haphazardly but applaud nonetheless. The president stood up and gave a slight nod then came out from behind his desk where Ron was already standing ready to escort him to his helicopter. Bradley grabbing his coat and scarf took the lead, a Ron with his coat already on followed with three secret servicemen in tow. Bradley stopped in front of a door down the hall and nodded at the secret servicemen; they immediately walked away then the president keyed in a code that only he and the past presidents knew (the code was always the choice of the new president) and he opened the door and entered with Ron close behind. Bradley flicked a switch as he closed the door that after made seven clicks each one a lock and then lights on the ceiling illuminated. Ron had never been in here before it was a long hallway with lights hanging from the ceiling every twenty feet. The president pulled on his long black cashmere coat and red scarf then turned towards Ron and said, "Shall we" as he motioned Ron down the hall. The two started walking and all that could be heard was them walking. Ron looked at the hallway as he walked, the ceiling was arched and the walls were a faded teal. The hall itself was long, so long in fact that Ron had no clue where the end was and even if he did he wouldn't be able to see it. Benches lined the way every so often and it was no wonder, Ron checked his watch and they had been walking five minutes and didn't seem to make any progress. The president looked at Ron as they walked "this hall was always here but no one knew about it except the president, I mean we have to have some secrets. It was an insurance policy in case someone was waiting to rub him out before he got to the west lawn." Ron responded in turn "I heard about this tunnel but I thought it was just a myth, a presidential legend" As they walked down the hall there was a definite chill in the air partially because there was no heat and the men could both see their breath as they walked down the hall. Finally Ron saw a welcome sight at the end of the hall, which was a dead end and a last bench by the wall. When they reached the bench the president stopped and pulled out a cigarette and once it was lit he sat down on the bench. Soon smoke filled the air as the president looked at Ron and in a very serious tone of voice asked Ron a question "So Ron how was I? Be honest now, none of that brownnosing tell them what they want to hear bullshit, give it to me straight". Ron took a moment and tried to figure out a response because in actuality he needed more time to really understand and critique what he had heard this evening. The president took a long drag off his cigarette, "well?" he said, shrugging his shoulders. Ron looked right at Bradley "to tell you the truth sir you really got everyone's attention, you really gave America a wake up call" The president stood up "you see Ron that's what I like about you, your honest, I just thought I scared the shit out of them and piss them off but I like your answer better" and with that the president dropped his butt on the ground crushed it out and walked down to the dead end of the hallway where there was another door hidden in the wall and it was equipped with a identification system the same as the front door of the hall, Bradley keyed in the code and opened the door. Ron walked out the door behind the president and was astonished where the door led. The door led into the presidential tea room and the door was concealed behind a large painting of President Washington. Right outside the tearoom at about fifty yards was a landing pad for the presidential helicopter. The president turned to Ron before opening the door and going to the helicopter. Putting his hand on Ron's shoulder he whispered to him "I'll take it from here". The president then shook his hand "have a merry Christmas and a happy new year my friend" and then he opened the door and took a few steps out turning to Ron "see you on the sixth" and with a wink he was out the door. Ron watched the president walk down the stone path to his helicopter turning as he entered and waving at the sea of cameras on the lawn. The door closed and the helicopter lifted off the pad and the president was off to the air force base to take a plane to an unknown destination for a vacation. Ron sat down on a chair close to the door and smiled uneasily and sighed, "I just don't know."

Christmas eventually came but it was anything but merry. The lines for food had grown, the unemployment rate was at an all time high, gas prices were still climbing and the whole country was in the midst of the worst depression since the "Dirty Thirties" or "The Great Depression as it was known, not only were times getting worse but peoples' spirits had been crushed. New years eve came and people were drinking and celebrating in America. After all it was a new year being ushered in, it was a clean slate for prosperity and a fresh start. In Aruba, safe and secure was the president, up to his chest in hot water with a drink in his hand, a cigar in his mouth and two beautiful women one on each side of him. As he watched the celebrations on television a smile came across his face as the sweat trickled down the side of it. Under his breath he muttered "hot damn a new year, this is my time, my era." Meanwhile the celebrations on

Arpad Horvath

Ron's television had gone unnoticed. A pizza box with a half eaten pizza in it laid on top of a coffee table with a half a bottle of scotch next to it. On the floor lay an empty bottle of scotch and in a leather easy chair Ron was snoring and enjoying probably the best sleep he had in a while, people celebrated as he slept.

CHAPTER 18

Turnabout Isn't Always Fair Play

On January sixth there was an emergency meeting of congress, and the first order of business was President Bradley's "land of the free and home of the brave" concept. There was not a lot of idle chatter since congress and the world had seen his speech. They got right down to business and voted, the answer overwhelmingly was a unanimous no. The president didn't get upset and thanked the house for their time and left the building as business continued as usual but couldn't help but wonder how the president remained so calm after he had really promoted his vision of the future.,

By January fifteenth the House of congress had another vote on Bradley's vision for America and voted in a landslide to endorse it, the speed with which voted was partially attributed to the deaths of ten of the house of congress who had all been in unfortunate accidents, the press got involved but details were held tight by the C.I.A as to the way in which they had died. When a reporter questioned the President, the president simply stated, "this is indeed a tragedy and a case for the investigators to investigate and now a new era is emerging". Another reporter asked the president when the implications of his vision would come into effect. The president cleared his throat and responded with only "effective immediately." Two days after the president's vision for a new America passed the president released a statement on national television once again from the oval office, only this time it was low key only with one camera, "my fellow Americans my vision for a better America, a stronger America has passed and as I Am speaking to all you now the government, my government has taken temporary control of every large freighter, airplane, train, bus and any other mode of transportation that is available to transport immigrants back to their country of origin or to where they can be picked up to be sent back, I will however give a six week grace period in which immigrants can say goodbye and pack up belongings or sell their house or what have you." The president then added "I would like the full cooperation of those going back to not hide or try to prolong your stay because if you don't comply, the military will come and collect you at your house, place of employment etc, and on a further note I' am pleased to say that our military forces abroad are coming home, thank you for your attention" and with that the expulsion of hundreds, thousands if not hundreds of thousands would soon begin. The next eight months saw the largest exodus of people in the history of the United States or for that matter the world. In Washington protests broke out and clashes between protesters and law enforcement whether it was local, state or military were extremely violent. The president had a five hundred yard perimeter established around the Whitehouse fence, which consisted of tanks, armored vehicles and military personnel so there would be a buffer zone between him and them. During the initial chaos that gripped the country Ron decided to take a three-week hiatus from work leaving his second in command, Horowitz in charge of the security for the president. Ron was only one week into his time off when there was a knock at his door at nine in the morning. As usual Ron never made it to bed, he fell asleep in his easy chair the result of going to a club ten years too late and trying to run with the younger crowd, drinking one too many mai tai's and thinking for a split second he could drink like the marine he used to be, he thought wrong. Another knock on the door and this time a voice from the other side spoke "Mr. Fuller are you there? It is very important we speak to you immediately". Ron's eyes opened slowly and his head was pounding like a jackhammer and the knocking on the door only made it worse. Slowly getting up from his chair with the speed of paint drying he shouted from his chair "who ever is pounding on my door better be dressed in a tuxedo and have a cute girl with big tits standing next to him with a big ass check because if not I' am going to be pissed". Ron finally made it to his feet and only wore jeans from the previous night before he approached the door and opened it. Outside were two men dressed in black suits and parked on the road was a black hummer. With as much grace as he could muster he went face to face with the one man and addressed him "pal" he said in a low tone of voice "I don't care who you and your buddy are but if you ever pound on my door like that again I'll break your goddamn arms... now who are you?" Within seconds the two men produced their identification agents Goodman and Dickson. "We are here at the request of the president and he apologizes for interrupting your vacation". Ron felt embarrassed and just stared at the floor for a few moments then looked at the agents. Ron sheepishly said "sorry gentlemen for being such a major league asshole, what does Bradley want to see me about?" Agent Goodman spoke up "it's a matter of national security". Rubbing his chin with a confused look Ron asked "national security? Why doesn't he take it up with homeland security or even the general or the C.I.A that's their department? I 'm just his personal security." The agents looked at each other for a moment and then agent Dickson answered "the president requested you specifically, now if you would get dressed sir we would appreciate it implicitly, we have a vehicle waiting". Ron walked upstairs, and put on a t-shirt and a hoodie, after all he was still on vacation. The ride to the Whitehouse was different to, instead of the standard black S.U.V they were transporting him in a black hummer and if that wasn't enough there was a hot cup of coffee and a crisp copy of newspaper. Ron smiled and spoke to the agents up front "is this French roast?" he said referring to the coffee. Agent Goodman answered "yes sir the president told us to treat you the way we would treat him, with respect". Ron smiled, sat back and enjoyed his coffee. As they neared the Whitehouse Ron was stunned at the mass of humanity that had accumulated over time after Bradley's vision was announced. The hummer stopped and opened the window; the agent showed his identification and waved through. A few minutes later Ron and the two agents entered the president's office. The president stood up from behind his desk with a look of relief on his face "Ron, good to see you, that will be all gentlemen please wait outside" and with that the agents left the room and closed the door. Ron walked over to the president who was now standing in front of his desk "sorry to bust up your vacation but we have a giant turd in the punchbowl, sit down... you want a drink cause I'm going to have one". As Ron sat down in a chair in front of the president's desk the president returned behind his desk and sat down. He pulled open a drawer and placed a shot glass on the desk, poured whiskey into it and quickly drank it, "whiskey before noon sir?" Ron said and the president responded, "It's five o'clock somewhere, last chance" he said, waving the shot glass Ron waved his hand and declined. The president put the shot glass back in the drawer. "Early this morning intelligence sent information that a radical groups based in several countries from from europe to Asia were very displeased about my vision and actions are planning to blow up one of America's premier monuments, Mount Rushmore, The Seattle Space needle, it could be anything" Ron had a look of concern on his face and asked "what does this have to do with me? I'm not the military or homeland security. I'm not even the secretary of defense" The president stared at him for a moment." You're right Ron but you have something I need" he said and then pointed at Ron's chest "the code key". Ron's silence spoke volumes and with that the president continued "that's right Ron all other options would be too slow" Fuller with a stunned and confused look on his face asked "Mr. President... Bob, why?" He looked at Ron with a stare that could cut lead "why? I'll tell you why because I' am the president of the United States, the most powerful man on the

The Silencer

planet and I will not be told by a group pissed off countries what I' am going to do and how I' am going to do it just because some of their fellow countrymen are being sent back! I want to send a message, now hand over the code key". Ron just stood in amazement at the behavior of the president "I can't do that sir I don't want to see millions of people die just because of a small faction making threats". The president was starting to get angry "really… ok let me ask you a question where were you on that September morning? Do you remember it? The screaming, the chaos, the destruction well I do and I say no more I say hit them hard and hit them fast." Then the president took a deep breath and calmed down and asked Ron again "I am ordering you as your commander and chief to hand it over now". Ron also took a deep breath and responded "I… I. can't in good conscience do it sir I just can't, there has to be another way somehow" Ron pleaded. Bradley was beside himself with anger "look you bastard! What you do now will define who you are and whose side you are on, so I'm ordering you one last time to hand over the code key right goddamn now!!" his face turning red and veins bulging. One last time Ron also tried to get the president to have a change of heart "Bob I'm begging you please use an alternative I know you can figure another route out of this please try for the love of God and all that is right… you could trigger world war three… please just think about the repercussions" he said with his hands folded as if he were praying. The president sat back down behind his desk and was quiet for a few moments as his face color returned to normal, then he slapped his desk an he spoke to Ron in a more civilized tone "you know what, your right there has to be another way" looking at Ron "I'll try and figure something out, in the meantime keep this little interaction under your hat and I'll get the agents who brought you here to take you home and just to show you no hard feelings take another week off Horowitz is doing a good job you just go home and relax". Ron was stunned by the quickness of the president's response. The president called in the two agents who were just outside the office door. No sooner did the agents come in then they left taking Ron home. On the way home the vehicle made an unexpected turn, Ron paid it little attention as he was enjoying a cup of specialty coffee, "what did you call this flavor again?" The agent Dickson turned back to Ron "it's called a Swiss mocha latte and if you wonder about why we turned we were just going to the gas station to fill up so enjoy your Joe and we will have you home shortly." Ron drank his coffee and found it kind of odd that they were going to stop for gas when he could clearly see the gas gauge showed well over a three quarters tank of fuel, but Ron figured the vehicle was new and they needed to get used to the gas-guzzler. The Hummer stopped at the gas station next to the pump and the agent Goodman got out. Ron finished his coffee and began to feel really dizzy and noticed everything around him started to slow down. Agent Dickson noticed Ron's behavior and started talking to him but everything he said slowed down to Ron and it sounded like Dickson was talking very slowly. By the time agent Goodman had paid for the fuel and got back in the vehicle Ron's eyes were glazed over and he looked like he was going to pass out which he did seconds later. Goodman looked at Dickson "let's do this" as the Hummer pulled out of the gas station.

CHAPTER 19

SCAPEGOAT TO THE SLAUGHTER

Sweat ran down Ron's forehead as he started to wake up, he rubbed his face as he noticed dried blood on both his hands, he turned his hands over and noticed that his knuckles were skinned and there was also dry blood on them as well. Slowly he got to the side of the bed and sat up, while sitting up he noticed his ribs on his left side hurt. Then Ron made another discovery his shirt was torn and when he looked at the mirror across from his bed on the dresser he noticed he had a black eye on the left side of his face. Something had happened but he wasn't sure what, he pulled his gun from his holster, which was always loaded and ejected the clip… it was empty. Ron tried to piece together what happened. Ron recalled his last memory, he left the Whitehouse with two agents, they stopped for gas and now he was here. He knew he was missing an element and then it came to him the coffee but before he could come to a clear-cut conclusion there was knocking coming from his front door downstairs. Ron slowly made his way from the bedroom and down the stairs clutching his ribs, which felt really sore. Ron turned the knob and from the sounds of the loud banging it was very urgent. The door opened and two local police, three military police and four agents barged in the door with their guns all pointed at Ron ordering him to pull out his gun and place it on the ground slowly, which he did then he was told to get on the ground on his stomach and assume the "spread eagle position" once again Ron did what he was told still not quite clear on what was happening to him. Moments later Ron emerged from the house with his wrists and ankles shackled taking small steps towards the end of his walkway where a government vehicle, an armored truck, was waiting to take him away. As Ron walked the pain of the shackles was nothing compared to the pain he felt walking down his walkway. His neighbors, friends and their children of some fifteen years watched, as he was led down the walkway it was the most painful, humiliating moment of his life. He was then helped up the three steps into the truck and the solid steel door was closed behind him. One of the neighbors asked a military officer what Ron did and the soldier's answer was cold and to the point "it's government business" and he walked away. After a bumpy, rough ride in a cold truck the doors opened at the back and Ron was hooded by an M.P and led out of the truck and into the unknown building. As they walked Ron just felt worse and worse, they entered an elevator and went down to the bottom floor. Ron walked for a few minutes and stopped, the shackles were released and the hood was taken off and Ron was shoved inside and to the cold hard floor. Ron pulled himself up and surveyed the area. The cell as it were was eight feet by eight feet solid concrete, no windows, there was a stainless steel toilet in the corner and a sink with a mirror over it between the toilet and the other corner on the back wall and of course a bank that had as much give as a cement block. Then he saw something that confirmed his suspicion of where he was: a twenty – seven inch television mounted in the upper left hand corner surrounded by steel mesh. Ron sat down on the bunk and tried, however hard it was, to figure out his situation. Then suddenly the screen in the corner lit up with an all too familiar image on it... the president. Ron sat back against the wall on his bunk he knew he was in for a performance, little did he know what he would hear would change his life and everything about it. The president started to say "hello Ron, you're probably wondering what you're doing in an eight by eight federal holding cell, and how you got here and for that matter why you're here well I'm gonna tell you so pay attention because I'm only going to say this once". Ron's eyes were totally focused on the screen as the president was starting to explain the situation "three hours ago a quarter of the middle east was totally destroyed, and what I mean by destroyed is an area five hundred miles either way reduced to a smoking crater, everything obliterated, buildings, men, women, children, nothing left and you made it happen, but I'm getting ahead of myself let me tell you how it all unfolded". The breath in Ron's lungs slowed, as his breathing became slightly heavier after hearing the president's opening statement and knowing he had more to say. The president continued, as if he were reading a news report "the agents drove you home and then you incapacitated them and drove the vehicle to our secret experimental military laboratory, which housed the XL 777 hydrogen long range missile, where you entered shooting seven guards and then going on to kill five engineers and two professors with your bare hands and the skills you acquired in the marines all before you entered the code to active the missile, set the course and target and plugged in the key to unlock the launch button, then with no remorse you pressed the button and unleashed hell on the middle east but since we got the tyrant who did the dirty work no counter attacks are planned by the middle east. Ron slouched against the wall as if he were shot and muttered "but I didn't do it". Then seemingly out of nowhere. laughing, Ron looked up at the television and saw that the president was slightly laughing but in Ron's opinion there was nothing funny about the current situation. The president soon explained his laughter "Ron I know you didn't do it, you're a real boy scout and your colors aren't red, white and blue it just plain yellow, you see I organized the whole damn thing, I found someone who had the guts to stick up for this country and he will also be my vice president." Ron glared up at the screen with a silent rage surging through every inch of his body, as he had to endure listening to the figure on the screen as it prepared to speak again. The president with a smirk spoke again, folding his hands in front of himself "ok son now I'll give you the skinny of what's going to happen to you, now pay attention because I'm only going to say it once." Putting on his half glasses he read off of a piece of paper to the screen "tomorrow morning you will be moved to Leavenworth military prison, in the afternoon, via satellite a judge will give the date for the trial, a six to eight month period but I'll speed it up and you will overwhelmingly be found guilty and I will personally make sure you will receive the death penalty and not a sissy lethal injection, you're going to ride Ol' Sparky, that's what I'll tell those non believers but in reality, you helped me out a lot so I'm only going to stick you in solitary where you can spend some alone time, or should I say a lifetime." Removing his glasses the president leaned forward "that's it, now I know that's a lot to think about but don't worry I'll make sure you have a nightlight and you'll have plenty of time to think, well good-bye son" the president paused for a moment then spoke as if he had something to add "oh by the way your fired, bye now" and the screen went dark. Ron stood up and punched the wall, this was a no win situation but Ron had been in situations like this before and with no gun and no plan Ron had to rely on one thing… Faith.

CHAPTER 20

BREAKING OUT AND MOVING IN

Lying in a rather uncomfortable bunk Ron stared at the ceiling trying to comprehend a plan of escape, but then that's what they would expect and shoot him, that would make Bradley happy, no, he needed a plan but none came to him. It was two in the morning as Ron stared at his watch. It was the only possession that had not been taken and he was glad it was a stainless steel marine issue watch he had received when he had left the marines to work in the pentagon it reminded him of where he came from. Suddenly he saw his cell door open slowly and instinctively he went for cover under the bunk. Then from under the bunk Ron saw a pair of combat boots enter the cell and stop just short of the bunk "Mr. Fuller" a voice called out and Ron slid out from under the bunk and stood up coming face to face with a figure dressed in black with a ski mask on. The masked man put a set of black clothes on the bunk "put these on" he said. "Who are you?" Ron asked. The masked man was silent for a moment then spoke, sounding quite upset "either we stand around playing twenty questions or you put the clothes on and we get out of here, it's your choice". Ron quickly put the clothes on and the two men left the cell with

135

great haste. After crawling through a five hundred foot air duct and down a rappel line to a waiting van the two drove off putting as much distance between them and the holding facility as possible. Finally the van pulled into a mall parking lot behind two dumpsters and stopped. Before the masked man could get a word out edgewise Ron turned to him "ok I thank you for getting me out and away from my tight situation but I need to know you a…" Before Ron could finish the masked man removed his mask to reveal himself. The look on Ron's face said it all. "I've met you before… From the crash site… umm Jake, John." The man next to him smiled "it's James, James Mass" Ron looked at him "that's right but what are you doing here? And why did you bust me out?" James lit a cigarette and was about to answer Ron's two questions with one answer "well Mr. Fuller" Ron stopped him immediately "call me Ron, Mr. Fuller was my father's name." James agreed and continued "Well Ron when the news broke about the countries that were unsettled about the prez's vision and when I heard you were locked up at federal slammer I got down here as fast as I could." Ron asked one of the original questions again "but why did you bust me out?" James paused for a moment and took a long drag of his cigarette. The smoke slowly wafted out of his mouth and nose as he answered "when I saw you at the crash site your eyes had passion, a passion for doing what you do best and I think you felt sorry for the assassin because you searched that limo very meticulously from top to bottom actually hoping he found a way out and is still alive, right?" Ron looked at James and smiled "in a roundabout way". James finished his cigarette and asked Ron "So where do you want to go?" Ron thought about it for a minute and then answered "Jersey City". Ron explained "in New Jersey I have a luxury apartment that I use when I want to get away, I also change my name and no one knows me… i totally disappear It's right off the grid" James checked a map and then spoke for a moment "Jersey City… no problem "and the two sped off. Destination: Jersey City.

The next morning the discovery of Ron Fuller's escape had been made. Helicopters, land vehicles and military personnel on foot were all dispatched along with a total shutdown of the area in which the federal holding cell was housed. When news of the escape had reached the president he tried very hard to keep cool under pressure as he made a statement a few hours after the escape "This morning it was discovered that Ronald Fuller the former head of presidential security and the individual responsible for the launching of an experimental weapon which caused chaos of biblical proportions in the middle east and furthermore we are making it our top priority to find him and with the blessing of God and the cooperation of the U.S treasury we have offered a cash reward for him in the sum of ten million dollars and no questions at this time thank-you." Then the president smiled and spoke once again "On an unrelated topic I have chosen the man who will stand by my side and help me help America become a better place for all generations to come". The president then turned to the man on his right and put his hand on his shoulder "Mr. Gene Horowitz". Horowitz raised his hand and waved, then spoke into the microphone "It is really an honor to be chosen as vice president and I will do my very best to help President Bradley realize his vision and make America the best country on the planet that it can be thank-you" and with that he shook President Bradley's hand while camera flashes lit up the room. Meanwhile in a small café in New Jersey Ron and James were finishing their coffee after a rather large breakfast. "I just want to thank-you once again," Ron said to James. James downed the last of his coffee "it's really no problem, it was only breakfast" he said almost laughing. Ron smiled back and shared the laugh "you know what I mean, breaking me out I just don't know how to repay you" James with a smile on his face answered Ron's dilemma "well first you can promise me you'll never try to cut your hair and shave in moving vehicle" James was referring to Ron's fast shave and a haircut to alter his appearance while on the way to New Jersey "and second I told you on the way here someday you can do me a favor ok?" Ron finished his coffee and stared directly into James' eyes "anything". James looked at his watch "I'll drop you off at that building that you told me about and then I have to scoot." So James paid the bill and they were

137

off. Twenty minutes later Ron and James were standing in a beautiful open concept apartment. As James looked around he commented on his surroundings "this is amazing" Ron nodded "yes it is and it's completely off the grid I purchased it while I was still in the Marine Corps, under another name of course just in case of trouble I was going to retire here and write my memoirs." James smiled "well you've got lots of time now" he said as he went out on the terrace and then he turned around and looked at the apartment from the terrace. It was an open concept with a small bathroom by the main door, the kitchen, bar and dining room on his left. In front were numerous couches, a tiger with a glass slab on his back and an oak table beside the door with a chessboard on it. And finally on his right was a fireplace a few feet from the bathroom by the main door and a few feet after that around the corner was obviously the master bedroom and to top it all off the whole apartment was done in outstanding hardwood. James then turned away to see an old rundown building blocking what was probably a magnificent view. "What's with the fossil?" he said referring to the building, which by his estimation went up three more floors. Ron joined him on the terrace and answered his question "you know, that building was here when I bought this place, the salesman said that it would be torn down in a matter of months and there it is, they should just blow it up and be done with it." James took one last look at the old building and walked back inside, Ron put his hand on his shoulder" you can crash here for a while if you like" Ron offered. James grinned, "no thanks, but I appreciate the offer I really do." Ron seemed curious, "what's your rush?" he inquired. James walked over to the door and turned to Ron "let's just say busting you out of a federal slammer isn't exactly my day job and we will leave it at that." Ron grinned approvingly "fair enough" and then took James' hand and shook it one last time "thanks once again and remember if you need anything… "James cut off Ron "yeah I know don't hesitate to ask, right?" Ron just smiled and gave a thumb up. James walked out in the hall and asked Ron to join him for one moment. Ron walked out into the hallway just as James entered the elevator. James turned to Ron. "Keep searching, he's alive, you know it and I know it." The elevator doors began to close, while Ron tried to contemplate what James had just said. James hit him with one more fact to think about "New York" and doors closed. Ron walked back into the apartment, closing the door behind him. Lighting a cigarette he sat down and finally relaxed "well if he's still alive and in New York, I'll find him, I've got to." Ron took a puff of his cigarette and blew the smoke straight up to the ceiling and watched as it dissipated when it suddenly dawned on him and his eyes widened "how does he know?"

(Sawyer's Voice)

"Change... it's inevitable, always happening everyday, week, month, year, decade and century, ... change is a constant.

"Some say change is good, some say change is bad, some fear it while others embrace it, in my opinion change is just confusing. It messes up things or tasks which were always routine, change is overrated.

"Darwin had a theory of evolution, depending on which side of the pew you're sitting on, but evolution was just another word for change, but did we really evolve? Did we really change? There is still killing and hatred, pain and suffering we are not evolving... it's all an illusion"

"The more things change the more they stay the same" is a quote that has been coined so many times it's lost all meaning, the only way, the right way to see if there really was progress in the evolution of mankind or society, if you will, is to see if (as most people from all walks of life say) it stands the test of time, and as for the last four years and the state of this union...

... Time's up.

December 22.... Four years later

CHAPTER 21

THE PRODIGAL SILENCER RETURNS

The snow gently fell from the sky as the Christmas rush was at its zenith. The hustling and bustling of the masses was evident from vehicles honking at each other and the electricity in the air. All through the shopping malls and throughout the city for that matter Christmas carols were being crooned by the time-honored masters, Sinatra, Martin, Cole and of course "Der Bingle" Bing Crosby sang the unofficial anthem of Christmas "White Christmas" as only he could.

America was going through a lot of changes, four years ago Christmas wasn't at all merry and the holidays were not happy. Americans had endured a lot of change in a short time and needed to get eased into the water as it were. This year however Americans were not only used to the water but they were rather enjoying it. Confidence had returned to the country along with a stronger economy due to more Americans going back to work and also filling jobs that were left when the immigrants were sent home. In Washington the hundreds upon hundreds of protesters who had survived brutal weather and the army had all disappeared in their place a much needed facelift for the white house along with two hundred foot bronze statue of president Bob Bradley pointing forward and winking with a big smile on his face and a quote or "catch phrase" as most people called it "I'm only going to say this once". The statue in a lot of citizens opinion was impressive but a waste of money, the president however disagreed and made a memorable quote at the unveiling of his monument to the ages "a statue is a lot more effective way to be remembered then stamps" and to cap it all off the president had announced that on new years eve at eight o'clock he would sign a proclamation that would declare that he was the president of the united states for life or until he could no longer carry out his duties in which case he could appoint a new president of his choosing, no questions asked, the whole signing would be televised and would be followed by a New year's eve gala the likes of which the world had never seen. Yes, America was in a very good position all the way around. There are of course two sides to every coin and some Americans lost the toss. For the Americans who were not so fortunate the usual charity and church run institutions were running at full capacity providing food, shelter and hope. Giving to the less fortunate at this time of year was a given and donations were collected in the malls and outside stores by volunteers who gave of their time to help at this blessed time of year. Another way some charities collected donations was with a volunteer dressed as the Christmas icon Santa Claus. Every year there were dozens of these jolly old elves all over major cities armed with their kettle and jingle bells drumming up donations as they had done since people could remember. In front of "Filbert's Fine Furniture" stood Santa Claus ringing his bell, wishing everyone a Merry Christmas and collecting donations in his kettle. In reality the man's name was Ben Hudson, city bus driver who for the past ten years stood outside this very store collecting for the less fortunate. Ben was a special Santa because he was of African American descent and there were not too many African American Santa's that he knew of but color was irrelevant when Christmas was concerned plus he had a hardy laugh and didn't need padding. The night was going well, donations were pouring in and handshakes and holiday washes were in abundance. Two men in their early

141

twenties approached Santa and demanded the money in the pot be handed over to them. "Hand over the money, fat man," the one man threatened. Ben responded "no, this is for the poor not for punks". The other man got right into Ben's face "we are the poor asshole!" Then without warning the man kicked Ben in the stomach, and he fell to the ground. Holding his stomach Ben asked for help but the small crowd that gathered around didn't possess what he was looking for. The two men continued to pummel the unfortunate volunteer while the people gathered around and still didn't even attempt to help the poor man. Then a knife suddenly appeared and the half unconscious volunteer in his tattered Santa suit smeared with blood could hear the man with the knife tell his intentions "let's carve this turkey, man!" Then from behind a voice spoke to the men in a calm tone "didn't your parents tell you not to play with knives, assuming you had parents." The man with the knife spun around and held the knife at the throat of what appeared to be a hobo. The point of the knife was against the hobo's throat "this isn't your business you old bastard, now turn around and walk away while I carve me some dark meat" The homeless man looked into the eyes of the man holding the knife and gave an unexpected answer "piss off you gutless little bastard!" Then with the quickness of his hands the homeless man disarmed the man and punched him once square in the mouth rendering him unconscious. Seeing his friend lying on the ground the other man scooped up what change he could and tried to run but the hobo emptied whatever was left in the kettle on the sidewalk. Grabbing the kettle by the chains that were used for hanging the kettle from the stand he started to spin the kettle around and around like a discus thrower in the Olympics. Finally after the last pass the hobo let go, sending the kettle soaring at the man running away with the stolen petty cash. The kettle flew and made a direct hit slamming into the back of the man sending him crashing to the pavement with change coming out of everywhere, kind of like a slot machine going off. The hobo ran over just as the man was gaining his composure and getting up, the hobo punched him knocking him out then dragging him over to his friend by his collar.

Ben slowly tried to get to his feet when he looked up and saw the hobo offering him a hand, but from the way the streetlight was shining behind him and the snow was lightly falling around him it gave him a almost angelic look and Ben took his hand and the hobo helped him to his feet. The hobo then set the kettle back on its stand and reached into his pocket and put a dollar in. Ben looked in the pot and never had he seen an act of kindness come from such a poor soul. Ben put his hand on the hobo's shoulder "god bless you son, you helped old Santa Clause out of a jam now what do you want for Christmas?" The hobo answered without reservation "I... I want to go home" he said with a sigh. The hobo shook Ben's hand "Merry Christmas Santa" and Ben answered "and a Merry Christmas to you" and with that he gave the hobo a hug so big he lifted him right off the ground. The hobo started to walk away when Ben shouted "I didn't catch your name", the hobo looked back and shouted "didn't throw it, see ya" and the hobo disappeared into the darkness and the lightly falling snow to the faint sound of police sirens approaching to clean up the mess he had left. Passing three city blocks the hobo walked trying to keep his coat closed to keep him warm on the count of the winds from the north were cold and shrill. Salvation came in the form of a demolished building site where the hobo saw two to three fire barrels going and walked over to a barrel, put his hands over it and felt the heat radiating from it breaking the chill that had become all too familiar to him. After a few moments of warming his hands he noticed, as well as the rest of people, a black Mercedes pulling over to the sidewalk and the passenger window sliding down. A voice inside the car said "you, in the car, now!" Six of the men around the barrel walked closer to the slick black car. The voice again spoke "no I want the guy who rescued Santa" The hobo stepped forward "So who are you?" The voice in the car responded sharply "It doesn't matter who I am, all that matters is you get in the car... now!" The hobo leaned on the open window "and if I refuse?" The voice inside the car was losing patience fast "if you refuse your cheating yourself out of a chance to make a difference!" The hobo ran his fingers through his long and somewhat gray hair "I don't know, what's in it for me besides the chance to make a difference "he said rolling his eyes. The voice in the car snapped "what's in it for you! What's in it for you?, you know what? screw you, stay in the streets you're in a better place you asshole!!" The hobo was still leaning on the open window when it started to close he removed his elbow and it still was closing. The window almost closed completely when the hobo put his hands on the top of the window and held it from closing. The hobo soon made his intention clear "ok I'll get in, jeez take a pill will ya'". And so the hobo got in the front seat and sat back as the car pulled away just as the skies were turning lighter and the stars were coming out. An awkward silence filled the car, the hobo nor the driver talked to each other, the silence was deafening. The hobo looked out the window as his hands covered the heat vents on the dashboard warming them. Then after silence had dominated the ride the driver broke the silence by asking a question "you're hard to find especially for a dead man, Sawyer." The hobo turned towards the window as he spoke to the driver "maybe I don't want to be found and as I recall neither do you, Ron" The silence returned once again neither man spoke all the way to their final destination, Ron's apartment.

CHAPTER 22

REUNION WITH A BANG

After parking in the underground lot Ron and Sawyer made their way up to the apartment still maintaining total silence towards each other. He fumbled with his keys once they arrived at the apartment and opened the door. Attempting to lighten the mood Ron started talking as he entered the apartment "So Sawyer what do you think, pretty nice huh?" Sawyer didn't answer and shut the door. Ron continued the running commentary "yep, this is the perfect place to hide, we are one hundred percent secure, so Sawyer honestly what do you think?" Ron stopped in front of a chair and turned around in an instant all Ron could see was a fist coming at him and then a white flash. Sawyer had caught Ron square in the jaw and he fell backwards over the chair and flipped onto his stomach. For a brief moment Ron laid face down on the floor, Sawyer standing with a clenched fist waited for retaliation, but to his surprise there wasn't any. Ron slowly placed his hands on the ground as if he was attempting a single pushup and got up from the ground shook his head twice and started walking towards Sawyer. As he walked to Sawyer he rubbed his jaw and responded to being punched "well I guess I had that one coming". Ron was almost near Sawyer when Sawyer drew back with fist clenched. In a heartbeat Ron pulled his gun from his shoulder holster

145

and pointed it directly at Sawyer "come on do it! Give me a reason!" Sawyer looked at Ron with a fire in his eyes "what? Do you think that pointing a gun in my face intimidates me? I hate to break it to you but it doesn't, wanna know why?" Sawyer was now in a rage "I'll tell you why, I have been gassed twice, took out some car dealer slash arms dealer and got ejected out of a fighter jet through a skylight then I traveled to Hawaii and found out at the last minute that I had been set up to shoot the goddamn president" Ron looked at Sawyer "I understand, you can stop now", but Sawyer wasn't quite done. He then continued like he was possessed "then there was swat cops trying to arrest me for something I didn't do, I have to hide under the president's casket just to get out of town, and if that's not enough then I drive a limo out of a fucking plane like some cartoon character and have to go underground then to top it all… the cherry on top of the sundae… off you come to New York looking for me and then when I give you what you deserve you point a gun at me and I'm supposed be scared of a forty-five in my face Well I don't think so you asshole, pull the trigger I triple dog dare you, you sackreligious sack of shit!!!" Ron slowly lowered the gun and his head as well. Sawyer on the other hand saw an advantage and took it. Quickly Sawyer hit Ron in the forearm as hard as he could, Ron's hand released the gun and Sawyer grabbed it and pointed it directly in his face. Ron stared at Sawyer in disbelief "feels like Air Force One all over again, what are you going to do now? Shoot me? I mean you didn't do it then and you won't do it now "Ron said with great confidence. Sawyer also spoke with a great deal of confidence "how can I shoot you Ron, I've been dead for four years "Ron rubbed his chin and nodded in agreement "well you've got me there" Sawyer lowered the gun slightly but kept eye contact "no, Ron my boy I'm not going to shoot you, not yet, we are both going to sit down and you are going to tell me what the hell has been going on for the past four years and clear some things up or I promise you I will end you." Ron could see by the sincerity in Sawyer's eyes that he was serious. Nodding once again in agreement "ok I'll tell you everything, I know you didn't kill Doyle but before I expand that and many other points of interest I'm thirsty I'll fix us some drinks" and with that he turned and walked over to the bar leaving Sawyer pointing the gun at no one and feeling rather embarrassed. Ron returned in a few minutes with two glasses containing crushed ice and the finest scotch in this part of the world, he also had tucked under his arm the bottle; this could turn out to be a long night. Two coasters had already been put out by Sawyer, Ron put a glass on each and the bottle in the middle then made a rather startling discovery his gun was laying next to the coaster. Ron sat down and slowly picked up the gun and looked at Sawyer "you got the clip right?" Sawyer shook his head side to side in response "see for yourself". Ron pushed down with his thumb the small lever on the side; the clip ejected and upon inspection was still loaded. With a puzzled look he asked Sawyer "why?" Sawyer picked up his glass and sipped the scotch which was as smooth as a velvet blanket "I hate to say it buddy but considering the circumstances you're the only one I can trust so…" Sawyer raised his glass "cheers" Ron slammed the clip back into the gun and put it down on the table, reached for his scotch and raised his glass "cheers" and with that a very unorthodox friendship was born. For the next several hours Ron spent unraveling the web of deception and lies to Sawyer who didn't speak once, instead he listened to every word that was said that he had been waiting four years to hear. Time slipped away quickly and it was nearing two in the morning, Both Ron and Sawyer had talked the entire time and with the exception of getting up to go to the bathroom, replenishing the scotch supply and answering the door for the "sub guy" they never moved from their seats. The clock on the wall chimed twice as Ron poured the remainder of the second bottle into his glass and then out of nowhere made a statement that got a double take from Sawyer, "I always wanted to be a mechanic". Sawyer looked at him rather oddly "and why is that?" Ron swallowed the last of his scotch and put the glass down "because my dad was one, my grandpa was one and my great grandpa was one" he said slightly slurring his words. "So it's all about carrying on a family tradition is it?" Sawyer asked, slightly slurring his words as well. Ron looked at

Sawyer and gave a small laugh "no man, when you're a mechanic or tradesman you don't get shot at or set up for something you didn't do" his voice raised slightly "All the generations of Fullers could walk down the street with their heads held high well into their old age and look at me I can't walk anywhere, I got a big bull's-eye pasted to my back!" he said as he ran his fingers through his hair. Sawyer looked at Ron with sympathetic eyes "don't beat yourself up man, let the world do it" he said with a smile and a laugh. Ron looked at Sawyer and laughed as he shook his head "you know Sawyer you're the first real friend I've had, thank-you and maybe someday when we get out of this I'll take you fishing and show you how the marines do it". Sawyer swallowed the last of his scotch "you don't even have a boat and furthermore..." Then Sawyer noticed as he was talking a red dot on Ron's ankle, which slowly made it's way up his leg. With as much subtlety as he could muster Sawyer calmly warned Ron of the impending danger, "Ron there's a red dot traveling up your leg". Ron who still had a half smile on his face responded comically "maybe it likes me". Sawyer noticed the dot was almost up to Ron's waist and dispensed with the subtlety "Ron there's a fucking laser sight traveling up to your head, someone on the building next to yours is going to pop you a new asshole in your forehead!". Ron slowly looked down as he saw the small dot coming up slowly then looked at Sawyer with a stone cold sober look on his face. He continued to say "ok on three jump to the side and hit the deck... three!" The two men turned out of their seats and hit the floor just as a hail of bullets started to shatter the windows. Sawyer and Ron were laying spread eagle as the seats they were sitting in only moments ago were being literally obliterated, as was the rest of the room. Sawyer looked over at Ron "what does he have? a Gatling Gun?, Ron where's your gun?" Ron answered back "it was on the coffee table." Sawyer peered around the side of the seat and saw the gun under the debris. Ron shouted at Sawyer "don't you have any weapons?" Sawyer angrily looked over at Ron "sure Ron, I've got coupons, maybe I'll throw some and he'll get a paper cut, you ass!! You pulled me off the street, remember!" The onslaught continued as glass,

The Silencer

plaster, wood and furniture stuffing filled the air as both Sawyer and Ron tried to come up with a plan. "Do you have anything we can use as a shield because these seats almost had it" Sawyer asked. Ron looked around as best he could from the floor for something sturdy until he saw it, "hey Sawyer you see that big oak table against the wall? That's it". Sawyer looked back as he was being covered in debris then turned to Ron "when this son of a bitch reloads we grab the table" Ron nodded back to Sawyer. In a few moments the firing ceased just as Sawyer said it would, now was their chance and they went for it. With the debris falling off of them they went over to the big oak table and pulled it forward then got behind it and pushed. Sawyer with a look of concern told Ron to hurry up because the reload would not take long. As soon as the table was almost on top of what was left of the plush seats they tipped it over and it landed with a resounding crash casting up a puff of dust and crushing the remaining frame of the seats. They quickly got behind the table and prayed it would give them more time to figure out how to get out of this mess. Once again the firing started and the table seemed to vibrate but the bullets never penetrated, the table was holding. Sawyer turned to Ron "what's this table made of besides oak?" Ron smiled "It has a steel plate between the layers of oak that make up the top, it was originally designed during the civil war for some general who's name I can't remember, in case of an attack it was a real steal I got it in an auction sale in..." Sawyer cut him off "I didn't ask for a fucking history lesson!" The room was starting to look more and more like a demolition sight but no one else in the building would have an idea what was going on because the apartment was sound proof and at the top of the building separate from the structure. Then he looked at the door, it wasn't far, maybe they could get to it and get out of here. "Sawyer, how about the door?"

Sawyer didn't even look at Ron, he knew the answer "not a good idea, this guy is a pro he probably rigged the door that's why he turned the apartment into a killbox to get us to open the door and take ourselves out it's called a lamb to the slaughter tactic, no we need a different way out."

Suddenly the shooting stopped, Ron and Sawyer looked at each other and tried to figure out why. "Maybe he's out of ammo?" Ron guessed. Sawyer shook his head" no, he's probably reloading." Ron looked over at the fireplace to his left, more importantly he looked at the leather case on the mantle, which contained his laptop. Looking back at Sawyer, Ron told him he needed to get his laptop before it was destroyed. Sawyer stared back at him with a small grin "you really are technology's bitch you know that? Here we are getting shot at and you're worried about your damn computer!!" Ron pleaded with Sawyer "you don't understand it's what's on it that matters, I need to get it now, I promise it's worth it I'll explain it to you in a less hostile environment, I promise". Sawyer bit his bottom lip "ok, it better be worth it, so what do I cover you with?" Ron pulled up his pant lag to reveal an ankle holster he pulled out the gun and handed it to Sawyer. Pulling back on the action Sawyer was amazed that he never figured Ron had a backup weapon "you son of a bitch, you had another gun all the time" Ron laying flat on his belly preparing to get his laptop looked back at Sawyer "I always like to be prepared". Sawyer shook his head "what were you a boy scout?" Ron smiled back at Sawyer "nope, door to door recruiter for the Marines in a low income neighborhood, now cover me". Sawyer turned and fired in the general direction of the shooting while Ron slid across the floor arm over arm pulling himself over to the base of the fireplace. Ron looked up at the mantle; he needed some way to reach the case without drawing attention away from Sawyer's decoy. He spied a poker beside the fireplace so grabbing it carefully, slowly reached up and hooked the handle, success was in his grasp. At that moment Sawyer ran out of ammo and quickly reloaded his gun. Ron had lowered the case down and was crawling back sliding the case in front of himself. He was only a foot away when he smiled at Sawyer proclaiming victory "I've got it" and in the same moment a shot rang out and Ron's smile disappeared and a look of terror now replaced it. Sawyer, realizing the situation had taken a turn for the worse, stood up and fired several more rounds in the direction of the shot then he grabbed Ron by the arms and pulled him behind the table. Sawyer sat him up and noticed Ron's hand covering a bloody spot on his abdomen but the blood was slowly running through his fingers. Ron looked at Sawyer "it's just a scratch I'll be ok". Sawyer knew a gut shot when he saw one and a grim reality set in that Ron's time was limited. Ron slowly handed the case to Sawyer and said "I'm screwed Sawyer so you have to do this for me." Sawyer looked at Ron who now had blood slowly running down the corner of his mouth "I'll do anything you ask." A faint smile came across Ron's face "good, everything you need to know is in the laptop hit "courage" and it will be self explanatory and everything you need to get the job done is in the case, the rest is in the trunk of my car here's the keys" The shooting ceased Sawyer figured the shooter probably thought he got his mark or he or she is just sitting in the weeds. The wound was taking it toll on Ron, he was starting to fade he asked Sawyer for the gun and Sawyer handed it to him with a disturbing expression on his face but Ron reassured him it was not what he was thinking "I'm not going to shoot myself I'm going to shoot that prick up on the roof". Getting up off the floor and squatting down he gripped the gun tight and slammed a fresh clip in the gun. He looked at Sawyer one more time and spoke with the blood flowing from his abdomen and his mouth "I may be gut shot and bleeding from the mouth, he may have taken my life from me but one thing that little bastard didn't count on "and at the risk of being shot Ron stood up behind the table and made a bold statement to Sawyer "once a marine… always a marine." And with that he walked out from behind the table and towards the direction from where the shots were coming from and raising his gun he fired as many shots as there were bullets in the clip. Sawyer watched from behind the table hoping his worst fears would not be realized… but they were. Ron's clip had run out and he was pulling the trigger only to hear a constant clicking, then the small red dot of the assassin's laser sight appeared and a shot was fired. Sawyer watched in horror as the shot that had hit Ron in the chest exited out his back, he felt useless, he had no gun he couldn't help, and all he could do was watch. A second shot then rang out hitting Ron in the shoulder but miraculously Ron was still on his feet "is that the best you got? you pussy!" he shouted with a tear in his eye, "come on you asshole finish the job!" A proud feeling came over Sawyer at that moment. Ron, a man who Sawyer didn't really know all that long or all that well had garnered Sawyer's respect but Sawyer knew the end was inevitable which made the proud feeling bitter sweet. A third shot hit Ron in the right knee sending Ron toppling to the floor for a moment. Laughter was heard by Sawyer and the assassin as Ron slowly, painfully stood up. Ron's laughter was half laughter and half crying but he stayed firm "Hey stupid" he shouted as a smile came across his face amid the pain that was eating him alive, "are you even trying? Do you know that marines can't be killed because we are immortal!!!" As Ron threw his head back and laughed he turned back towards Sawyer and winked at him, Sawyer's eyes were misting up he was witnessing an act of courage the likes of which he had never seen. Ron then turned back just as a forth shot was fired. The shot was straight to the skull and on target. Ron fell to his knees and then fell forward onto the ground and to the debris covering the floor, then silence. Sawyer waited for a few minutes as the wave of emotion he had experienced passed then he stayed low and ventured out. He looked around the aftermath of the attack then walked over to Ron and kneeled beside him. Sawyer turned him over, Ron lifeless eyes were still open and Sawyer promptly closed them by sliding his hand slowly down the length of Ron's face. Sawyer then slid Ron's U.S Marine Corps watch off his wrist and put it on his own and just as he started to get up he noticed something very odd. Sawyer noticed the chards of glass near Ron's body and the glass on the floor in general was turning a glowing red. Sawyer turned to where the windows used to be and saw a rocket heading straight towards the room Sawyer stood up and turned to run but it was too late. The rocket slammed into the wall of the apartment with such force that it threw Sawyer into the oak table and slid the whole table towards the door. The heavy legs of the table on the right side crashed through the apartment door setting off an explosion that Sawyer had foreseen and would now experience. The force of the explosion

The Silencer

sent the oak table along with Sawyer skidding along the floor once again; when the tables snagged another piece of furniture, it stopped flinging Sawyer onto the floor. Sawyer laid face down in the debris for a moment then slowly raised his head a few inches and watched the shadowy figure on the top of the building across the way vanish.

CHAPTER 23

SHOWDOWN PART I...

Every muscle, bone and follicle of Sawyer's being was aching but he slowly managed to get up on his feet. When Sawyer was finally erect he could hear a creaking sound and knew that his troubles weren't over, the floor was going to collapse soon. Sawyer walked back a few steps and picked up the laptop case by the strap and slung it over his shoulder then he saw the fire escapes on the other building, one for every room and that gave him an idea. Walking back a few more steps he knew if he wanted to get this assassin time was crucial and he also had a gut feeling that after the rocket had hit his location that the floor wasn't going to last much longer. Sawyer concentrated and then started running as fast as he could towards the remaining piece of the balcony. Dust flew up with every step Sawyer took, he then was at the edge of the balcony and led off with his left foot launching himself across the alley between the two buildings and stretched out his arms getting ready to grasp the fire escape railing. The railing was in reach and Sawyer... missed. He fell and managed to catch the third railing down, the force of the sudden stop was so abrupt that Sawyer swung into the small fire escape landing face first. Sawyer hung there for a few moments to try and endure the pain then pulled himself up onto the small landing, then proceeded to climb up until he

154

reached the last one and climbed up a straight ladder to the roof. Once he had climbed to the edge of the roof he slowly crawled up onto the roof and lay on his stomach in the cold snow. Sawyer stayed low and could see the silhouette of the assassin on the far end of the building against the lights of the city below. Having no weapon Sawyer would have to approach with caution so he quietly got into a crouching position and slowly advanced towards his target using the massive air conditioning units on the top as cover. As he approached the last unit. The assassin turned his back towards Sawyer, this was his time to strike he had to take it. Sawyer spied a short piece of copper pipe and picked it up, his idea was a long shot but it was his only option. Stealthily Sawyer snuck up on the assassin and stuck the pipe into his ribs. He had caught the assassin off guard "now drop your weapon and raise your hands slowly or I'm going to blow a hole so big in you that you'll look like a tunnel!" The assassin dropped his weapon on the ground then raised his hands. Sawyer pushed the pipe in tighter and spoke into his ear "that's good, now tell me who are you? Who do you work for? Who sent you?" The assassin stood silently then started to laugh a little, this only enraged Sawyer further "what? You think this is funny? Let's see how funny you think it is when I toss you off the fucking building, now start talking!" The laughter stopped and the assassin said "I wish you would make up your mind, first you're going to make a tunnel out of me now you want to throw me off this building" he turned his head slightly "what's the matter, copper pipe ran out of bullets?" Sawyer was amazed that his bluff was actually called but he also lost his train of thought for a moment. All of a sudden the assassin caught Sawyer in the jaw with a hard elbow and knocked him back. Sawyer quickly tried to gather his composer but he wasn't quick enough. The assassin spun around and as he did he pulled something from his pocket and jammed it into Sawyer's abdomen. After a few seconds Sawyer felt an incredible surge of electricity racing through his body then in the speed of a heartbeat Sawyer fell backwards landing hard on the snow. The attacker took a few steps forward and looked down at Sawyer and raised an eyebrow "a copper pipe?" he said as he picked up the piece of pipe. Sawyer tried to move but he couldn't, he looked up at his attacker "a taser?" Sawyer's attacker smiled broadly and walked around Sawyer "here I stand over "The Great Silencer", the icon, the legend, the man, only to be confronted with a copper pipe, I mean I give you an "A" for effort but a "F" for results… look at you, your on the ground in the snow without little or no effort on my part you really got to work on your game." Sawyer, eyes still looking at his attacker, asked, "Who are you anyway?" The attacker answered apologetically "oh, where are my manners, I' am… the Messiah", then he looked at his watch "but we will have to talk another time" The Messiah picked up Sawyer from behind dragging him back a few feet then laying him on the ground. "Are you going to kill me like you killed Ron?" Messiah looked down at Sawyer and shook his head" no, I'm going to put you under this old air-conditioned unit so in five minutes when a police helicopter flies over it won't see you because if it sees you that will just…" Suddenly a police helicopter came out of nowhere to the Messiah's surprise, he in turn aimed a weapon hanging on his shoulder which fired a small rocket out of the bottom barrel obliterating the helicopter upon impact in a brilliant ball of flame. As the charred wreckage began to fall the Messiah turned back to Sawyer and finished his sentence as if nothing had happened "make things real complicated and who needs that", and then he rolled Sawyer under the old air conditioner unit. The Messiah then turned and started to walk over to the edge of the building when Sawyer shouted "why did you kill Ron you sadistic son of a bitch!" Messiah stopped at the edge of the building and started to put on a harness, which he would use to repel down to the ground, but he didn't acknowledge Sawyer's question. Sawyer then shouted louder "why don't you kill me too and get it over with you asshole coward!" Messiah walked over to Sawyer "I don't have a lot time here to play twenty questions but since your so damn curious I'll tell you quiz kid, Ron was a tool I took a hell of a risk breaking him out of the clink but I knew it would pay off, in short I used him to smoke you out and it worked." Helicopters could be heard in the distance and Messiah when over to the edge once again to attach the cable to himself but he kept talking to Sawyer "Secondly I'm not going to kill you right now because that would rob me of the spectacular finale" Sawyer confusedly asked "what do you mean finale" Messiah shook his head and smiled "the finale, the crescendo, two guys, high noon, black hat, white hat, the final showdown" Sawyer then asked sarcastically "how do you know there will be a showdown and that I'll even show up?" The Messiah was now on the edge of the building facing Sawyer, the helicopters were fast approaching "you'll be there... Sawyer" Sawyer's expression turned blank "you know my name?" he asked. The Messiah smiled like a Cheshire cat "of course I do I created you" he then looked down then back at Sawyer "oh by the way Merry Christmas" and with that he disappeared over the side of the building into the darkness. Within minutes Sawyer could hear two helicopters coming directly overhead and then pausing over the building. Bright spotlights shone on the top of the building, Sawyer didn't even breathe. Just then the reminisce of Ron 's apartment collapsed in a ball of flame and debris, the helicopters shut off their spotlights and moved on, Sawyer started to breathe again. An hour later the paralysis effect of the taser wore off and Sawyer experienced a rush of feeling coming over him and the cold slowly chilling him, it was a good feeling. Sawyer, making sure the focus was on the smoldering apartment and not on his present location slowly, using the fire escapes, made his way down to the ground. Keeping to the shadows he made his way into the parking garage below Ron's apartment building, found Ron's car and started his trek back to New York.

CHAPTER 24
THE VOICE OF DIVINITY

December 24 Christmas Eve

The snow slowly fell and covered the city of New York in a blanket of white on one of the holiest nights of the year. The once busy streets were silent except for a few odd taxis and people going to church or loved ones. Christmas could be a happy time, and a lonely one. In the attic of a condemned church two candles flickered as a solemn figure sat in silence. Christmas eve used to be the highlight of Sawyer's year, but for the past four years there was nothing really merry about it. For these last four Christmases were spent the same the way, go to the mission, pick up Christmas "good will" platter, come back to the church, eat, sleep, wake up go to mission again for "goodwill" breakfast and then come back to the church, feel miserable and fall asleep, Christmas was indeed not merry. This year however seemed different however, Sawyer didn't know why, it just was. The church Sawyer resided in was slated to be demolished six years ago, but as everyone knows when the words "church" and "demolition" are in the same sentence it can be quiet an awkward situation, with religious groups, historical groups and what have you, the fate of the church was in limbo and that's where it would remain now and probably for a while yet. Sawyer knew this and was content to live in the attic of the church, rent-free with running water and electricity, and keep it company. Sawyer sat behind an old oak desk on a hard oak chair, before was a foil wrapped platter he gotten at the mission, a bottle of 1968 merlot which be took while a truck was unloading at the liquor store, actually he had taken a case but this was the last one and a small plastic wine glass he had in his bag which he had gotten on the plane to Toronto four years ago. Sawyer sighed as he peeled back the foil, alone once again for Christmas. The smell of the food permeated the attic overpowering the musty odor that was the standard throughout the year. Sawyer looked at his meal, a meager feast yet well appreciated, it was hot and a decent portion, even for a handout. Sawyer produced a corkscrew and grabbed the bottle, inserted the corkscrew and started to turn it. The sound of a popping cork made Sawyer grin and smelling the cork took Sawyer back to a time when he ate and drank and the finest restaurants in whatever city he happened to be in. Sawyer put the cork down and filled the small plastic wine glass, he then raised the glass to the darkness of the high ceiling "Merry Christmas Gwen, I really miss you and I hope someday we can be together again, I know I' am in deep but you'll see I'll get out of this, I promise". A single tear rolled down his cheek as he swallowed the wine in one gulp. Grabbing the bottle once again Sawyer refilled the glass and raised it to the ceiling and talking as if he were at a funeral "Merry Christmas Ron, I didn't really get to know you, but I wish I did, you were the very epitome of what a person should be and I considered you my friend, thank- you". Once again Sawyer drank the contents of the glass in one gulp. Sawyer pour himself one more drink and ate his rather brief Christmas meal, then once he was finish he was about to pour another drink he stopped and raised the bottle to his lips "sipping wine my ass" and he drank from the bottle and watched the candles burn low, he then finished the bottle and went to bed where he stared at the case containing the laptop but he couldn't bring himself to open it, he slowly fell asleep as the soft glow of the city lights was filtered through the stain glass windows and the image gave Sawyer comfort, for a reason, after four years, he still couldn't explain.

December 25 Christmas Morning.

Christmas morning had arrived, the one morning of the entire year that parents didn't have to coax their kids into getting up early and also the morning responsible for increased coffee sales worldwide. The sun beamed through the stained glass windows in the attic of the old church where Sawyer lay in bed. The taste of sour wine slowly awoke him from his slumber and he rubbed his eyes and put his hands behind his head staring up at the ceiling, despite the cobwebs, the architecture and the materials (mostly oak) still looked in pristine shape. The ceiling wasn't really what Sawyer was focusing on, instead his mind was wandering back to a time when Christmas morning was magical. He thought of the food, the presents, the music, basically the whole of the atmosphere that made up the season but especially the family and friends but soon the whole illusion vanished and the ceiling was all he could see so he decided to get up. The bells were ringing at the church across the street; Sawyer walked over to the window and opened the bottom portion to have a look outside. The sight was indescribable, along with the bells ringing, white doves were flying in the air, people dressed in their best were shaking hands and hugging whilst filing into the church, Sawyer felt as if he were in a Christmas card. The cold air started to chill Sawyer as he continued to stare "I haven't missed it" Sawyer said, doing his best impersonation of Scrooge from the Dickens' classic "A Christmas Carol". Sawyer then closed the window and sat back down on his cot. He stared at the case containing the laptop and it seemed to stare back, for some reason Sawyer felt something was missing that wouldn't let him open the case, but he didn't know what. Then at that moment it was as if someone had turned Sawyer's head and he was staring at a stained glass window, the only one on that wall. The picture in the glass was one of Jesus coming out of his tomb three days after the crucifixion, a story related usually at Easter but for all intents and purposes it didn't matter when the story was told. Sawyer gazed at the window, almost mesmerized; it spoke to him and awakened his senses. He stared at it for another moment and then as if a switch went off in his head something clicked, he looked at his watch "there still might be enough time", he had found the missing piece and it was time to see if it fit into place.

"Everyone please rise for our opening hymn" everyone in the church rose to their feet for the opening hymn and while the hymn played the priest followed by four alter boys walked down the aisle to the altar, turned and joined in the singing of the hymn after which the congregation sat down and only the priest remained standing. Sawyer sat in the far left corner of the last pew next to an elderly gentleman. As the mass proceeded Sawyer looked around an observed the people that made up the mass and listened to the priest speak of Mary and Joseph and the birth of Jesus Christ and later in the mass, for the first time in a long while Sawyer walked up the aisle and excepted the host and was astonished when he walked back to his seat that despite the old suit he wearing that he found hanging in a closet in the church attic that no one looked, pointed or laughed at him he was accepted and not judged, that alone was refreshing to him. The mass was drawing to an close and while the priest was making the congregation laugh which final comments about eating too much and kid hopped up on sugar, Sawyer's eyes were fixated on the crucifix with the replica of Jesus hanging on the wall high up behind the altar and for a moment nothing mattered, not how rich, poor or powerful a person was because here was a man who didn't have anything and sacrificed everything for the good of others, Sawyer bowed his head, closed his eyes and prayed for no apparent reason. The mass ended and the people slowly filed out as Sawyer sat still and once again fixated on the crucifix. The church was soon empty as the priests made their way back in from the sunny yet cold morning air outside. He looked to the side and noticed Sawyer sitting quietly. "Was I that boring?" he said as he looked over at Sawyer. Sawyer looked back at the priest with a smile "no, actually I was very taken by your words, father".

The priest made his way over to Sawyer and sat next to him "good, for a moment there I thought you were asleep and I know your not here for the fruitcake because just between you and me" he said lowering his voice to almost a whisper "it tastes bad and could probably used as a weapon, I think the secret ingredient they're always bragging about isn't love it's titanium" and he put a finger to his lips. Sawyer smiled and laughed a little. The priest extended his hand to Sawyer "Father Graham Keep" he said as Sawyer shook his hand and answered in turn "S.B". Father Graham looked at Sawyer and asked "so why are you still here? I mean it's Christmas morning after all." Sawyer looked at the ceiling and scratched his head. Father Graham gave a small smirk "ok out with it I don't usually talk shop on Christmas morning but I sense you have a problem or a dilemma so I'll make an exception in your case" he said looking at his watch "you have ten minutes... go".

Sawyer took a deep breath and spoke to the father "well father I recently lost someone, for whom I had a great deal of respect and trust in a friend really and he had a last request. It was a bit of a tall order, but he sacrificed and I feel I owe him the request..." Sawyer said lowering his head "I... I don't know if it's right or wrong and then I thought I'll come here and maybe I could find the answer." Father Graham sat back in the pew and pondered the statement for a few moments then looked over at Sawyer and folded his hands "that's a real head scratcher S.B, who's to say what's right or wrong, if this person was good friend and sacrificed for you then his request, whatever it was is warranted" Father Graham paused for a moment and then went on trying to avoid sounding like he was preaching, "if the request sounds and feels right to you then it probably is regardless what other people or society thinks, you have to make a decision, move forward and never look back". Sawyer with a solemn expression on his face nodded in agreement "thank-you father" he said. A wide smile came across Father Graham's face "it's what I do" he said as he raised an eyebrow. Standing up Father Graham shuffled over to the aisle "I'll walk you to the door" he said motioning Sawyer over. The two walked to the

The Silencer

door and stopped. Sawyer turned to Father Graham and shook his hand "once again thank-you father for your help and guidance" Father Graham, almost looking bashful as he tried to return the pleasantry "your welcome S.B and god bless you wherever you may go." Then he closed his eyes and made the symbol of the cross over Sawyer's head "now go in peace." Sawyer turned and made his way down the steps of the church when father Graham called out to him. Sawyer turned around and looked at the father "yes" he answered. Father Graham looked at Sawyer "I almost forgot, have a merry Christmas and a happy new year" he said and raised his hand and waved. Sawyer waved back "same to you father, same to you."

CHAPTER 25

FROM THE GRAVE

Stopping by "the mission" to pick up the traditional Christmas breakfast Sawyer went back to the church attic with a renewed sense of confidence. After eating breakfast Sawyer took the lid of his coffee and placed it down on the desk then he took a deep breath as he prepared to take out the laptop. Slowly Sawyer opened the leather case, Ron's blood still stained the case, which gave Sawyer a slightly queasy feeling but in spite of it he pulled out the laptop and placed it in front of himself. Sawyer then opened it up and turned the power on. While the laptop was starting up he got up from the desk and turned with the leather case in hand putting it down on top of his bunk. Then a ghostly voice chilled his blood as it said "hello Sawyer", it was Ron's voice Sawyer froze, then slowly he turned around and faced the desk but there was no one to be found. Then Sawyer noticed the image on the screen of Ron, who was still speaking but Sawyer was so stunned by the image he didn't hear a word. Sawyer sat down in front of the laptop and slowly closed it then sat back and caught his breath it was as if he had just run a marathon. Finally catching his breath Sawyer opened the laptop and once again turned on the power. In a few moments the almost haunting image of Ron came on the screen and this time Sawyer would listen to every word he had to say.

164

After a moment Ron spoke "hello Sawyer, if you're watching this I'm probably dead, otherwise I would carry out the mission myself." He sipped his coffee slowly wondering about what mission to which Ron was referring. Ron continued and Sawyer made a conscious decision to not think, just listen. "Now before I tell you too much and get you too involved a screen is going to pop up with two boxes one to agree to take this mission and the other to decline it, now I know you've been through a lot and I will understand if you decline, but if you decline and touch the icon the laptop, program and everything else will fry and that will be the end of that, so go ahead and choose". Sawyer put his finger on the little touchpad to control the arrow, which would touch the icon and accept or decline the mission. Back and forth, forth and back Sawyer was hard pressed to make a decision, he had promised himself a long time ago to never put himself in a position that meant choosing one or the other of anything but he needed to make a decision. A few minutes went by and Sawyer was still at the crossroads, what was right? What was wrong? Sawyer's head was throbbing and no clear answer was in sight. Getting up out of his chair he paced back and forth looking at the image of Ron and two boxes from which he had to choose, it was as if the laptop was teasing him, daring him to make a decision. Finally Sawyer calmly sat down, closed his eyes and moved the arrow to a box on the screen and clicked on it. Sawyer slowly opened his eyes and looked at the screen, the image of Ron remained but the small boxes were gone, Sawyer made his decision and he would see this mission through to the end. Picking up his coffee which was now lukewarm at best Sawyer took a sip and nearly spilled the rest on himself when the image of Ron spoke, "I thank-you Sawyer, A nation thanks you, or at least it would if it knew what you were about to save it from" Ron paused then continued "If I've already told you about what's going on, fine I' am going to tell you again and you may be surprised or pissed off at facts I may have omitted, remember I wanted this mission". Sawyer clicked on pause and sat back in his chair, he knew he was getting in deep and he also knew he could still walk away; after all it was just an image on a screen? Now whether it was his sense of right and wrong, or just plain old guilt Sawyer found himself clicking off the pause and listening to every word Ron had to say. He started to speak and Sawyer could feel a weight already being placed upon his shoulders. "President Bob Bradley is a cancer to this country, he has given it a false sense of pride and confidence. Americans have been blinded, sure he has brought back jobs to hundreds if not thousands but at what cost? Strap yourself in, Sawyer it gets rough from here." Sawyer drank the last of his coffee and was now totally fixated on the computer screen. Ron now almost took the tone of a narrator chronicling President Bradley's strategy for America as well as being president. "I learned a lot of things Bob wanted to do when the smoke cleared after four years. He wanted to turn country against country, upset the balance of world politics, in short, world domination... a world, like America that he envisioned." Sawyer was hearing Ron's words but had trouble believing that this one man could take the world's most powerful nation and turn it into the world's most powerful dominating nation. "He must be stopped at all costs because if he is not, the world that we love, that we fought for and many died for will be pushed all the way back to the Hitler era, an era of dictatorship, communism, oppression, a giant shadow of darkness will be cast across this nation and around the world that once in place will change the outcome of history not just for years or decades to come... but generations." Ron's words hit Sawyer with such impact that the weight he had been feeling on his shoulders just got a lot heavier. The image of Ron on the screen smiled "no pressure". Sawyer smiled almost feeling like there was no screen between him and Ron; it was as if Ron was right there. "Sawyer, I'm going to lay everything out for you, it won't be simple but I know you can pull it off so just listen". Sawyer watched as Ron explained everything in full detail. "As you may have heard from me or the media Bradley is going to sign the ' Declaration of Presidential Independence' which for the first time in history will make him president for life, it's actually quite simple he will be president for as long as he can until by illness or design he can't be president he will turn the seat of power over to his second in command which he will have hand picked as well as his administration, no voting, no muss, no fuss." Ron then stopped for a moment and lit a cigarette, then he looked at the screen "like it's going to make a difference" he said referring to the cigarette squeezed between his two fingers. He then took a drag off the smoke and continued, "On December thirty-first at eight o'clock he will sign the document, fly to Massachusetts and celebrate New Year's Eve at an exclusive party in Martha's Vineyard while his vice president will be off in Tahiti getting boozed and screwed." Ron face turned now turned serious, "ok Sawyer here it is in a nutshell, on December thirtieth by midnight the entire Whitehouse will be vacated by order of the president, on December thirty-first Bradley and five of his top bodyguards will go the Whitehouse where they will wait in the lobby while Bradley goes up to the oval office and tweaks the declaration until it is just the way he wants it, then he will sign it just incase someone tries to stop him to stop him". Ron stopped and crushed out his cigarette then sat back and continued "Sawyer what you need to do is technically real simple, if Bradley has signed the paper destroy it, burn it, eat it if you have to, but if he hasn't signed don't let him, the unsigned paper can be used as evidence against him." A befuddled look came across Sawyer's face and he raised his index finger as if to ask a question to the screen, Ron beat him to it. Sitting forward again he explained "now I know you're asking "what good is evidence if the mark is eliminated?" well there's the twist I don't want him killed, it might be hard for you to understand why but let me indulge you for a moment" and with that Ron lit another cigarette. Sawyer, with a slight look of disdain was prepared to listen to Ron anyway, Ron, with a far off stare started to speak "back when I was in the corps we had a mission in West Africa, a group of rogue militants had taken over the munitions depot and had become a real concern to the local government, there were five of us sent in, among them was my commander, a sergeant, myself and two more marines, we were told the force at the depot was minimal which meant five, six guys at most with small arms." A cloud of smoke wafted through the air as Ron blew smoke skyward and then he continued with a much somber expression on his face "we were dropped ten miles from the depot and got into our light armored vehicles which were dropped an hour previous to our arrival, myself and my commander drove in one and the sergeant with the two marines in tow commandeered the other one." Once again Ron sat back looking rather uneasy "as the depot came into sight the vehicle with our three brothers in arms exploded into the air and came down big ball of fire, we swerved and jumped out just before our vehicle explode into the air also, it twisted in the air for a few moments crashed to the ground, they knew we were coming and to make matters worse there weren't five or even six guys it was more like ten to twelve." A single tear rolled down Ron's cheek and before he could continue he wiped it away with his hand, a cigarette squeezed between his fingers "we were down to two, the other guys died on impact and the charred ruins spoke for itself, however my commander and myself managed to slide behind the twisted mass of metal that was once a fine vehicle and tried to form a plan... fast." Ron stopped and took a sip of water then continued "yeah we were in really deep shit and to make matters worse my commander took some shrapnel when the vehicle exploded and was bleeding bad but he was one tough son of a bitch and he never complained, the shooting stopped, the bastards knew they had was where they wanted us or so they thought. My commander pulled out a pair of field glasses and slowly looked over the situation then turned to me and said something that has stuck with me to this very day he said "son, give a man enough rope and he can lasso the moon give him too much and he'll hang himself" I really didn't understand what he meant but then he showed me. He reached into the back of the vehicle and pulled out one undamaged R.P.G (rocket propelled grenade) then he reached in once again and found a launcher, he loaded, stood up and fired straight at the depot, you should have seen that son of a bitch explode it was like three fourth of Julys all rolled into one, as for the twelve guys... obliterated totally obliterated." Ron laughed, then with a smile he finished the story "yep I knew what he meant then, we all received the

The Silencer

Congressional Medal of Honor... all of us, we all sacrificed... some gave all." Ron lowered his head for a moment as Sawyer was left breathless as if he were there during the mission, it was quite sobering. Ron then raised his head "well Sawyer that 's the end of the sermon as for what you need for this mission or job or whatever you want to label it is in this laptop the password to access the program is "courage" something you have in spades and you can then download all the information into an Ipod which is in the trunk of my Mercedes along with everything else you'll need which I'm sure you keep in pristine shape" he said clasping his hands almost begging him "call it my last request... damn I love that car". he then paused, "Actually, Sawyer I do want you to do one thing when this is all over I want you to make sure that everybody knows that I did not knowingly have anything do with the plot to assassinate President Doyle and that I also didn't launch a missile at Iraq and that I was set up and that I love this country and would never try to harm it." Ron stopped for a moment and there was an awkward silence then he took a breath and continued, "One last thing, I want to be buried in Arlington cemetery next to my brothers in arms." Ron then cleared his throat and returned to the tone of voice which he started out with "good luck Sawyer I know you can do this, you're the best, you're the Silencer, God bless you my friend, and If you screw this up I'll see you soon" he said with a smile and then snapped a to attention and saluted "dismissed" and with that the image froze for and minute then faded away replaced by a white screen with the words "enter password now" in the center.

169

CHAPTER 26

LAYOUT

Sawyer sat for a moment, his eyes still glazed over, still trying to fathom what he had just seen and heard. Finally he took a deep breath and entered the password the screen turned to a light blue color and then a index came up of every room in the white house listed individually also camera locations, electrical schematics, telephone lines, then Sawyer saw what interested him most on the list: itinerary, it gave a detailed outline of Bradley's whole day and a blueprint on which to build his strategy. Sawyer was puzzled as to why all the rooms in the Whitehouse were listed and he would soon get his answer. Sawyer clicked on the first words under the index marked "program information" and the blueprint of the white house popped up with a familiar voice doing the narration… Ron. He started right in "if you're wondering why there is a blueprint of the Whitehouse let me simplify it, the whole program is locked into the Whitehouse which basically means that you have the power to shut down any room, elevator, camera, etc." As Ron explained the sections of the blueprint were highlighted as he continued "just point and click it's that simple, but just make sure of two things, one: remember to download the program on to your phone and two: after this is over destroy everything, the laptop, clothing, everything, we don't need some punk ass little shit getting a hold of it and playing with it, ok that's it." Ron then smiled and added "try not to screw it up ok?" After introduction to the program Sawyer had no problem interpreting Ron's plan with the exception of the "rope speech "as it came to be known by Sawyer later on. For the next several days Sawyer studied the program over and over getting every aspect and detail down to a science, down to a point where it was as natural as breathing. The Mercedes containing the rest of the gear Sawyer would need was stored in the small garage beside the church. Sawyer popped the trunk and saw the duffle bag but didn't bother to inspect it, if Ron said everything was in it, who was Sawyer to doubt him. He closed the trunk and covered the car over with a dirty old tarp then threw junk and garbage on it, he didn't need someone to accidentally find it.

CHAPTER 27

WAKE, EAT, ... LAST SLEEP

December 29

Sawyer woke up and made his way down to the mission for the last time, he knew that after he accomplished his objective in the nation's capitol he couldn't come back, in essence this would be like his last meal. He walked in the front door and was immediately immersed in the sights, smells and sounds that made up the place that he had come to for the past four years. Sawyer walked up and received his last meal of potatoes, corn, pork and beans and roast beef with gravy (or a reasonable facsimile thereof). He went over to a table and sat down, at the table were five men who Sawyer affectionately referred to as "the boys". They were here when Sawyer arrived and they would still be here after he was gone. After finishing his meal he started towards the door and the one thing Sawyer took from the place, aside from memories, was a business card from a small plastic tray screwed to the wall. Maybe sometime, somehow he could repay the generosity shown to him… maybe. The rest of Sawyer's day went by quickly, it was basically getting his head and face shaved also a shower at the local gym. Sawyer then returned to the church to get packed up. With his bag packed and having gone through the plan again

172

The Silencer

on the laptop, darkness once came over the city. Sawyer sat on his bunk and looked around the room, he remembered how scared and curious he was when he first arrived and how melancholy he felt now. Sawyer could feel his confidence coming back slowly… but it was definitely there. He laid down to catch a few hours of sleep because he knew the next twenty four to seventy two hours were going to be sleepless.

CHAPTER 28

LOCATION, LOCATION, PREPARATION

December 30 3:00 am

Sawyer awoke and sat up on the edge of his shaking the cobwebs loose from his mind. He put on some relatively clean clothes: jeans, a t-shirt and a sweater; black running shoes completed the ensemble. Making his way down two sets of creaky, old unstable stairs Sawyer made it to the bottom floor. Sawyer, bags in hand, made his way to the door to the garage when he stopped. To his right was the cathedral, now he hadn't set foot in it once since he had come here other than a quick glance now and again while he was leaving for the mission. Sawyer put his bags down and entered the cathedral. A weak hinge supported the only door on the double door entrance Sawyer walked through. It was an amazing sight set before him, amazing yet sad. The church had been set ablaze six months before Sawyer arrived and the cathedral took the brunt of the fire. Sawyer walked in. Lights from outside illuminated the room though the windows that held a few chards of stained glass and everywhere he looked blackness and destruction. Sawyer made his way up the aisle to the reminisce of what once was a pew and sat down. Sawyer took another look around and shook his head at the lightly snow covered floors and damage over every inch of the room. He then dropped to his knees, hands clasped, and he started to pray his way. He looked up at the altar and then behind it to the wall and up to where the crucifix should have been hanging but wasn't, all that was left was a perfect outline surrounded by smoke damage. Sawyer maintained his stare and began to speak, "I've never really been the religious type lord, but I think I need your support, now I know I've done some bad things in my life and I... I' am willing to repent and change my ways as best I can, I know you can see right through the bullshit and if this whole thing doesn't workout so good for me, try and be flexible, I never killed anyone who didn't deserve it." Sawyer then bowed his head and prayed silently for a few moments after which he raised his head "and by the way lord" he added, "I haven't sold my soul to the company stove. I hope that counts for something, thanks for listening". Sawyer then got off his knees and sat back on the pew looking around once again. In his mind Sawyer couldn't believe how people could degrade a church by trying to burn it down, spray painting the outside. Then Sawyer looked on the ground next to him and saw what appeared to be a couple of used condoms and beside those needles. Sawyer shook his head and looked at the altar "what's this world coming to, I mean condoms and needles in the house of the lord, this is evolution? What a degrading way for a church to go out" he said with utter disdain. Sawyer stood up and bowed in the direction of the altar and headed for the door with a small smile on his face "don't worry I 'll give you a proper retirement, I'll give you back dignity". After his prayer session Sawyer went to the garage and removed the old auto parts along with the tarp, which protected the car and left it practically dust free. Sawyer put his bag and the laptop in the backseat of the car, and then he slowly started to drive away. He got five hundred yards from the church he pulled a small detonator and using his teeth pulled the antenna out, then he pressed the red button on the center of the controller and all of a sudden the entire church exploded into a big ball of flame and black smoke Sawyer glanced into his rear view mirror couple of times while driving away "now you have back your dignity". Then slowly, the further he got the better he felt, it wasn't that he hated church after all it gave him shelter and sanctuary. Sawyer, in his mind, saw by blowing up the church with his last bits of plastique and detonators. The way Sawyer saw it he released an old friend from a cruel fate of sitting lonely. Sawyer felt as if he took someone dear and unplugged the life support system. Sawyer felt a small amount of guilt for all the joy of weddings to the sorrow of funerals the church must have had in its hundred and twenty year history. Sawyer kept driving to his next destination: Washington. Driving for almost the entire duration stopping only once for breakfast Sawyer made remarkable time. Once in Washington Sawyer consulted his Blackberry and under the heading of "Accommodations" the name of the hotel, the location, and the alias he needed to use also the reservation was already made so Sawyer didn't need a credit card, which was provided in the suitcase in the trunk, "Ron didn't miss a trick so far" Sawyer said "I hope he has plenty more in the bag. When Sawyer arrived at the hotel the check in he was a bit hesitant but after a few brief moments at the check in counter Sawyer's hesitation was put to rest and the check in when extremely smooth without a hitch and the next thing he knew he was in a beautiful suite fit for a king or a celebrity. In a few moments Sawyer's bags arrived in the room, he tipped the bellboy and then before shutting the door he hung the "do not disturb" sign on the handle. Sawyer made his way to the window and looked out, from his room he had a perfect view of the Whitehouse which could have been more than six or seven blocks away; far enough that it wouldn't that the hotel wouldn't be suspected for housing the aggressor and close enough that it was in walking distance where on the way a person could easily lose themselves in a crowd. The suitcase that was in Ron's trunk was hoisted onto the bed and opened. Inside the suitcase was a black suit, white shirt, black tie and black Italian dress shoes. "Ron had good taste," Sawyer thought. Removing the suit and hanging it Sawyer looked back into the case and noticed an envelope, he took it out, the front of the envelope read

"Sawyer after this is over," Sawyer then felt the envelope had some keys inside, then it all started to make sense. Ron wasn't going to go on the mission Sawyer was and he knew it all the time; the envelop, the Italian shoes, it all clicked and probably the keys and whatever paper was inside was to a locker box in some train station with case in it, Sawyer had to give Ron an "A" for planning. The suitcase was snapped shut and slid under the bed; the envelope however was put in the room safe located in the closet, for safekeeping. Sawyer clicked on the television and sat down, the show was about fishing or something Sawyer didn't know, he lay back on the bed and was asleep in second, the batteries were worn down, it was time for a recharge… sleep, beautiful sleep. The next morning or early afternoon as the sun beamed through the open blind and directly into Sawyer's eyes. Slowly he awoke and sat up on the edge of the bed, his mind still working feverishly on how he would access the Whitehouse. He knew that once he was it in the plan could go forward, once he was in he know what to do, but getting access was the wrinkle. Pacing around the room, Sawyer hoped that a plan would come to him, and a plan wasn't just going to fall in his lap or was it. Sawyer noticed on the desk a bunch of assorted pamphlets of landmarks and monuments in Washington, things like the Washington monument, the Lincoln memorial and most importantly of all the Whitehouse, Sawyer looked at the bottom of the pamphlet of tour times then he looked at his watch, it was almost two o'clock and there was a tour starting at three, Sawyer first needed to get some inconspicuous clothing so as not to stick out in the crowd. At approximately two forty-five Sawyer arrived dressed in a black tracksuit and fanny pack just to add the tourist flavor to the whole ensemble. Three o'clock and a slender young lady cupped her hands around her mouth and announced that the tour of the Whitehouse was about to commence. The tour itself lasted only thirty minutes due to the fact that several sections of the Whitehouse were off limits to tourists, and Sawyer was no further ahead then when he started and he still needed a way to get in he knew the reason Ron didn't mention how to get in because he would have simply have used his credentials to get in. Sawyer sat down on a bench for a moment and tried to sort things out. A few moments later he was still drawing blanks until the answer became apparent. A man dressed in white coveralls pushing a buffing machine came in, plugged in the machine and began to buff the floor and then another man also dressed in white coveralls walked towards the men's room and went in. Sawyer had seen all he needed to see and made his way to the front doors. But not before he got a close look at the coveralls and the logo on the back. Sawyer went to the hardware store and got the supplies he needed so he could make a pair or coveralls exactly like the cleaning staff. He wouldn't need it long because Sawyer also checked on the iphone for the layout and location of the president's secret elevator which was located only fifty feet from the men's room on the main floor. The elevator was not only concealed by a giant plant, but there was always a security guard posted there. Sawyer knew that tomorrow there would only be five secret service men in the whole building, but what five? and where would they be posted was the question, he would have to use all his skill to get in the Whitehouse and then past the muscle to the elevator, get to the president, somehow destroy but not kill him and save America from screwing the world and itself. With these thoughts in mind Sawyer left to Whitehouse and hailed a taxi all the while he couldn't help but think that Ron and God were having a cold beer-watching him with great interest to see if he could actually pull it off and all Sawyer could do was smile and shake his head as he instructed the driver to take him to a pub… a curtain pub. After a short twenty-minute ride the taxi pulled up in front of the pub, Sawyer paid the driver and got out. It felt like old times and he hadn't even entered the pub. Sawyer walked in and over to a corner booth; the same booth he used to sit at almost every night after work, it seemed surreal. The name of the pub was "The Lincoln Lounge" it had been around since the early nineteen- fifties and had served literally generations of government workers and citizens of Washington D.C The most famous moment for this particular establishment came when president John. F Kennedy and Frank Sinatra came in for a drink just after Kennedy and the first lady had taken in Sinatra performing in Las Vegas at the Dunes hotel and casino and at the behest of Kennedy, "Ol Blue Eyes" and the rest of the "Rat Pack" came back to Washington with him. The two went and called ahead and got a very private area in the pub, it was so private that no one even knew they were there. The president, the "Chairman of the Board" and the boys drank for a while, so much in fact that they had run up a bar tab that was so high it still stood to this very day and a picture of the crooner and the politician hangs very proudly over the bar with the two of them an arm on each others shoulders and on the bottom signed by both of them, yes this bar had history and Sawyer felt like he was home. As Sawyer looked around the room he saw laughing, talking and a real kinship between all patrons in the pub, no negativity at all. That sight that puts everything in perspective. A beautiful young lady was helping a soldier on crutches; the soldier was missing his left leg. As Sawyer watched as the two sat down at the other side of the pub and the young lady kissed the soldier on the cheek and rested her head on his shoulder. Sawyer sat silent, then signaled the waitress to come over and Sawyer ordered a double scotch neat. When the waitress brought his scotch over Sawyer also asked, "So what's the damage, love?" As the waitress tallied up his bill he drank the scotch in one gulp. The waitress turned to Sawyer with the total "eight twenty-five sweetie". Sawyer reached into his pocket for his money clip and gave the waitress fourteen dollars and asked her "you see that soldier with that young lady on the other side of the bar in the booth?" The waitress nodded, Sawyer continued, "what are they drinking?" The waitress answered "a beer and screwdriver (vodka and orange juice), why?" Sawyer put his hand under the waitress's hand with the money and closed her hand "I want to buy them a drink, ok?" The waitress answered back "ok, but this is too much money". Sawyer responded "it's the total for the drinks and a little something extra for you, and tell them the drinks are from a friend." The waitress smiled and left the table. The drinks arrived at the table across the pub for the soldier and the young lady, the waitress told them whom it was from, but by the time the soldier looked over to raise his drink, Sawyer was gone. After leaving the pub he made a quick stop at the hardware store to pick up supplies and another at the costume shop for a disguise and then he returned to the hotel room to make his final strategies for tomorrow. It was going to be an extremely long day... the longest he'd had in a while.

December 31st 4:30 am

CHAPTER 29

GAME DAY

Lawyer awoke, he was noticeably tired after going over the plans for the mission, in fact he had gone over it so many times that it was almost as natural as breathing. The smell of freshly brewed coffee filled the room as Sawyer stepped into the shower, the only place he felt he could truly think. The hot water ran down Sawyer's body as he tried to clear his mind and concentrate on nothing but the hot water and the steam, which filled the entire bathroom. He needed calm before the storm. No sooner did Sawyer emerge from the bathroom wrapped in a towel then he poured himself a cup of black coffee and turned on the television to watch the international news channel. Time was on Sawyer's side. According to Ron's plan The President would not be arriving at the Whitehouse until five o'clock and he would leave at seven thirty which gave Sawyer most of the day to prepare, his first action in preparation was pouring another cup of coffee. A few hours later at president Bradley's compound in an extremely well protected area, President Bradley ate breakfast on the terrace and watched the television. He was most interested in watching the preparations for the New Year's Eve gala at which he would unveil his "declaration of presidential independence." The president had almost finished his breakfast when Vice President Horowitz came out on the

181

terrace, hot cup of coffee in hand and sat down. President Bradley turned to him "what brings you out this morning Horowitz?" he said as he took a bite of toast. Horowitz sipped his coffee and replied "I just came by to wish you a happy new year because in two hours as you know I'm flying to Tahiti." Bradley smiled, "good for you, have a nice time." Horowitz went quiet for a moment and then spoke "I'm also here because I would like to see the "Declaration" for a moment "Bradley turned to Horowitz in disbelief "you want to see the declaration… why?" Horowitz replied rather apprehensively "well I saw the first draft, but that's not good enough. I would like to see it first hand… please after all, I'm the vice president and we should be on the same team… right?" Bradley looked at Horowitz with an ice-cold stare and a scowl. Bradley took a sip of his coffee and addressed the request "now you listen here, you little asshole, the only reason you're the vice president is because you did what I wanted, how I wanted it and when I wanted it done, that's all." Horowitz should have stopped talking but something inside of him was forcing him to ask again. Clearing his throat he tried reasoning with an already upset president "I' am not asking to change the declaration I just would like the opportunity to read it and share my thoughts, after all what kind of Vice president would I be if I didn't ask?" he said with an uneasy smile. Bradley, still with a chilling stare answered the query "what kind would you be? You would be the unemployed kind, that's the kind you would be!" Bradley wasn't finished yet, he was just getting started "I can see the papers now" he said as he held an imaginary newspaper in front of himself "Vice president indicted after intelligence discovers that he was behind the assassinations of President Doyle, and senior adviser Ron Fuller, along with condemning a man for a crime he didn't commit and the genocide of a nation with the push of a button." Horowitz sat and stared at Bradley for a moment, but there was a little more Bradley had in store. "And another thing there a lot of people who jump at the opportunity to be at my right hand if something happened to you, look your next in line and you have the world at you feet as it stands don't fuck it up, now stand up and let's try this whole thing again, only this time keep it simple and to the point." Horowitz stood up; at first he didn't understand what the president meant but then he caught on. Another sip of coffee and Bradley stood up with a smile and faced Horowitz. "Good morning vice president Horowitz, what brought you here this morning?" Horowitz, as if he was reading a script "I just came by to say good-bye and good luck tonight". The president stood up and extended his hand, Horowitz took it. As the two shook hands the president talked as if Horowitz had been there only a few moments disregarding the time already spent. "Well thank you son that means a lot, now I don't want to hold you up but don't you have a plane to catch?" Horowitz hung his head and responded "yes I have a plane to catch and I do have to go, once more Mr. President good luck tonight," and then he turned "good bye". Bradley finished up his breakfast and drank his coffee as if nothing happened. The vice president however walked away as if had been raped, raped of his dignity and pride but he took consolation in the fact that Bradley wasn't a spring chicken anymore and when he checked out he would check in, "in for a penny in for a pound" he thought as he made his way to the front door a small smile unseen by Bradley crossed his face. Sawyer stayed in for the day ordering his breakfast and lunch, he'd often look over at the clock on the wall and watch the minutes ticking by slowly. It was tedious and it was only one fifteen in the afternoon. With his mind trying to find a way to relax for the next two hours, at least. Then Sawyer remembered a way. Sawyer was on a job in Florida and stayed in a two star motel that had a pool outside that is where he met Jackie "The Magician" Miller an old time hitman who was now retired but was dubbed his moniker by making people disappear without a trace. After a few days by the pool with him, Sawyer got to know Jackie quite well and when they both had discovered they were in the same business… A convenient coincidence or the hand of fate, either way both men were on the same page. Sawyer must have heard hundreds of stories from the man but there was one conversation that stuck in his mind and that was when Sawyer asked him how he stayed so calm and loose. Jackie tilted his straw hat and told Sawyer "the way to stay calm is to find a way to let go entirely I take a swim on the day of a big job, the water relaxes me in a way that nothing else can, it's like lying in God's hand and letting him take you for a guided tour of heaven itself and when I'm done I feel like I'm reborn and that my boy is the key to staying loose and calm, of course it varies from person to person, you know dealer's choice." The flashback then faded away and it made Sawyer feel better at least he knew what he needed to do. Sawyer went down to the overpriced souvenir shop and bought a pair of swimming trunks and for the next hour he went to the hotel pool and swam. When Sawyer emerged he felt like a new man, refreshed, focused and totally relaxed.

CHAPTER 30

EMPIRE FORWARD...
GAME DAY PT 1

3:00 pm President Bradley's Compound.

President Bradley had just finished his shower and emerged from the bathroom. The steam from his shower vented into the room and hung in the air. At the press of a button and music filled the room "The Three Tenors live" as Bradley walked through the massive closet, which had everything in it from suits to shoes. After making his decision and laying the suit on the bed Bradley got dressed and when he was finished he looked into a full-length mirror at himself and smiled combing his silver hair and striking a pose identical to the statue in front of the Whitehouse. Bradley then walked over to a painting of himself posed in front of the American flag; his fists clenched on his hips in almost a "Superman" pose with the word "pride" in big, bold letters across the bottom. He ran his fingers along the right side of the frame until he felt a small switch and with his index finger he flicked it up. The painting slid over to the right and a vault was revealed. President Bradley placed his thumb on a small pad located in the middle of the vault door; there

185

was no dial on this particular vault, just the identification in the center. A small stream of red light passed over his thumbprint on the pad and within seconds a voice stated that the print was authentic and accepted, the vault door swung open with ease. The contents of the vault varied, from one hundred thousand dollars in cash to ten bars of solid gold bullion to a thick stack of documents which no one had seen except the president himself but there was one document that piqued his interest at this very moment, "The Declaration of Presidential Independence". President Bradley pulled the large, brown envelope which was on top of the stack of documents and placed it in a black briefcase on a small table beside the wall then he closed it and locked the two combination locks on the front. Once the vault was closed President Bradley slid his finger up the side of the painting once again and flicked the small switch down, the painting slid back into place and there was a short silence. Looking into a full-length mirror President Bradley ran his fingers through his lush, gray hair then secured his wrist to the suitcase with a handcuff, he then pressed "1" on his cell phone and contacted his driver "Fred, we will be taking the company S.U.V. today, I don't want to attract attention so warm it up son, I'll be down soon, we have to make a few well wisher stops, you know the bullshit where I get photos and donate money to charities and stuff and then it's off to the Whitehouse and after this day is done I'm giving you the month off, now like I said warm up the vehicle I'll be down in ten".

CHAPTER 31

SILENTLY STORMING... GAME DAY PT 2

5:00pm The Whitehouse

The company S.U.V. had just pulled up and entered through the back entrance where no one could see him come in… that is no one but Sawyer. Sawyer had been sitting in a van that he acquired for nearly three quarters of an hour, he'd sit for another fifteen minutes, by then President Bradley should be in the oval office. The president entered the Whitehouse flanked by his "personal security force, five men, the best of the best, precision trained in hand to hand combat, weapons and tactics. The president approached a secret elevator behind a large plant then stopped and turned to his men "gentlemen, I'm going to be a couple of hours, I've got some items that need to be attended to before the New Year's festivities and some loose ends to tie up so I want you men to let no one in and be extra vigilant is that understood!" The men nodded their heads in agreement and then one spoke "Mr. President, sir, we have been informed that there is an electrician coming soon for some minor work, just wanted to let you know… should we just tell the electrician to leave? or let him do

187

his work." The president nodded "That's ok, just in and out no screwing around" and with that the president walked over to a giant pillar behind the plant in the corner and pressed a small controller he had in his shirt pocket, the pillar turned revealing a single person elevator. The door opened and the president got in. He turned around facing the men and addressed them one more time before closing the door "and unless a war breaks out I don't want to be disturbed!" Then the pillar turned once again and the president was whisked away to the oval office while his men settled in. Fifteen minutes had passed as Sawyer slipped his phone into his pocket and left his van which he had driven in five minutes after the president had arrived with the help of a coded security card which Ron used for access when he was on better terms with the president. In his hand a black electrician's bag which contained everything he needed to accomplish his mission on the bottom, on the top tangled up wires, cutters, several different types of tape and other tools of the trade in case he needed to show security so that he could remain legitimate and keep his cover intact. There were so many variables he tried not to think of a worst case scenario and finally a five foot folding ladder which he picked up at the hardware store just before he borrowed his transportation. Sawyer walked through the service entrance and up the stairs to the first floor at which point he was greeted by one of the members of the presidential security force standing at the top of the stairs. When Sawyer got to the top the agent introduced himself "hello, I'm agent Diaz commander of the presidential security force, I was notified you were coming and may I ask how long will you be here?" Sawyer looked up in the air to give the impression that he was trying to figure out a time frame for the job. Sawyer, finishing up his time estimation, answered the agent "about fifteen to twenty minutes… half hour tops." The agent nodded and led Sawyer to the washroom's location, he turned to Sawyer "a half hour, tops?" Sawyer looked back at the agent before entering the ladies room "you have my word, now if you'll excuse me I'll get right to work." The agent once again nodded and Sawyer turned his attention and entered the ladies room. He walked around the

The Silencer

ladies room for fifteen minutes trying to kill time so at least the agents outside thought he was doing something, if he came out too quickly they might become suspicious. So Sawyer used the time to apply more make-up glue to his mustache and fix his shoulder length hair. A shock was in store for Sawyer when he emerged from the ladies room, Sawyer expected the agents to be eyeballing him until he came out, instead he saw the five agents sitting around a table playing poker "is this what presidential security has come to?" he thought. When the agent noticed Sawyer and looked over, Sawyer nodded and said "one down and one to go" much to the joy of the agent who nodded back and continued to play cards. Sawyer then entered the "men's room". There was not much he could do for the moment, he needed to play the waiting game, only this time he needed to spend enough time in the washroom so an agent would come in that way he not only improved his odds for success but he might be able to catch them by surprise… time would tell. Twenty minutes had passed and the agent in charge started to wonder about the status of the electrician. The agent folded his hand and called over to another agent who was sitting on a bench down from the game, he had been cleaned out in the game and had retreated to lick his preverbal wounds. The agent shouted, "Hey josh! Go in the shithouse and see what the hell sparky is up to?" The agent sighed, then got and walked over to the men's washroom and entered. Looking around the agent called out to Sawyer "hey where are you?" When there was no response the agent pulled his gun from his shoulder holster and walked cautiously around the washroom, "I say again where are you?" There was no visual or sound, the agent was getting nervous. "Where are you? I'm not going to ask again", but again there was silence. All of a sudden a voice called out from inside one of the stalls "here I 'am" the voice called out, the agent walked toward the voice and when he came to the stall where he heard it he inconspicuously looked under the stall and saw a pants and coveralls lying on the floor wrapped around the electrician's ankles. The agent smiled "oh sorry, had to go huh?" The voice answered him back "yeah I wanted to finish one job before I started another one, know what I mean?" The agent returned the gun to its holster with a laugh and walked over to the sinks "you ok in there?" Sawyer replied back "yep, just doing a little intestinal yoga, I'll be out in a couple of minutes." Turning the cold water tap on, the agent replied, "It's ok, finish your job before you finish the job." The agent cupped his hands under the tap, the cold water felt good on his face and he splashed the water on several times, but as he dried his face with a few paper towels he noticed someone standing to his left in a dark suit with a smile. The agent was so surprised his reaction time was slightly compromised and Sawyer struck fast and hard. Putting his two hands on the edge of the sink next to the agent he swung both his legs and caught the agent in the back of the head with enough strength to send his head crashing into the edge of the sink and then to the ground, Sawyer put a finger on the agent's throat, he was alive which was a real relief he didn't want to leave a trail of carnage. Sawyer quickly dragged the agent to a stall and propped him up on the toilet then opened his bag and took out a roll of black electrical tape. So Sawyer commenced taping the wrists, ankles, mouth and eyes then Sawyer taped the agent to the tank. He then climbed up on the toilet tank in the next stall and sliding a ceiling tile to the side he put the bag up in the ceiling and carefully slipped the tile back. No one would know and it would be easy to access just in case things went sideways. The agents outside the washroom maintained playing poker and were completely oblivious to the absence of their colleague, poker was where their attention lied. With the washroom door facing Sawyer dead in the face the adrenaline started to flow from his heart to his toes and then he pulled back the door and went out of the washroom. As soon as Sawyer set foot in the main hallway, he couldn't help but notice time slowing down. At first the agent's playing cards didn't notice Sawyer in the hall but when one noticed they all locked eyes on Sawyer. "Where's Josh?" one of them asked. Sawyer looked back "He's taking a nap, but don't worry you're all paid by the hour anyway." As the agents got up they knocked over the table and the cards and chips started falling to the ground. Sawyer noticed that he could hear the cards flutter to the ground and the chips fell with a distinct tone. The four agents walked towards Sawyer with their guns drawn. Sawyer drew his gun also and he and the agents walked towards each other. In Sawyer's ears he could only hear an electric guitar and a harmonica. The whole scene of Sawyer and the agents approaching each other, guns drawn played out like a scene from a Sergio Leone spaghetti western but then as all parties were at least five feet from each other the music stopped playing in Sawyer's ears. The lead agent was now a mediator. He looked at Sawyer and took control of the situation "put the gun down or else we will be forced to take immediate action!" Sawyer smirked, "What are you going to shoot me?" The agents looked at each other, Sawyer knew he was on to something and he needed to roll with it. Sawyer continued to talk hard and fast "let me get this straight, it takes four of you, armed to the teeth to take down little old me?" Sawyer rolled his eyes, "you guys are pathetic." He then looked at the agents and grinned "I thought you guys were precision trained and yet you pussies need guns… sad" The lead agent turned back to the other agents who were holding position with their guns drawn and locked on Sawyer "he's right guys" he said in a convincing tone "we don't need weapons, we are weapons!" Sawyer then smiled "That's the spirit boys, you put away yours and I'll put away mine, then you can show me you're not a big bunch of lunkheaded pussies, c'mon gentleman earn that government cheese".So the lead agent put down his gun as did the rest of the agents. Then the four agents all took defensive stances, tight fists getting ready to strike. Sawyer had been up against multiple opponents before but never ones as experienced, Sawyer needed an edge, he reached into his shoulder holster and produced his weapon. The agent's look of confidence suddenly vanished and was replaced by looks of curiosity. Sawyer smiled and laughed, "You didn't think I was going to try to fight all four of you, did you? Because that would be stupid." Sawyer pointed his weapon at the agents and instructed them to go towards the men's room. The agents started to enter the men's room in single file when the lead agent who was in front of Sawyer suddenly swung back with a hard elbow which caught

Sawyer by surprise not to mention flush in the jaw and sent him skidding across the white tile floor. The agents quickly came over to where Sawyer was and surrounded him. The lead agent snickered "Well I guess we get that fight after all" Another agent looked over "shouldn't we call the president you know keep him in the loop?" The agent looked at him "no, you remember what the man said, I think we will turn this problem into ground chuck." Sawyer made two fists then put them down and addressed the lead agent yet again. The lead agent was starting to get annoyed but said he would listen to what Sawyer had to say but this was it. The lead agent asked "what?" Sawyer reached into his front jacket pocket and pulled out his phone "are you going to text for some help?" he said laughing. Sawyer laughed as he looked at the agent "no, I just wanted to tell you that I do my best work…" and then with touch to the screen the entire bottom floor went dark. For next few minutes nothing could be heard but the sound of punches connecting and bones breaking and when the lights came back on there was only Sawyer standing alone while all the agents were spread out on the floor, Sawyer looked down at the lead agent who was lying face down on the floor and finished his sentence "in the dark." Sawyer dragged the agents into the men's room where he propped them up on toilets in four individual stalls and then proceeded to tape all the agents to the toilets leaving the noses free to breathe. When the last agent was taped Sawyer looked at his watch he had time but in twenty minutes time would get tighter and then the pressure would be on.

CHAPTER 32

IS THE PEN MIGHTIER THAN THE SWORD? GAME DAY PT 3

President Bradley sat in the oval office behind his desk with the most important document in the history of America and the world eventually sitting in front of him. He had been sitting at his desk looking at the document for the last ten minutes, he was mesmerized by it in the fact that a small piece of paper would soon have such a huge impact; he was truly standing at the cusp of history in the making, his type of history. The pen he had also been holding in his right hand quivered a bit, he wasn't so much hesitant about signing the paper, which he would do later at a fake signing at the New Year's Eve gala, a moment with passion a real adrenaline rush. President Bradley sat back in his chair, took a deep breath, clinched the pen he was about to sign when he heard someone outside his office, he put the pen down and administered a tongue lashing right from his desk. The scowl on the president's face was without compare "I don't know if your deaf, dumb or just ignorant but I specifically said I didn't want to be disturbed unless we are under attack and obviously we are not, so I suggest you turn around and piss off or in the new year you'll find yourself unemfuckingployed! Do you hear me? Unemfuckingployed!!!" There was then total silence; the president breathed a sigh of relief and picked up the pen once again attempting to sign when suddenly he heard a sound that surprised him. President Bradley had the old door on the oval office replaced with a door of solid steel kind of like a door on a vault with seven locks and only one man had the code to get in and he also controlled the door with a remote under his desk, a small button. to be exact. The door was painted a slick white with all the workmanship from the first door initiated into it; the original door was donated to the Smithsonian Institute.

President Bradley sat behind his desk with almost a glazed look on his face as one by one the locks started to release and after the last lock released the door slowly swung open. From what President Bradley could gather the figure entering the oval office was one of his own men, but as the figure drew closer the president then realized it wasn't. Just then the door slowly swung shut and the plethora of locks could be heard, once again locking the door the office was now solitary confinement. President Bradley knew he was outmatched so he reached for the red telephone on his desk. Bradley picked up the receiver "Eagle one has been compromised! I repeat eagle one has been compromised!" he shouted but no one was there, the phone was dead. Bradley looked at the figure standing in front of the door and began to shout, "what the hell did you do to my phone and who the hell are you!!!" The figure walked in a few more steps and answered the questions "your phone has been cut off although your power remains on I want you in private and as for who am I well you see..." he took two steps closer "I'm the ghost of Christmas past" The president looked closely and then as if a light had gone on in his head he smiled slightly "I know who you are" he said with astonishment "your Sawyer Briggs, you're the guy that Ron hired to rub out President Doyle". Sawyer stood quietly as the president went on "but tell me something son... how in the name of modern physics did you manage to drive a limo out of a plane, plummet more than thirty two thousand feet and survive?" Sawyer answered being rather abrupt "how I survived is neither here nor there I just came here for one reason only" President Bradley looked at his watch then at Sawyer "well if that reason is to shoot me or get some kind of payback you'd better do it now because I have a schedule to keep and if I don't the entire Whitehouse will be crawling with the nation's finest from every direction, one of the perks of being the boss." Sawyer shook his head in response "no, it's nothing like that, I just want to talk." President Bradley had a puzzled look on his face, he never saw that one coming "you mean to tell me, all this preparation and planning just so you could have a chat with yours truly?" Sawyer nodded his head. The president's eyes narrowed "are you wearing a wire?" Sawyer just shook his head "On my honor as a gentleman I'm wearing no wire, I just want to know the truth and how I fit in, that's it." Leaning up against the front of his desk President Bradley then asked "alright, but what's in it for me?" Sawyer shrugged his shoulders, pulled his gun from the shoulder holster and pointed it at the president "well for starters I won't kill you... yet" The president folded his arms "awww, son you're gonna have to do a hell of a lot better than that, I've been held in two P.O.W camps and held hostage for four days in 747 on the runway at an airport in Israel, death has lost it sting with me." Sawyer was amazed at the cool demeanor of the president; he needed a new plan and fast. After a minute or two of awkward silence Sawyer had a new plan, one that would appeal to the president's ego "ok. how's this, you tell me everything I want to know and when it's all said and done, I'll hand you my gun and you can point it at my head and walk me out telling everyone you took me down without the assistance of bodyguards, what do you say?" President Bradley looked at Sawyer with a sincere look on his face "you're on... but no bullshit bate and switch" he said. Sawyer agreed "no bullshit bate and switch... you have my word".So that being said President Bradley walked over to a big globe with a ring around it. Sawyer watched him walk over and asked, "What are you doing?" The president looked back at him, "well if I'm going to talk to you for a little bit I refuse to do it dry." The president put his hand on top of the globe and pulled back, it opened up to reveal a fully stocked bar, he poured himself a scotch and then asked Sawyer if he wanted a drink, Sawyer declined, "suit yourself" said president Bradley. Then he leaned against the front of his desk, scotch in hand ready to talk. Taking a sip the president made a small request "you can put that gun away I'm unarmed" Sawyer put his gun back in the holster and had a feeling in the pit of his stomach that told him to check the president but Sawyer dismissed the thought as being over cautious. The president took a sip of his scotch and started to say "I'm not going to beat about the bush, I hated Doyle, at first he was ' America for Americans' and I was taken in by it but towards the end of his first term he had gone soft." Then President Bradley pulled out a cigarette, lit it and continued, "he was all like ' were all in this together' and we need to embrace our fellow man today for a brighter tomorrow' what a load of horseshit." President Bradley took a puff of his cigarette and the conversation really began to heat up. "I figured after one term the old boy would retire, but now he had a vision for the future, I wasn't having any of his vision for the future shit, I needed to eliminate the problem and I got someone who could get the job done!" Sawyer noticed Bradley was starting to sound angry but then he calmed down, crushed out his cigarette and carried on "I needed someone who would get the job done quickly and quietly so I asked Ron Fuller, a man who had been with me since I was a senator, he was a good man" The president stopped for a moment and stared at the ceiling, he seemed to be reminiscing it only lasted a few moments. President Bradley took another sip of his scotch "yep, I told him I wanted the best of the best so he found you I don't know how but he did it, now I figured a man of your experience who left his chosen profession for seven years really didn't want back in so I sent Ron out to find me an insurance policy just in case you decided to have a change of heart... which you did." President Bradley swallowed the last of his scotch and in doing so he walked back over to the bar and refilled his glass. "Sure you don't want that scotch now?" Bradley asked. Sawyer politely replied "no, I'll get around it later, don't worry." The President closed the lid on the bar and walked over to his desk, sat on the edge as before and was ready to talk some more. Placing his glass next to him he continued, "It was money well spent, considerably less money than I offered you" he said with a wink. The President laughed for a moment and then continued with a smile on face like a Cheshire cat "after that everything was gravy, the loose ends I was somewhat concerned about worked themselves out and were all tied up, I mean Doyle was dead, my guy got shot and the money disappeared and you... well you dove out of a plane the hard way and before you could say "hail to the chief" I was bigger than Jesus, my god isn't timing wonderful". Sawyer looked at President Bradley with disdain and disgust "all the loose ends huh? Is that why you killed Ron Fuller? Was he the last loose end? You self-righteous son of a bitch!!" The president downed his scotch and slammed the glass down on his desk "just what is being insinuated here son!?! Do you think I killed Ron Fuller?" Sawyer answered without hesitation "you're goddamn right I do!" The president raised his voice "Ron Fuller was a boy scout from day one if he knew about the plot to kill the president he would have busted me and I would have spent my twilight years at Club Fed, he had no knowledge, he thought I was having a drug dealer taken out, you see he didn't mind if the bad guys were being rubbed out and he thought we were taking out drug and arms dealers when we were really taking out my competition so in conclusion to your question I did not have Ron Fuller terminated, exterminated, eradicated or whacked." Sawyer kept pressing "but you did set him up to believe he blew up a quarter of the Middle East didn't you?" The president fired back "yes I did, I would rather have him in solitary lockup then have him dead, he didn't deserve it and you can take that to the bank!!" he said slamming his fist on the desk. For the first time Sawyer actually believed the president telling the truth and did feel some remorse. The president stood up, straightened his tie, smoothed his silver hair and spoke in a calmer tone of voice "so are we ready to go?

CHAPTER 33

MASS DISRUPTION GAME DAY PT 4

'll just get my document and then it's Showtime." Then suddenly closet doors burst open and a figure emerged brandishing two automatic weapons and firing them at the ceiling. Tiny pieces of mortar fell from the ceiling and a light dust hovered in the air as the figure came forward. Sawyer and the president were at a loss for words but the aggressor had plenty to say. Both guns swung freely from the straps at the sides of their attacker as he applauded "what a performance, what a performance you guys were amazing!" he said emphatically with the energy of a film critic. Sawyer and president Bradley looked at each other dumbfounded. Their attacker or critic as it were continued with praise "I mean the power, the passion it was all so moving, black hat, white hat, high noon, middle of the street it was gold, when all is said and done you guys should have this made this whole dramatic situation into a book, a movie, a video game something because that was the performance of a lifetime, bravo, bravo" he said applauding once more. For a moment there was an awkward silence and then the president, looking a bit agitated, said "alright I'm just going to come out and say it, who in the blue hell are you?" The figure looked

198

over at Sawyer for a moment "pushy isn't he?" he said with a smile. Then he answered the president back "I'll tell you that after both of you relinquish your weapons." Sawyer threw his gun down. The attacker looked over at President Bradley "you too Mr. President" he said motioning the president to lay his weapon down. Sawyer looked at the attacker and smirked "he's got no weapon" he pointed to the president and then asked confidently "do you?" President Bradley sighed and pulled up his pant leg to reveal an ankle holster with a small gun in it. President Bradley took off the gun holster and all and tossed it over to the side. Sawyer was immediately outraged, "you son of a bitch, you had a gun all the time!" President Bradley looked at Sawyer and confessed "yes, yes I did have a gun. What did you expect a politician to tell the truth, come on, it's dangerous out there and a guy with my status needs to be protected, I'm a damn celebrity." The attacker looked at president Bradley "so you want to know who I am, you mean you don't remember me?" President Bradley looked at the man's face and shook his head "sorry fella I can't say that I do." The attacker smiled "I didn't expect you too, you see I'm dead, I'm the ghost of Christmas future, I'm James Mass better known in some circles as The Messiah, now do you know who I am champ?" The arrogance and sarcastic demeanor of the president left as soon as he heard the name and was replaced by whitening of his facial color and not much talking. Mass looked over at the bewildered head of state and bared his teeth "you remember I know you do, all the thick, brown envelopes dropped off in fast food trash cans, phone booths, the mail and I suppose you don't remember New Mexico, Guatemala, Ecuador, Chicago, L.A or any other of the many places I went to rub out anyone who gave you grief or competition as that was your term of choice i believe." The president rubbed his chin "yeah I remember a James Mass but you aren't him, he's dead, he blew up in a..." Mass cut off the president "in a propane explosion, right?" A puzzled look came across president Bradley's face "that's right, he's dead." A smile covered Mass's face "your right, in a manner of speaking, Mass is dead but the Messiah was born... I rose again and I thank you, considering you were the one who ordered to have my house blown up all because you didn't want to pay me for my last job and so I wouldn't squeal on you." The president lit another cigarette and blew the smoke up in the air. "it wasn't personal, it was business, you were a liability and I couldn't afford to keep you around... to make a long story short you served your purpose." Sawyer sat quietly and saw the smile almost instantaneously disappear from Mass's face and a cold feeling came over him knowing full well that this particular individual holding the automatic weapon was unstable and could snap at any moment. Sawyer didn't know how right he was. Mass pointed the gun at the president and spoke in an angry, loud tone which filled the room "you used me!! You're a user!! You used me, you used him!" he said pointing at Sawyer "you used Fuller, hell you used the whole United States of America!!" Mass was starting to turn a light shade of red, but the president just took another drag off his cigarette and blew it skyward then said in a very calm way "shit happens that's just the way it is." The automatic weapon was raised and several rounds were fired into the ceiling then was lowered but the loud address from Mass still continued "Business?!? Is that what you call it? Business!?!" The president nodded. Mass looked at the president "you ruined my life, I lost my house, my girlfriend who was in Dallas at the time, my car, everything." Mass stopped talking and calmed right down "but I got my pay in Hawaii" he said with a smile "that's right I wanted to kill the little puke you sent to kill me so I tracked him to a small shit hole bar in Chicago but just as I was going to take him out when I saw Ron Fuller walk in I laid low he was only there for ten minutes and then he left so I decided I was going to be Eli Rose's shadow which lead me to Hawaii, which in turn lead me to my final pay and I got to exterminate that little cockroach Rose in the process, it was a win win situation your presidentship." The president looked at Mass "ok so you have your money and your revenge and Sawyer has the answers he was looking for, so if you gentlemen don't mind I would like to finish my work here I have a" he stopped to adjust his bowtie "gala to attend." Mass cocked his head to the side and smiled "oh ok sorry about the ceiling and taking

200

The Silencer

up your time but I have one little piece of business to attend to" he pulled back the action on the side of his weapon and let it snap back then he aimed it at President Bradley. The president assessed his predicament and smiled "c'mon let's cut a deal son, surely there must be something you want, I mean hell I'm the most powerful man on the planet if you want something, anything I can make it happen" he said with a definite air of confidence. Mass lowered the weapon "anything at all?" he queried. The president looked at him and said "try me". Mass's smile increased and he took a breath. "Well there are a lot of things but one thing in particular." President Bradley clapped his hands together "now we are cookin!" he said as he got behind his desk. A pad and a pen were quickly produced and the President was ready to put pen to paper, he didn't even sit down he just stood behind the desk ready to take down the request. Mass looked at the president and gave his request "could you please tell Elvis I think he is still the undisputed king of rock and roll and I loved all his music even the movie stuff he did… well it was ok" then he raised his weapon and pointed directly at the president "good- bye Mr. President" A look of sheer terror came over the president's face "nooooooo!!!" he shouted as Mass squeezed the trigger. Now in the assassin's profession a mark is usually taken from a distance and in some cases if a mark is taken at close range the way about handling him or her that is employed is stabbing, strangulation, suffixation, being tossed out of a window (preferably a high one) or the time honored bullet to the head, but in this particular instance all the employed tactics were laid to the side. A much talked about but rarely seen almost mythical scene was about to unfold. Mass squeezed the trigger and a flurry of bullets ripped into the president's chest, shoulder and abdomen. What took no longer than twenty seconds felt a lot longer in Sawyer's eyes. As Sawyer sat he witnessed what in the assassin's world was called "the dance of death" or "the death dance" or more commonly referred to as "the last tango". "The last tango" was when an automatic weapon was fired from close range and the marks body would actually flail back and forth from the sheer force of the automatic weapon and the bullets slamming into the mark. As

201

Sawyer watched, the president's body flailed from the force being thrust upon it, first the right shoulder went back and the left shoulder came forward and then the left shoulder went back and the right came forward so that it seemed as if a dance was taking place. Sawyer could not believe the sight unfolding in front of him and the look on the president's face as countless bullets perforated him alive, it was a sight that would be burned into the annals of Sawyer's mind forever. In a few moments the sound of popping and shell casings hitting the floor stopped as the automatic weapon's clip had been emptied. As soon as firing stopped the empty clip was ejected from the bottom and started to fall to the ground as did president Bradley's body, if anyone was to place a wager on which one would hit the floor first it would be a photo finish. Sawyer noticed that Mass was still standing and pointing his weapon to where the president stood only moments ago, the barrel still smoking, it looked as if Mass was in awe even of himself, Mass raised the right side of his lip and pointed both fingers in the direction of the fallen president and did his best Elvis impersonation "Thank you... Thank you very much."

CHAPTER 34

SHOWDOWN PART II...

A s this was going on Sawyer used his foot to pull his gun closer so he could grab it using all the subtlety he could muster. The gun was finally close enough and Sawyer reached down for it. He just got his hand around the grip when he could feel some heat of the automatic weapon's barrel, which was pointed right at his face. Mass squatted down so he could see Sawyer better "Do you seriously want to shoot me?" Sawyer pulled no punches "well that was kind of the plan" he said still in the reaching position and his back starting to ache ever so slightly. Mass still squatting "yeah I figured that, but not before you know the truth of how I created you, it burns you up inside you just have to know" and with that Mass stood up and walked over to the president's desk. Sawyer with the grip still in his hand slowly released and sat up. Mass casually flipped open the lid of a wooden box on the corner of the desk and pulled out a cigar, he ran it back and forth under his nose, then bit off the tip and spat it onto the floor and lit it. Sawyer sat and watched which in all reality was all he could do "smoking a dead man's cigars isn't that just a tad unclassy?" he asked. Mass turned to him a small plume of smoke rising above his head "no" he answered and made his way over to a big globe situated in front of a full size painting of Abraham Lincoln. Sawyer watched Mass look at the globe "master of all you survey?" he asked. Mass turned to Sawyer with a half smile on his face and the cigar between his teeth, he opened the globe revealing a fully stocked bar "something like that." Mass put two glasses on the edge of the bottom half of the globe and pulled out a bottle of scotch, he looked at the label "well I'll tell you one thing Sawyer my boy Bobby had excellent taste" he complimented and the opened the bottle and filled each glass half full and then added ice which was in the center of the globe giving off a light mist. There was silence in the room except for the clinking of ice cubes in the glasses of scotch when Sawyer decided to keep heckling his aggressor because if he was talking he was still alive. The drinks were poured and Sawyer released a crusher "my god man don't you have any decency, I mean smoking cigars ok but drinking out of the bar, c'mon man that's just sick". Mass took a sip of his scotch and "Sawyer, these items weren't his," he said pointing to the corpse behind the desk. Sawyer asked, puzzled "then whose were they?" Mass puffed his cigar and answered Sawyer "they are yours and mine. In fact they belong to America" Sawyer looked at Mass still puzzled "what exactly are you talking about." Mass's head fell and he sighed then took a sip of his scotch and explained his philosophy on the whole thing "you see Sawyer the government takes our money in taxes and it intern pays for these fat cats to have the finest booze and cigars but we paid for it so call smoking cigars and drinking the president's booze a tax refund" He walked over to Sawyer with the glass of scotch, his weapon dangling precariously from the shoulder strap. As he approached Sawyer a plan began to form in Sawyer's mind how he would disarm and incapacitate Mass at his most venerable, he would hit him in the throat then kick him the nuts and take control of the situation but, as soon as he received his drink the plan disappeared and Sawyer then realized he needed to keep a cool head and look for a positive opening. Then Mass returned to the president's desk and sat on top. Sawyer took a sip of scotch and asked Mass "when do I get to hear how you created me even though we only met once on the rooftop the one time". Mass smiled and drank down the contents of his glass then he coughed a couple of times and cleared his throat as if he were given a state of the union address "did you ever try to do the right thing and get shot down by life? Well I did." Sawyer took another sip of his scotch "yeah, but your story is much more tragic I'll bet." Mass looked at Sawyer "damn right, I trained at Fort Bragg and became a green beret, I went on three tours to the middle east and did over twenty-five covert missions for the United States, I received a purple heart and the C.M.A that's right, the congressional medal of fuckin' honor, I soon got tired and of all the military shit and applied to the government for job and do you know where they placed me?!"Mass asked. Sawyer answered "not really, the C.I.A? F.B.I?, What?" So Mass explained in as calm a tone as he could "at Interpol behind a desk" he said slamming his fist on the president's desk "a small cubicle with a computer screen and not much more than top secret documents to process, a fucking decorated legend like me… in a cubicle!!… now that's bullshit." Another sip of scotch was in order so Mass refilled his glass and then continued "and you know what the worst part of it was?" he questioned. With wondering eyes Sawyer answered "I can't possibly imagine". Mass now locked his eyes on Sawyer "I had to listen to the accolades day in and day out of one person and it made me sick!" Having worked at Interpol himself Sawyer decided to ask who the agent was that Mass obviously had a vendetta against, perhaps he knew the agent, "and who was this one person who pissed you off so much?" Mass with his eyes still fixated on Sawyer pointed his finger directly at him "You, just you." He said in a calm, almost eerie voice. Sawyer sat up and with a puzzled look on his face and tried to get some clarity on what Mass was talking about "me" he said pointing to himself. Mass nodded his head "that's right superstar, you, it was like the little comic strip, you know the one where the big guy kicks sand into the little guy's face on the beach and then the little guy goes, and for four bucks, gets a book on how to train then he goes back to the beach and kicks sand in the strong guys face, do you remember that one, do ya?" Sawyer smiled slightly then dropped his head for a moment and then looked at Mass "so this is all about jealousy, killing Ron, the president and now me? Just plain jealousy?" Mass with an uneasy look on his face nodded slowly, Sawyer seemed almost embarrassed "oh bitch please give me a fucking break." Like an eight year old trying to defend his point over who the best ball player was. Mass spoke abruptly with a scowl forming on his face, "Well no not exactly, I wasn't jealous of you it was just having to hear it all day it got to me, I mean here I was a loyal employee and decorated war veteran and not a promotion in six years it was a big load of crap." All Sawyer could do was shrug his shoulders "you can't win them all". Once again Mass got a twisted smile on his face "oh, but I did, you see one day I got called to the Senator's mansion and he had gone over my records and was impressed, so impressed that the senator offered me a trial job which was to take out his accountant who had been skimming funds of the top and charging him high rates in turn he would give me fifty large, so I found the accountant's home and took him out in his washroom at three hundred yards, got paid and that was that… or so I thought". Mass then finished his scotch and went over to the bar, poured another and returned to his place and continued his story. "I hadn't heard from the senator in a week until he called me at Interpol and gave me another mark and twice the money and from there on in I was rolling in the cash with minimum risk to myself for almost three years until he was going to move up to be Doyle's running mate and that's when things got sour." Another swallow from his scotch and Mass spoke again "The senator called me up one last time and told me that since he was moving up to be Doyle's running mate he would be watched a lot closer by the media so our relationship would have to be dissolved but he had one last job and he would give me a cool two million dollars on completion." Sawyer, who was not interested in the mass's story, asked, "What job was that?" Mass puffed on his cigar "my mark was Juan Perez he was wanted by the C.I.A, F.B.I, Interpol and the D.E.A for dealing drugs, prostitution, extortion and arms dealing, a real big dog in the yard. I went down to Mexico on the next flight out, it took me less than a day to find him, he owned half of Mexico." Sawyer started to recall in his mind this particular individual; he used to be one of the top five most wanted in North America. Mass continued talking oblivious to Sawyer's recollections "I got a meeting set up he'd give me a briefcase with eleven million dollars and I would give him a briefcase with a single piece of paper and on that piece of paper were the names of all the agents working in his vicinity, the plan was simple until all of a sudden all main branches of the U.S law enforcement showed up, it was a set up." Mass swallowed his drink and walked over to the bar and this time brought the bottle of scotch back with him and topped up Sawyer's drink then topped up his own and put the bottle on the corner of the desk and then leaned against the desk. Mass took a puff on his cigar and a sip of scotch before speaking again, all the while Sawyer tried to figure out a plan but was so intrigued by the situation being presented before him that he kept his ideas in check until Mass finished his story. Cigar smoke hung heavy in the air over Mass's head as he continued his story "with all the heat coming from everywhere I knew there was only one way out, one winning way out that is." A smile had returned across the face of Mass as he continued, "I pulled out my .38 special and shot the three body guards Perez had and then I shot that big sack of shit pig right between the eyes and he fell to the floor, then I grabbed the briefcase with the list and the other with the cash and went out the kitchen door and into the ally, sounds like the perfect getaway but it was far from perfect" Mass sipped his drink and continued "I ran down the alley as fast I could until I heard a popping sound behind and then my left shoulder felt really hot and I noticed bloods coming from the front of my shirt, I had been shot!" Sawyer noticed a pent up aggression in Mass's face that was being released with every word he said and move he made, in fact Sawyer noticed a slight shaking in Mass's hand as he held his drink. Mass then finished his drink rather abruptly and placed the glass on the desk and opened up "well, I hit the ground like a sack of spuds but before I did I grabbed my gun and held it against my chest who ever shot me was coming up to me in a slow deliberate way figuring I was a sure kill, I felt a hand turn me over and I could feel the heat from the sun being blocked out, I pointed and fired at where I thought the face should be I didn't even look at it when I heard it hit the ground, I just grabbed the cases jumped in a cab and got the fuck out of there as fast as I could and got as far as I could." Mass picked up the bottle and poured himself another drink, he didn't look like a man in control. "After taking the cab as far as it would go I crossed some river and then hopped the fence back into the U.S.A, then I hotwired a ride and took off checking into the first shit hole motel I could find." All the while Sawyer kept his eyes focused on his gun on the ground waiting for another opportunity, but he didn't realize that what he would hear next would consume him entirely. Mass picked up the stubby glass from the corner of the desk and downed the drink as a single tear ran down his cheek. Sawyer didn't like the direction this story was going to take. Mass relit his cigar and continued talking after a satisfying puff on his cigar "So I checked into a hotel somewhere near the border in Texas, I didn't realize how fast new traveled, I flicked on the television and the whole story of what happened was on CNN, it didn't surprise me much cause I was there" he laughed but only for a moment then his face returned to the somber expression that it was in a moment ago "but then I heard something I didn't expect the reporter said the name of the agent who I shot in the alley, it was agent Gwen Briggs, your wife." Sawyer's eyes teared up and his face filled with rage as his hands gripped cushions on either side of him he looked like an enraged pit-bull ready to strike "you motherfucker, you bastard, you prick, you killed my wife, you killed my wife!!!!!!" Mass tried to console Sawyer to no avail "I'm sorry, I didn't mean for it to happen, I was on the run, but you had to know and now that you know" he said sliding off the desk "it's time to put you away, once again I 'm sorry and this time I'm going to make sure you stay there…" Mass stared down at Sawyer, and then pointed his weapon directly at Sawyer. It was at this point Sawyer needed to think on his feet or his toes would be pointing up from them. Sawyer had to appeal to the obvious obsession Mass had to destroy him and be the best, he had to shake his confidence and challenge him. A sneer came across Sawyer's face "so that's it? You're just going to shoot me." Mass looked at Sawyer a little confused "yeah that's the general idea." He said with a hint of sarcasm. Sawyer gave a half smile "then how will you ever know?" Mass started to look a little annoyed "know what?" Sawyer now gave a full smile "If you were the best" Mass looked at Sawyer with a sarcastic grin "well let's see" he said taking on the tone of an adult addressing a child "I have a gun pointed at your head, and you are totally defeated, uh I think that makes me the best, duh." Sawyer needed to keep punching "sure, you have me defeated and you could shoot me but, tomorrow the next day, the next year, hell, many years down the line you will still ask yourself the same question over and over again" Sawyer stated raising his voice "was I better then him, was I beyond a shadow of a doubt the absolute best? The question will haunt you for the rest of your life, in fact the Russian's, the Chinese and anyone else you used to work for you used to call you a rent-a-thug because you were expendable, you were small time you were a gun toting freelance thug with a big gun and no brains you were quantity and I was quality you asshole!" For a brief moment there was silence then Mass began to laugh "I know where this is heading, you're trying to draw me into a physical confrontation, you want to fight, is that Sawyer, are you spoiling for a fight?" Sawyer, despite the threat of an automatic weapon pointed at his face, stood up and looked directly into Mass's eyes and answered "you're damn right I' am." Mass looked back at Sawyer and nodded with a look of admiration "well if that's what you want" he said and he turned away and then in a heartbeat turned back swinging his right arm with the weapon in hand he hit Sawyer across the face cutting him in the process "then that's what you'll get" he said as he swung his right arm back and again connecting with Sawyer's head and face cutting him once more. Sawyer had been so hard and so fast that he had no time to react; he tried to clear the cobwebs in his head as quick as he could but it would take a few moments; he had sustained two major blows to the head. Mass basked a tiny bit in this victory and then spoke to Sawyer who was still fuzzy "so you still want to do this, shooting you is much quicker" Sawyer straightened himself out, blood running down his face from the laceration on his forehead he told Mass "is that the best you got? Hit me with your best shot!!" Mass looked at Sawyer and smiled "lot's of stamina" and then in the same breath Mass delivered a spinning roundhouse kick which sent Sawyer flying over the couch flipping and then landing on his stomach. After a few seconds Sawyer was on all fours shaking his head trying to revive himself when Mass came around the couch and sat on Sawyer's back. Sawyer could feel the weight of Mass on his back but that was the least of Sawyer's problems. Sawyer felt something else which took his mind off of the weight on his back. Mass put the strap of his weapon across Sawyer's throat and pulled back on it like a jockey pulling back on the reins of a horse. Two index fingers were all Sawyer could put between his throat and the hard leather strap cutting off his oxygen. The next couple of minutes were excruciating aside from the sound of Sawyer trying to breathe. The room was silent. Then as Sawyer was seemingly passing out Mass leaned down beside Sawyer's ear and talked in almost a whisper tone. Mass spoke as Sawyer had no choice but to listen "how does it feel Sawyer, like you're breathing through a straw? How does it feel to feel your heart slow down? Not so good huh?" Sawyer' s eye's started to glaze over, and images of his wife, Fuller and his life flashed before his eyes in brief, short spurts. Mass's premonition was coming true but Mass wasn't done with him quite yet. Mass continued talking and as he did so he jerked the strap so Sawyer would fall asleep and slip into a coma "you know Sawyer I want to tell you something before you go" he jerked the strap again feeling Sawyer's body going limp "stay with me now buddy it will only take a minute, you see I'm not sorry for what I did to Bradley, Fuller or your wife, especially your wife, you see you weren't there for her and she died and Fuller... well ya dropped the ball on that one too, huh amigo? You know what your problem is? you're too damn slow, too damn old and you're a fraud and when they pick your body up and make me into a certified hero for desperately trying to save the Prez's life I'll tell them you were easy." Mass jerked the strap one last time, he wanted to be positive Sawyer heard his last words before he entered the great beyond "tonight my boy The

Silencer becomes The Bitch... ... my bitch." At that moment it was as if a flame was ignited within Sawyer, all of a sudden breathing was a little easier, the glaze over his eyes started to clear and his heart rate started to speed up and Sawyer slowly he got to his feet with Mass still pulling back on the weapon strap for all he was worth, to no avail. Once on his feet Sawyer started to walk backwards and in the process push Mass backwards into the wall as soon as Sawyer knew they were up against the wall he went forward a few steps pulling Mass forward with the strap on his neck then quickly backing up into the wall with Mass exposed to the full brunt of the blow. Again and again Sawyer slammed Mass into the wall and with every hit the strap loosened off of Sawyer's throat. With the strap loosened and Sawyer's pushing Mass against the wall Sawyer bowed his head forward and the threw it back several times into Mass's face until Sawyer could feel the strap go totally loose and he also felt the cartilage in of Mass's nose crack against the back of his head and the warm blood flow down the from the Mass's crushed proboscis. Then finally Sawyer pulled forward away from Mass's grip and fell to his knees as the oxygen that had been momentarily depleted from him began to flow again like a mighty river and Sawyer took it all in. "Is that all you got?" a voice said from behind him and Sawyer got to his feet a bit dizzy but otherwise stable and slowly turned around. The sight he would witness would put no doubt in his mind that he might have met his match... and then some. Mass stared at Sawyer with a rather twisted grin indicating that pain to him was not an issue "Sawyer, you've got heart and this ain't over just give me two seconds and we will get back at it". Disbelief was the word that crossed Sawyer's mind as he watched Mass take his index and middle finger and stick one in each nostril, once the initial pain had passed he slowly moved his nose to the left and then quickly to the right, a cracking sound echoed through the entire oval office. A small stream of blood trickled from Mass's nose "is that the best you've got because if it is you should have let me strangle you" he said laughing. Sawyer gave a very serious stare to Mass which took the smile right off his face and then stated, "If I gave you my best you'd be dead" then a moment of silence and he continued, "It's time for you to die, you bastard!!" A smile returned to Mass's face as he slightly bowed his head to Sawyer "then let the games begin, let's see if you're really that good." For the next several minutes, which seemed like an eternity, both men fought fiercely using all the skills they had in their respective arsenals. After a short while of intense fighting both men, realizing it was a stalemate and that this situation wasn't getting them anywhere. Mass looked at Sawyer and gave him a compliment, in a roundabout way "you fight pretty good for an old man." He said with a small grin on his face. Sawyer returned the favor "yeah, and you fight good for a half-ass rent-a-thug". Mass smiled and walked over to the wall on his right and pulled down a foil which was the type of sword used in fencing, then he looked over at Sawyer "let's spice it up, old boy." Sawyer looked around the room for a weapon when he spied a bag of golf clubs leaning against the wall, he walked over and pulled out a nine iron then addressed Mass one more time "this is silly why don't you put down the sword and I'll lay the club down." Mass pondered Sawyer's request for a few moments then answered by holding the sword in front of his face and responding "on guard!" Sawyer shrugged his shoulders in disappointment "oh well, four!!" Once again both men were locked in combat. Though the sword and club made contact several times they also made contact with each other's opponents. Mass swung the sword at Sawyer cutting the front of Sawyer's chest, the blood coming through his white shirt in two neat red lines. Sawyer held the club with two hands as if it were a broad sword and swung at Mass with no regard. The club caught Mass with more blows than he could handle, blows to the ribs, the head, and the back were hard and constant. Sawyer handed the upper hand and played it to the full, with one powerful blow Sawyer knocked the sword out of Mass's hand and to the floor, victory was at hand. Mass looked at Sawyer and knew this was the end. Sawyer heaved back the club for a final blow and... tripped over the oval office's flagpole, which lay next to the desk, Sawyer fell backwards and bumped his head against the solid oak desk of the president. Mass, seizing the moment, took two steps forward and jumped in the air and came down as hard as he could on Sawyer's ankle and to his satisfaction heard a snap. Sawyer yelled out in agony and put his hand on his ankle, the pain was overwhelming as if his ankle had been set on fire. Seeing Sawyer was hurt badly was a great relief to Mass as he dropped to his knees totally spent. Mass looked at Sawyer "you have to be the toughest son of a bitch I have ever come across, but…" Mass winced in pain as he got to his feet, the fight had taken more out of him then he had anticipated. "I won and all I need to do now is put the exclamation point at the end of the sentence." Looking around, Mass spotted one of two automatic weapons he had brought in and bent over to pick it up which caused him an almost intolerable amount of pain. Sawyer watched as Mass slowly walked over and lowered the weapon pointing directly at him. "Ok Sawyer, I'm a fair man, where do you want it? the heart? Or the head." Sawyer sat back against the desk, hands at his sides "make it the heart, it was ripped out the day you killed my wife you might as well finish the job, you cocky son of a bitch." Mass looked down at Sawyer with a smirk of confidence "how romantic." Mass pulled back on the action of the weapon and pulled the trigger. "Click" then silence, once again "click" then silence, Mass pulled the trigger a few more times wondering why Sawyer's head wasn't blown apart. Sawyer smiled for unbeknownst to Mass the clip in the weapon had been knocked loose when he struck Sawyer with it and the loaded clip was underneath Sawyer, he had fallen on it, but he wasn't telling. Sawyer looked at Mass "having a little trouble rent a thug?" Sawyer said with his smile still intact. Mass smiled right back at Sawyer "nope, just a little rut in the road". Mass looked around again and spied what he was seeking and once again bent over with the pain shooting up his spine and picked up the item. Sawyer watched mass walk over to him again, only this time he had in his hand Sawyer's gun. Mass pointed the weapon directly at Sawyer "now this is poetic justice, shooting you with your own gun". Suddenly Mass lowered the gun "wait a minute" he said with a hint of sympathy in his voice "this is a waste, I mean here we are two of the best at what we do and if I shoot you it will just be me, right?" Sawyer's pain in his ankle subsided for the moment as he tried to contemplate what was being said and after a minute or so he was drawing a total blank" what the hell are you trying to say? You illiterate boob". Mass raised an eyebrow at Sawyer's comment then continued "well I think we should team up, I mean think of the possibilities, what do you say? It's a lot better than dying." Sawyer slowly moved his head side to side and then looked at Mass and nodded his head "not in a million fucking light years you hack, I'll take dying thanks." Mass raised the gun to Sawyer again "ok if that's the way you want it, do you have any last words or a request before I blow your stupid head off?" Sawyer nodded and with his left hand reached up on the desk and pulled the president's cigar box off, it crashed to the floor sending cigars everywhere. Sawyer picked up one of the cigars and bit off the tip and spat it in Mass's face. The mix of saliva and the tip of the cigar ran down the side of Mass's face as he calmly said "last words?" Sawyer placed the cigar between his lips "light me, bitch." Mass was a little confused by the request, but it didn't matter to him, he was going to kill Sawyer and that's all that mattered. Mass pointed the gun two inches from Sawyer's face, he wanted maximum carnage. Slowly, savoring the experience, Mass pulled the trigger and instead of a round penetrating Sawyer's skull, a small flame came out of the barrel of the gun. Sawyer leaned forward and lit his cigar, knowing full well that Mass was going to lose it any second, but to Sawyer's surprise, he didn't. Mass tossed the gun or lighter as it was into Sawyer's lap and with a small smile shook his head "I just can't catch a break, my clip is empty, your gun is a lighter and I couldn't strangle you, what should I do Sawyer?" For a moment Sawyer was silent then laughingly suggested to Mass "why don't you try and find a gun that say's "bang" when you shoot it and maybe it will actually kill me". Rubbing his chin Mass Replied to the statement "no I have a better idea" and with that Mass kicked Sawyer as hard as he could in the stomach, Sawyer held the cigar firm between his teeth and doubled over in pain holding his abdomen. Mass looked down at Sawyer and waited until he sat up then kicked him

The Silencer

in the ribs and once again Sawyer went down, doubled up and tried to catch his breath. Mass squatted down, his pain still there judging by the look on his face, he said to Sawyer "not so funny is it?" Sawyer looked up "fuck you, you parasite." Mass then spoke again "let me tell you dazzle you with a fast fact, I almost made the U.S world cup football club or as everyone here calls it, soccer team back when I was a little younger, I was a striker and by the look on your face, I've still got it" Sawyer painfully tried to talk as he held his stomach "and so what has this got to do with me?" Mass looked at Sawyer "everything, you see my friend. I can't find any guns that work so I'm going to back up and run at you and with one kick I'm going to shatter your world by shattering your skull and you can try to stop me… keeper." As Sawyer watched, Mass backed up to the door leading to the secretary's office and tapped his toe on the ground three times and looked at Sawyer. "Good bye, Sawyer, and hey look at the bright side, I'm not wearing my cleats." As Sawyer listened to Mass he knew he needed some line of defense on the count of his head that would resemble a piñata. Suddenly Sawyer made a life saving discovery on his right side was a flagpole and on the very end was a brass tip which was shaped like a spear head and it gave Sawyer an idea that just might work. He pulled the flagpole over to him and rested the butt against the desk that seemed to be bolted to the floor, which indeed it was. On the other end of the room Mass started his run, he knew he couldn't get much speed build like on the football pitch, but with the speed he could build up he would have no problem caving in Sawyer's skull with one strike. As Mass got closer, Sawyer's fingers wrapped around the pole, timing was of the essence and Sawyer was ready. When Mass got closer he let out a scream that seemed like a war cry, his eyes were now affixed on Sawyer's cranium and how he could shatter it. Then suddenly when Mass was in very close range. Like a knight of old Sawyer raised the flagpole on an angle right at Mass who was coming as fast as he could. When Mass saw the pointed brass tip on the flag pole he tried to slow down but a small section of hardwood flooring was exposed and Mass's feet could not grip on it and he was thrust onto the point. When the flagpole made contact with Mass's chest it instantly ran right through it and came out of his back, shattering part of his spine, Sawyer could feel the impact as the pole reverberated down the flagpole and through his hand. Mass looked at Sawyer as his blood slowly began to escape his body through his ears, nose, and mouth and of course his chest. Sawyer looked at the site before him, a once tough yet calculating adversary and now he was reduced to a human shish kabob impaled on a flagpole. Assuming Mass was dead Sawyer made an attempt to get up. Suddenly Mass raised his head slightly and opened his eyes as Sawyer stopped the attempt to stand up and looked directly at him. Mass, with his last bit of strength snickered, laughed a little and attempted to say something as Sawyer listened intently. With a pool of blood formed under him and his eyes watering, Mass made one last statement "you're the.... best... but... Bradley, he was just a cog in the wheel" he said as his voice started to fade fast and his eyes began to slowly close "a... cog... in... the... wheel... axis..." and with that his eyes closed, his head dropped and he was dead leaving Sawyer with a cryptic message he would need to give thought to but that would have to wait as Sawyer picked up a cigar laying next to him, lit it with his gun, it was the best cigar he ever smoked.

CHAPTER 35

CLEAN UP... OVER AND OUT

awyer looked at his watch, which was still in surprisingly good shape considering the beating he had just taken. The time was now 7:40pm. Sawyer knew that if the president had not been heard from by eight o'clock, the Whitehouse would be crawling with agents, military, etc, he needed to get going. Turning his whole body with the cigar clenched between his teeth, Sawyer reached up to the top of the desk with one hand then the other and slowly pulled himself up, then as if he were praying on the desk he pressed down on his arms and hoisted himself up to the point where he was standing straight up and then he turned and leaned up against the desk taking a minute to rest. Sawyer limped over to the couch, with the aid of the golf club he had used as a sword, where he had been sitting and picked up his leather bag then slowly made his way over to the full-length painting of George Washington. Sawyer stared humbly at the portrait in awe of its mere presence in the room. Then after the slight glaze in his stare wore off Sawyer looked at the words emblazoned across the center of the picture in big, bold, black print "I Cannot Tell a Lie." A few moments passed and Sawyer looked at the words closely, and then he saw it, the button to open a secret door. The button itself was not even a letter at all; it was the dot on top of the letter "i". Sawyer had found it and immediately pressed it. A low clanking sound erupted, and then another and another, until finally the low clanking sound disappeared and was replaced by a slick banging sound which sounded (at least to Sawyer) like a vault opening. Silence gripped Sawyer for a moment as he heard the last noise of a lock opening and the secret door swung open. Sawyer turned and took one last look at the oval office, the carnage and the destruction, "what a way to end the year" Sawyer said as he shook his head and walked into the long secret corridor. The door with its many locks slowly swung shut, as the picture of George Washington almost seemed to have a small smile knowing all would be well again and that was no lie. Eight o'clock came and when the President had not been heard from, the military responded by not only showing up at the White House in full force but locking down the entire building tight. Embarrassment overwhelmed the secret service men when they were found duct taped to the toilet seats in the men's washroom, once released they provided little vital information and it was surmised that they simply had their ass's kicked and were taped to toilets. When the door to the "Oval Office" was broken down and thhe area was secure the men were surprised and shocked at the sight of the office busted up, a man impaled on a flagpole and the badly bullet ridden body of President Bradley crumpled up behind the desk. Sawyer, who'd since returned to his room at the hotel, was all settled in with a glass of scotch in one hand, an icepack on his ankle and the television on a news network watching what had just unfolded at the white house, in all reality every channel in the United States was following the story. Sawyer sat and watched as he sipped his scotch. The C.I.A and F.B.I stayed tight lipped about what had occurred and no doubt there would be a lengthy investigation in which the entire event would be blamed on terrorists because no one would suspect an American of killing their fearless leader, but Sawyer was about to put a stop to that. Sawyer stood up after enduring another half hour of re-chewed reports and old footage from a few years ago and limped over to the desk and sat down. Putting down the now empty glass he opened up the laptop that was sitting on the desk in front of him. Sawyer turned the power on and watched as the screen lit up. As soon as everything was going, Sawyer clicked on "documents" and then when the second screen came up he clicked on a new file, which was entitled "The Prez" and closed his eyes and waited for the file to open. Sawyer smiled as he slowly opened his eyes. The file he opened indicated that there were two substantial attachments that had come in fairly recently and all Sawyer had to do was download them onto the file. Sawyer knew full well what the attachments contained and downloaded them immediately. As soon as the download was complete Sawyer took a swallow of his scotch and opened the first downloaded attachment. A black screen appeared and then the image of President Bradley explaining what his intentions were for America. Sawyer watched intently as his plan work while keeping his honesty intact, the reason being that when president Bradley asked Sawyer if he was wearing a wire, he wasn't, the wreath on the lapel of Sawyer's coat was a mini camera which was connected directly to the laptop, whatever the camera recorded was put in directly as an attachment. And it was wireless. Sawyer moved ahead and found the second attachment was recorded after Mass entered the room. A cold chill went up Sawyer's spine as he once again saw Mass. The footage was all there, the talking, dark humor and the slaughter of Bradley. Sawyer watched all the footage of both lengths and deleted anything that had his name mentioned, after all, he was dead and he wanted to keep it that way. Looking at his watch as he completed the editing job of what he considered a masterpiece, he drank the last of his scotch and rubbed his eyes. The minute hand ticked ominously as time was winding down, the time was five minutes to eleven and Sawyer poured another scotch and watched the five minutes tick away to eleven o'clock. At precisely eleven o'clock Sawyer put his head in his hands and then rubbed his head. What he was about to do would make everything he had done, not just in the recent years but his entire life pale in comparison. Sawyer went on to the "Youtube" website and with the click of a mouse Sawyer released all the footage, he knew that on this night, in the age of technology there were a lot of young and middle aged men and woman who lived in their parent's basement and would rather surf the net and play online games then celebrate New Year's eve by going out, drinking and with some luck getting laid, not only did he know this but he was counting on it. After the footage was downloaded Sawyer removed a memory stick from the side with all the information and then he hobbled over, with laptop in hand to the balcony door and opened it. The air was raw and the sky was crystal clear as the stars twinkled up above. Sawyer walked out onto the balcony and broke the laptop over his knee then tossed the two sides of the laptop over the side of the balcony. Watching the two sides of the laptop plummet through the air gave Sawyer a sense of satisfaction and a small smile came across his face as he turned and walked back into the room. The warmth of the room immediately permeated Sawyer as he made his way to the edge of his bed and sat down. All of Sawyer's bags were packed and by the door, he was playing the waiting game as he watched the television. He knew that before the stroke of midnight the information would make the news and slightly after it would be worldwide. Sawyer changed the channel on the television to another New Year's Eve celebration this time from Las Vegas to prove a simple point. He got up one more time and hobbled over to the mini bar but this time instead pouring another shot or even a half glass with crushed ice Sawyer simply grabbed the bottle and made his way back to the edge of the bed where he unscrewed the cap off the bottle and threw it over his shoulder, then took a good long gulp of the scotch "fuck educate" he said knowing full well that scotch was made for sipping. Then as Sawyer had predicted The show that was currently on was interrupted by the three words on the screen "special news bulletin". A blonde woman, the news anchor, sat looking directly at the screen and got ready to speak. Sawyer took another long gulp from the bottle in his hand, and then focused as the woman spoke "A few minutes ago the world media community has received word that Robert "Bob" Sutton Bradley, the president of the United States is dead, there are few our details being released on how the president met his demise." Sawyer took another drink from the almost empty bottle of scotch "wait for it" he said as if someone were sitting right next to him. In a few moments as Sawyer had foreseen the anchorwoman put her finger to her ear as she was receiving another report, Sawyer smiled "told you so". The anchorwoman took her finger away from her ear and stared directly at the screen "I have just received word that a few moments ago full length footage has been released on social media of not only the what would appear to be execution of president Bob Bradley but also what appeared to be an interview before his death of the framing of a former aid, and the plot to assassinate president Doyle, all laid out in chilling detail." A smile began to grow on Sawyer's face as he took the last sip of what drops remained from the bottle, which was now empty "c'mon tell everyone the rest." The anchorwoman put her finger to her ear once more briefly and spoke "the footage also been said to contain a confessional from the actual assassin, government sources now say the information cannot be contained because it has been accessed by anyone with any kind of media outlet which has risen to one million viewers worldwide and is climbing, but one question remains who took the footage? The C.I.A and F.B.I are collaborating in a joint investigation as we speak, the entire White House is on lockdown until further notice, details available as we get them now back to New Years in Time Square." A full-blown smile was being worn by Sawyer and from the bed he looked at the mirror over the desk as he spoke to the reflection "you did it you son of a bitch, you actually did it!" Sawyer let out a huge sigh of relief and stared up for a moment "at ease" he said and gave a small salute in honor of his fallen comrade Ron. His attention returned to the screen as the big ball came down to usher in the new year "five... four... three... two... one... and in a burst of glory friends, lovers, acquaintances, and celebrities wished each other success and happiness in the new year all set against the backdrop of lights, fireworks and loud choruses of the time honored classic "Auld Lang Syne." Not everyone knew what had transpired tonight and maybe it was just better that way, Sawyer knew that after the hangovers, late night lovemaking and multiple parties, not just here but around the world, slowly but surely the events of tonight and the last four years for that matter, would take center stage and be talked about for the months to come as investigations took their course. Sawyer turned off the television and slipped under sheets setting the alarm clock for five am. He wanted to start the new year off right like the Bing Crosby song, by being as far from here as possible.

CHAPTER 36
REARVIEW MIRROR

The morning came quickly and at approximately five am the alarm sounded. An annoying D.J's voice came on just as he was trying to tell a joke, and at this hour any joke would not have gotten a lot of laughs. Sawyer had gotten up before the alarm had gone off and by the time it did and the annoying voice was trying to be entertaining he was already showered, shaved and had cut his hair down to it's original look with the help of a small electric clipper and a pair of scissors. His face was out of the mainstream media and he wasn't worried about being spotted. Sawyer gathered up the hair in the bathroom and put it in a bag just in case something occurred he didn't want to leave a trail. Looking at the watch he still had some time so he sat down at the desk. Taking out his pen he wrote a letter and stuck it in an envelope, the letter wasn't very long but it was right to the point, he could have just as easily emailed a letter but Sawyer found emails impersonal, rude and just plain lazy. He sealed the envelope and put a stamp on, which the room provided and put it on top of his bag. He got dressed in casual clothes which included a black hoodie, a far cry from the designer suits and clothing he used to wear not all that long ago. He just wanted to blend in and not attract attention, there was a one in a half million chance that someone would recognize him and that was even too great a chance for his liking. At five thirty Sawyer took one last look around and made his way to the front desk to check out and then it was on to the parking garage where he could finally begin his journey. Listening intently to the radio as he drove, all he could hear was report after report about what had transpired on New Year's eve at the white house, so much that Sawyer turned the radio off. After driving for a while with little to no traffic the state line was coming into sight just as the sun started to peak over the horizon. Sawyer was about five miles past the state line when he pulled the car to the side of the road, stopped and shut off the engine. Sawyer got out of the car and opened the trunk, leaned in and opened his bag looking inside for an item he would need. Pulling out of the trunk Sawyer had a key in his hand along with a folded piece of paper he quickly shut the trunk and got back in his car, the temperature still being frigid, Sawyer was getting cold. Sitting in the car warming up Sawyer placed the key on the dashboard and unfolded the piece of paper and what was written on surprised Sawyer. On the paper was written a security code, the name of a town somewhere in northern British Columbia and instructions where to go once the town was reached. The piece of paper also contained a small message "everything you need is in the trunk, use the key that was with the laptop to access it, … Thanks. R.F". Sawyer sat for a moment almost breathless and smiled "he knew he wasn't going to make it to the job, somehow he knew it… it… was all planned, I'll be damned" All Sawyer could do was shake his head in amazement and smile. After a few moments Sawyer opened the truck once again and got out grabbing the key off the dashboard. Looking inside the trunk Sawyer saw a small metal box in the far end of the trunk he pulled it towards him, it was a little bit bigger than the size of your average safety deposit box. He put the key into it and turned, he heard a small "click" and the top of the box flipped open. For a moment Sawyer just stood and stared at the contents of the box. Inside the box were a few assorted items, a portable G.P.S system with a piece of paper stuck to it with the word "preset" stuck to it and although the car had a G.P.S system he decided he would probably go with this one.

There were five other items in the box, each would be more than useful for Sawyer, and they were a 9mm handgun with one loaded clip, two passports (one Canadian and one American both ready for a picture and information), twenty thousand dollars in cash and a few keys on a ring. Sawyer took out the G.P.S and placed it in his coat pocket then shut the box and held it under his arm as he closed the trunk. Once Sawyer closed the trunk he went and placed the box in the back seat and sat down in the driver's seat and closed the door. After starting the car and cranking up the heat, Sawyer took the portable unit from his pocket, it had a small pull out stand on the back and two small suction cups on each corner of it which held it in place on the dashboard. Once he had affixed the unit to the dashboard he turned it on. Almost immediately the screen lit up revealing a map and a highlighted line traveling all through the screen showing a direct route to his final destination or at least to the state line of the next state and after that it would show the next one and so on until he was to where he was supposed to go. Sawyer fastened his seatbelt, put the car into drive, slowly pulled onto the road and began to pick up speed. As the sun dawned on a new day Sawyer looked into the rear view mirror and bid a fond farewell to an old friend "good-bye Sawyer, see you around" and indeed he might, he just might.

6 months later

Spring was slowly starting to wrap up as summer was just over the horizon. America was still in the process of trying to repair the damage caused by four years of infamy. The country had been healing from the inside out since that fateful night in the oval office on New Year's Eve. Internal investigations by all branches of the government, the F.B.I, C.I.A, and any other investigative branches the government had at its disposal, all the branches even called agents out of retirement to assist. Hearings and inquiries were being held more than ever before and there were no favorites. Senators, Governors, Congressmen and even the entire Bradley administration would be on trial. Bridges that were burned between America and Europe, the Middle East and Asia would, through negotiations, conferences and concessions be rebuilt, slowly but stronger as time went on was the direction they were hopefully heading in. The new President, General Austin Dwayne Olive (retired) reviewed the footage from the Oval office and after viewing it several times realized that Bradley was a manipulative and condescending traitor who used anybody who had experience and wanted to reach a higher level in the government, Bradley would offer advancement that he never delivered on just to get what he wanted.That being the case it was the new President's decision that everything that had transpired in the last four years was all President Bradley's fault and he just used people to get to his prime objective, the domination and emasculation of America and possibly in time… the world. The President, being an old military man himself decided to right a wrong, he personally had the remains of marine corps officer Ron Fuller exhumed from a regular public cemetery to Arlington cemetery in Washington D.C with full military honors bestowed upon him for all around bravery in the field or wherever it took place he would be remembered as a national hero. The president in a surprise move, which was somewhat shocking, not only gave a full pardon to Sawyer Briggs, not knowing that he and the country owed him a lot more but he put a memorial headstone, in spite of the fact that there were no remains to bury right next to fullers grave. It was the fourth of July when the President delivered a speech that would be seen and heard across the country and around the world by every form of communication on the planet. The set for the speech was different from when Bradley gave it. The oval office especially looked different because behind the president's desk was a large American flag, also the desk which President Bradley sat behind was replaced with the original desk that was a part of Oval Office's history. At precisely seven o' clock all television networks and radio stations were preempted so that the address of the President would be seen and heard without distraction or delay by everyone. The president took a few sips of water, cleared his throat and began to say "Good evening my fellow Americans, tonight we write a new

The Silencer

chapter in what has been four years of an America that I didn't recognize as my own and neither did most Americans. Prosperity did cross the land but at what cost? Dignity, equality, integrity, inclusion which is the very fabric of which this country was founded on, the price was indeed high my friends." The President paused for a moment and sighed then continued "There were many caught in the crossfire in the last four years and both citizens and countries suffered dearly." The President once again paused and this time lowered his head and removed his glasses, he then wiped his eyes, which could visibly be seen shedding a tear or two, and then painstakingly he continued. "My tears do not show a sign of weakness, they show a sign of passion, the passion I had for this country when I fought in many wars for it, the passion I have for this country now that I' am leading it and the passion I will show this country as I try to help with healing process that will take time but in the end it will be time well spent." The President then stood up, took his glasses off and tossed them on the desk; "In closing, my fellow Americans my friends I vow not only as it's president but as a retired general, son, father, husband, grandfather and citizen of this great nation that I will do everything within my power and this government's power to restore this country's pride and integrity so that once again we the people may rise up and salute the flag that shows we are one nation under god, indivisible with liberty and justice for all, may god bless America and all of you, good-bye, good night and thank-you." Once the cameras stopped rolling the president collapsed into his chair and opened up a bottle of water he had on the desk. He had never given a speech like that, not even to his troops at the eleventh hour. He was not a talker, he was a man of action and he was tired. His Whitehouse aide came up to him and asked him if he was ok, the president looked at him, took a sip of water and in a rather depressing tone of voice said "man, I'm getting soft."

CHAPTER 37

LAST CHAPTER OR FIRST PAGE...?

Somewhere in Northern British Columbia, Four months later.

The sun slowly started to ascend over the tall pine trees as the distant sound of a loon could be heard echoing through the bush and along the twisting banks of a secluded river that ran, quite literally for at least one hundred miles or better. Through the light mist on the water came a small canoe with a small outboard motor on the back that hardly made a sound. As the canoe slowly and silently broke through the still water a very calm and content figure sat in the rear controlling the throttle effortlessly taking in all the scenery. Sawyer had indeed found his own utopia amongst the rugged terrain of the Northern bush. He had been here four months and in that amount of time his blood pressure dropped along with his stress level and he had not only found the rest and relaxation he had been craving for the last four years but also he had found total a deep undeniable inner peace. When Sawyer had arrived he wasn't quite sure what to expect. All he knew was that he was going to be alone and it was going to be quiet. The cabin itself surprised Sawyer and exceeded even his expectations. It was a big, rustic log cabin. On the outside was a porch, which stretched across the whole of the front with the exception of the opening for the front steps and had four wooden chairs in the front, which gave it a friendly and inviting appearance. One key, the only key Sawyer had for the cabin, was placed in the keyhole and turned, cautiously he entered the cabin. Amazed, he looked around and all he could say in a low tone was "wow". He walked around much like a real estate agent would walk around a house with a potential buyer; Sawyer checked every nook and cranny. Then after his impromptu inspection was done, he went over to the fireplace and turned a big chair around in front of it, the kind of chair that everyone had seen in old movies, with the red leather and the big wings on both sides along thick rolled arm rests, all that was missing was a pipe, slippers and a newspaper. Sawyer sat down slowly and sank into the chair, he looked at the whole interior and what it offered. The interior was incredible. It was an open concept cabin with all the accessories found in a home. The interior of the cabin had the essential appliances that you would find in any home. It also had a bathroom, which was, although a little snug and was just the right size for a single individual occupying this cabin. As for the rest of the cabin it had a rustic yet cozy feeling with it's big stone fireplace, warm deluxe king size bed in the bedroom, and a loaded bar, a flat screen television with satellite and the softest chair and couch Sawyer had ever encountered. The cabin also had efficiency with its high-speed Internet access and uplinks with everything from the Whitehouse to the Pentagon and all points in between. The whole cabin was powered by a generator with a lithium core, no fuel was needed, a government perk. Everything was ready and waiting. All Sawyer had to do was order food and on the desk next to the window was a handwritten list with all the numbers to call, it was as if Ron wanted to just come to the cabin and hide away from the world. The food would come in within a day or two of a call or email via floatplane and Ron also had on the list approximately how much supplies he would need for at least four to four and a half months (a typical winter in those parts... sometimes longer... sometimes shorter) when the river was frozen. The last feature of this hidden Valhalla was what sold Sawyer on it... the boat and dock. When Sawyer first arrived he parked the car at the landing, which was where all boats launched from and also where the float planes took off. There was a quaint motel with eight rooms and a bar downstairs which doubled as a dining room during the day, the motel was never really busy with the exception of deer, moose and bear season when hunters would flock to the motel sand bring in a steady flow of income for the two elderly owners of the motel who also were married with three sons who flew the planes just like their father in his hay days. Sawyer handed a slip of paper to the owner, Wayne was his name and he pointed Sawyer over to the dock where he saw a two-man boat with a small engine on the back. Sawyer went back to the car, opened the trunk and removed a giant green duffle bag and his bag, returned to the motel front desk and handed the keys to the car and said only" take care of her for me". Wayne could see Sawyer's car glistening in the sun then looked back at Sawyer and smiled "like my eyes" and with that he turned to the boat, started the engine and made his way up river to his way to a new life, a fresh start, a second chance. The cry of a loon brought Sawyer back to reality and he shook off the moment of reflection. Sawyer's pier could be seen from about fifty feet away and as Sawyer approached the pier he slowed the motor down to a bare crawl. Sawyer looked through his binoculars, which he always wore when he went fishing for observing wildlife when the fishing wasn't any good, and through the light mist Sawyer saw a boat much like his tied to the pier, it appeared to be empty. Immediately Sawyer opened his tackle box and removed the first tray, underneath was a handgun with a loaded clip. Sawyer's defenses were up as he took out the gun and stuck it in the back of his pants. The pier was in plain view as his boat slowly approached. The second his boat touched the dock he looked all around, taking in every detail of his surroundings and looking for the ones that didn't belong. Sawyer stepped out and tied his boat to the pier then he walked over to the other boat and looked inside. The other boat was almost like Sawyer's with one outstanding exception, the letters "U.S.M.C" were boldly emphasized on both sides and it had the same gray color tone as most navy issued boats, ships etc. Sawyer took a few more steps towards it to get a better look, when suddenly he could hear someone shouting at him. He looked up to the front porch of his cabin and saw a rather large man stand up from one of the two chairs located there. Once again the man shouted, "Catch anything??" Sawyer heard the question and responded by lifting his chain from the edge of his boat and shouting back an answer "nope not really" which was evident when on his chain were two, small, pathetic fish. The figure once again shouted down to Sawyer, this time cupping his hands around his mouth "too bad… If you want some, take a few from my chain, I can spare some, help yourself" So Sawyer walked over to the other boat and started to pull up the chain with one hand, when he realized he would need two hands to complete the set task. When Sawyer lifted the chain out of the water he was quite impressed to say the least, dangling from the chain were a dozen fish. Now under normal circumstances he would not accept the generous offer but he did, for two good reasons, he was hungry for fish and while he was fooling about with the chain he tried to get a better look at the figure that was on his porch but he was too far and just got the overall shape. Sawyer stood with the two fish one in each hand and walked over to his boat and put them on his chain then lowered them into the water. A deep cleansing breath now filled Sawyer's lungs as he slowly stood up, turned around and made his way up the stairs, which led to a flat in front of the cabin. When he had reached the flat the figure stood up from the chair and both he and Sawyer sized each other up. The figure then said "well are you going to come here? Or are we going to make pretty eyes at each other." Sawyer walked up the five wide, wooden steps to the porch and stood face to face with the stranger. Trying to act as casually as possible Sawyer started the conversation "thank- you for the fish and if you don't mind me asking you, who are you?" Not knowing what the response would be, he remained cautious. The stranger took steps back and then standing somewhat rigid, almost at attention he answered "Master Gunnery Sergeant Harold Robert Crosby United States Marine Corps Retired." Sawyer was quite stunned by the rousing title and now he quickly took an assessment of the man in front of him. The man in question was six foot two inches with a silver crew cut; a stern face, which looked like it, was chiseled from granite, in fact the entire man looked like he was chiseled from Granite, he wore a red Hawaiian style shirt, light brown khaki shorts and sandals, to Sawyer he kind of resembled John Wayne, big and barrel-chested a sight to behold and it only took Sawyer twenty seconds. The mountain of a man extended his hand to Sawyer "you can call me Gunny everybody else does and you are?" Holding Gunny's hand Sawyer used his previous alias and just hoped that this particular individual never heard it before "Wyatt Brown". Gunny released his rather crushing grip and seemed somewhat disappointed in the answer he had just received and sat down in the deck chair behind him. Still standing he was confused and a bit more on edge although he didn't let it show. Gunny looked up at Sawyer "it's very interesting" he said as he rubbed the predominant cleft in his chin. Sawyer sat down in a deck chair next to him "what's very interesting" he said as he slowly placed his arm on the arm of the chair so that if need be he could defend himself. Gunny looked over at Sawyer "your name, Wyatt, what with that English accent and all, I'd accept Neville, Nigel, or even Goddamn Bond, my name is James Bond, but Wyatt, that's just too funny, You want a beer?" For a moment Sawyer sighed an internal sigh of relief then addressed the question as he looked at his watch. "Umm it's nine-thirty in the morning." The massive hand of Gunny reached into a small cooler beside him and pulled out two cans of beer, the ice dripping off of both of them and handed one to Sawyer "yeah I know but it's five o'clock somewhere, know what I mean?" Sawyer accepted the beer and nodded his head. Taking a sip from the ice-cold beverage Gunny spoke "yep, there's a lot of history here, did the real estate guy tell you anything about it?" Sawyer shook his head trying to make the whole real estate scam look legitimate "no "he replied. Gunny took another sip of beer and started in "well sir I'll tell ya' the previous owner served under my command in the United states marine corps for six years, he was one of the good ones, smart, quick, good in any situation." Gunny pulled out a cigar from his shirt pocket, bit off the tip, spit it on the ground and lit it, and then he looked at Sawyer "you'll get one after my story." Thick smoke surrounded Gunny's head as he continued "so anyway, after countless missions and tours we became friends and after a night of drinking in Bangkok, I think it was, we came to the realization that we should enjoy life instead of risking it all the time, so we made a pact, wherever the next mission is, regardless where on the globe it might be, we would both retire and go live life to the fullest." Emptying the remainder of his beer down his throat, Gunny grabbed another beer from the cooler, "how's your beer holding up?" he asked Sawyer. Looking back at Gunny he replied "I'm good" to which Gunny took another puff of his cigar and laughed as smoke billowed out of his mouth "goddamn tea totaling limey" he said as he gave Sawyer a small wink as he pulled the tab on another brew. Taking a sip of his beer, which was almost half the can, Gunny continued telling his story after very loud and pronounced belch "the last mission was coming up, so true to our pact we came to British Columbia and bought two plots of land side by side and hired the same contractor to custom build our two cabins almost identical, we spared no expense, of course we wouldn't see them until we got back but we could wait to get back, any job worth doing is worth doing right." He stared at Sawyer and asked "right?" Sawyer raised his can of "amen" he announced. Another plume of smoke rose into the air as Gunny proceeded "well, a month and a half went by and we finally returned, the mission was a success and we got metals pinned on our chest's by the president even though I had a shade more on my chest it didn't matter because it was our last mission." Swallowing the remainder of the beer and crushing the can with his massive hand Gunny puffed his cigar with a more somber look coming about his face as he went on "we both came out here a week after coming back and were we impressed not only were the cabins done and docks to boot but the higher ups in the marine corps caught wind of our plans and fully furnished everything from furniture to boats, and all the equipment we would need, and they also set up an account for us so if we needed anything Uncle Sam would pick up the tab, it was a sort of retirement gift, a sweet deal." Nodding his head in approval Sawyer inquired about the whereabouts of his friend "so, where is your friend if everything was such a sweet deal?" Gunny took a deep breath then sighed "well, everything was going great for the first year or so, we hunted and fished and had no cares in the world, we even had women flown in on occasion" he said looking at Sawyer and raising and lowering his eyebrows quickly "yeah life was good." Grabbing another beer from the cooler Sawyer sat back in his chair, opened the can and listened to Gunny's every word, he was quite intrigued by the whole story. Gunny hung his head and concluded the story "after the first year and a bit my friend got a phone call from the Pentagon to come work for them in a special branch, he couldn't turn it down and I didn't even want him to turn it down, I wanted him to have all the success in the world, he really deserved it." Gunny then reached into the cooler for another beer and as he did so he kept speaking "oh, I heard from him from time to time but it was always brief, I heard a lot more from him during his tenure with president Bradley and also after, he also kept me in the loop about his pursuit of you." Gunny took a long sip from his can of beer and took a puff off his cigar, blowing the smoke in the air. Turning towards Sawyer "I know who you are" he said with a broad smile. Almost immediately Sawyer went into defensive mode, sliding his right hand back behind himself and gripping the handle of the gun he had brought as a precaution. Firmly Sawyer gripped the handle and was about to pull it out when Gunny raised his voice, which seemed to stop him cold, "Now wait a minute I have been watching your right hand slide back slightly ever since I started talking to you and I know you have a gun stuck in the back of your pants pointed down the crack of your ass and I also know that if you shoot me you'll accomplish nothing but kill an old man who served his country, now do you really want that on your conscience? Do you?" Sawyer froze and slightly dropped his head as Gunny continued "look I have been watching you since you moved in and if I wanted to hit you on the head, stuff you in a sack and deliver you to the authorities I could have done it, you dropped your guard so many times it would have been easy." Slowly Sawyer removed his hand from the grip and felt a little embarrassed. Gunny knew he had Sawyer's attention and that he was not going to harm him. Gunny stood up and faced Sawyer who also stood up not knowing what was going to transpire. Looking straight into Sawyer's eyes Gunny cleared his throat and snapped to attention just as he did when he introduced himself the first time, "I'm Master Gunnery Sergeant Harold Robert Crosby United States Marine Corps retired." Standing at attention Gunny extended his hand "and you are?" he asked. Sawyer hesitated then took gunny's hand and held it "I' am Sawyer Francis Briggs head of the espionage and terrorism division for the International Police... umm... deceased?" and then he shook Gunny's hand as he laughed "deceased" and shook his head. They both sat back down as Gunny finished another can of beer "you see" he said to Sawyer as he crushed the empty can in his hand "that wasn't so tough even though you deserve more than a handshake for what you did." Knowing what he had done Sawyer remained silent and handed Gunny another can of beer from the cooler. An awkward silence then arose as Sawyer and Gunny sat staring out at the calm water flowing by. "So "Sawyer said as he tried to start a new conversation "it's really peaceful up here, isn't it?" Gunny smiled "yes, it sure is." Sawyer then took another can of beer from the cooler and kept the conversation going "it must get awfully lonely at times." He said as he opened up the ice-cold can. Gunny nodded his head "well, you see Sawyer at times it gets lonely but..." Just then a plane with floats on it similar to the one that brought in supplies roared overhead cutting off Gunny in mid sentence, the plane turned in the air and headed back dropping altitude quite rapidly as it was preparing to land. The two of them watched as the plane touched down on the water making a picture perfect landing. Sawyer commented to Gunny "that guy sure knows his shit" As the two of them watched, the plane slowly floated to the end of the dock and stopped broadside, hardly touching the side. Gunny and Sawyer both stood up as the door on the plane opened and the pilot stepped out and stood on the pontoon. A smile came across Gunny's face and in moments Sawyer found out why. "Are we still on for breakfast, Gunny?" the pilot shouted. For a second Sawyer thought his hearing was off, the voice of the pilot sounded like a female. Taking a closer look it was a female, a voluptuous female about fifty years of age, with bright red hair wearing an orange jumpsuit unzipped midway down just beginning to reveal her breasts. Gunny cupped his mouth and shouted back "yeah, I'm heading out soon, the door's open." She smiled "who's your friend?" Gunny's massive arm laid over Sawyer's shoulder "this is my new neighbor" Then Gunny looked at Sawyer "well, don't just stand there waving at her." So Sawyer awkwardly smiled and waved, to which she waved back. Blowing a kiss to the both of them she got back in the plane, started the engine and slowly taxied away from the dock and up the river. As the sound of the engine faded the two of them sat back down, Gunny turned to Sawyer "sometimes it does get lonely... and sometimes it doesn't" he said followed by a hardy laugh and a slap to Sawyer's shoulder. Sawyer sipped his beer and made a statement to Gunny "I bet she doesn't let you get cold in the winter, it must be a bastard up here." Gunny, still staring out at the water, answered back "who? Her?" Sawyer nodded as Gunny continued "she's just a friend besides I don't stay up here in the winter, I do what all good senior citizens do I head to Florida or maybe Cuba or Colombia for that matter I could be anywhere in the winter and sometimes if I'm not busy fishing or doing other things" he said raising and lowering his eyebrows quite quickly, "in the summer." Sawyer looked at Gunny with a rather puzzled look on his face but before he could even ask a question Gunny explained it to him. "You see a few guys I commanded ended up in high end jobs much like Ron, you know F.B.I, C.I.A national intelligence, stuff like that." Sawyer still looked somewhat puzzled. Gunny took a deep breath and continued, "Well they sometimes need an average Joe, you know your typical tourist type to do a little sightseeing and tell them what they saw." Sawyer developed a small grin "what you mean to say is intelligence agencies are using you for reconnaissance missions am I close?" Gunny nodded and answered "more or less, but it's a great gig. I get all my expenses paid by the government, food, booze, hotels, you name It." Then Gunny looked over at Sawyer and rubbed his chin. "Hey, I could tell the boys I have a buddy who could be part of the team and together we could cover more ground, we could travel together, were neighbors so why not be a team, think of the adventures we could have?" Sawyer now had a big smile on his face and even laughed a little "look, Gunny thanks for the offer but I was on the run from everybody from hit men to bounty hunters and government agents and the last thing I want in this whole world is adventure, so once again thanks… but no thanks." Gunny sighed as he crushed his beer can and dropped it on the porch "well I can respect that, but if you change your mind come on down to my cabin we can talk about it over dinner I'll supply the fish, you supply the refreshment" he said as he winked at Sawyer and with that Gunny stood up and he and Sawyer shook hands. Gunny slowly made his way down the stairs as Sawyer thought about the offer and looked up "Gwen, this will be the last time I swear it, the offer is good I take some photos and get free vacations in the process, what could go wrong? Sorry, I love you." Gunny was just stepping on to the dock when Sawyer cupped his mouth and shouted down "Gunny!!" Gunny stopped, turned around and shouted back to Sawyer "I like beer with my fish and it better be cold." he uncupped his hands from his mouth and smiled as he leaned against a post on the porch as he watched Gunny in his boat slowly leave the dock and then watched as disappeared out of sight, he then sat back in his chair and grabbed a cold beer from the cooler opened it and raised it up "well… it'll beat fishing anyway."

Sawyer's Voice

> "Human nature is a strange thing, it has been contested, researched and debated since the time of philosophers and prophets and they could not even figure it out."

"Why is it when a human, whether man or woman gets into a situation (cheating, extortion, robbery, etc) they try to get out as quickly and cleanly as they can say they will never ever do it again if they get out… But then as soon as they are out and time passes they are right back where they started, crazy, isn't it?"

"It just doesn't make sense, I mean a person would have to be a complete idiot to escape a violent, and possibly life threatening situation only to go back to it again, a person would have to be an utter and complete jackass to want to return to something of that distinction"

"Well then just give me a sugar cube. HeeeeeFuckin' Hawwwww!